Readers love
KATE SHERWOOD

In Too Deep

"This story captured my attention immediately and I was completely immersed until the very end."

—It's About The Book

"This is an intense and truly magnificent novel… This is a story that touched my heart, and it's definitely being added to my favorites."

—Rainbow Book Reviews

Chasing the Dragon

"*Chasing the Dragon* by Kate Sherwood is an intense emotional ride. A story of twists and turns and heart stopping moments that grabbed me and wouldn't let me go."

—Prism Book Alliance

Riding Tall

"It was beautiful and I was completely satisfied."

—Boys in Our Books

By KATE SHERWOOD

All That Glitters
Beneath the Surface
Chasing the Dragon
The Fall • Riding Tall
In Too Deep
Lost Treasure
More Than Chemistry
Shying Away • New Tricks

AGAINST THE ODDS
The Pawn
The Knight

DARK HORSE
Dark Horse
Out of the Darkness
Of Dark and Bright

Published by DREAMSPINNER PRESS
www.dreamspinnerpress.com

Kate
Sherwood

All That
GLITTERS

Published by

DREAMSPINNER PRESS

5032 Capital Circle SW, Suite 2, PMB# 279, Tallahassee, FL 32305-7886 USA
www.dreamspinnerpress.com

This is a work of fiction. Names, characters, places, and incidents either are the product of author imagination or are used fictitiously, and any resemblance to actual persons, living or dead, business establishments, events, or locales is entirely coincidental.

All That Glitters
© 2018 Kate Sherwood.

Cover Art
© 2018 Adrian Nicholas.
adrian.nicholas177@gmail.com
Cover content is for illustrative purposes only and any person depicted on the cover is a model.

Trade Paperback ISBN: 978-1-64080-526-2
Digital ISBN: 978-1-64080-525-5
Library of Congress Control Number: 2018930562
Trade Paperback published June 2018
v. 1.0

Printed in the United States of America
∞
This paper meets the requirements of
ANSI/NISO Z39.48-1992 (Permanence of Paper).

CHAPTER ONE

LIAM MARSHALL hadn't had a destination in mind when he left the city. He'd just been driving. He headed north because—well, because he hadn't wanted to deal with bridges, maybe, and he could go a long way north without hitting water.

He hadn't *consciously* known where he was going until he was driving through the park on the way to the Bear Mountain Bridge. Because that was, obviously, a bridge, so if his navigation was based on avoiding bridges, he was doing a shitty job of it. Pretty clueless if he couldn't avoid a river as big as the Hudson. And he really didn't think he was that bad at navigating.

At other things, though— But he cut that thought off before it got too far. He was driving to clear his mind, not to wallow.

He buzzed his window down and took a few deep breaths of clean spring air. Clearing, clearing, clearing. Nothing to think about, no scenes to replay.

Except…. *"We're all so excited to be working with a fresh new name! Please join me in congratulating Allison Sutcliffe, the lead architect for the Taybec Briggs Foundation! Allison, come on up here and share your vision for this project."*

And Liam had been standing at the front of the room, unable to escape. So sure he was going to be the one chosen—because of *course* he'd be the one chosen, he always was, and always would be—so he'd found a spot right beside Tristan McTighe, the visionary behind the firm where Liam had been working for the past decade. Liam had been at Tristan's right hand, where he damn well belonged. And then Tristan had said her name. Allison Sutcliffe.

Young.

That's what Liam had thought. She was so damn young, too young to be in charge of such a prestigious, significant project.

But she was twenty-nine, only eight years younger than he was, and older than he'd been when he'd gotten his first lead job.

But that had been different. That had been *him*....

Shit.

He pushed down on the accelerator, went into the huge traffic circle way too fast, and pulled out of it even faster. It wasn't cheap, keeping a car in New York City, and he hardly ever had a reason to drive anywhere. But this? This freedom, this power—it justified the expense, absolutely.

He saw the flashing lights behind him and took his foot off the gas. He wouldn't actually hit the brakes, wouldn't stop the car, wouldn't acknowledge that this had anything to do with him. Not until he absolutely had to.

Yeah, keep fooling yourself. Keep pretending you're something special. Go ahead.

He kept driving, pulled over only when the cop car drove up beside him and the driver started waving in a threatening manner, and then, shockingly, Liam found himself close to tears.

Tears. Like, he was going to *cry* because he was getting a speeding ticket. Jesus Christ, he was falling apart.

The cruiser parked in front of him and the cop swaggered back. Yeah, swaggered. He'd pulled over a Mercedes sports car; he was going to swagger a little.

But he's not going to shoot you, asshole, so maybe you can ease off on the poor-little-victim routine.

"Do you know how fast you were going?" the officer demanded. Then he bent down. "Holy shit. Liam? Is that you?"

Liam looked at him blankly.

"Oh. Are you—you're going back for the funeral. Damn, man, I'm sorry. I didn't know you guys were that close."

And there was a moment of near panic. Someone was dead. Someone Liam had known, possibly? Someone he might even have been close to. It couldn't be—no. He wasn't really in contact with anyone in North Falls, but he wasn't hard to find, and someone would have tracked him down for *that*. Whoever was dead, it wasn't—who he'd first thought of.

Then came a brief moment of wondering if he could play this. Of course he could. The grief had been too much for him, he'd been feeling desperate, but he'd absolutely be more careful in the future. Thank you for the warning, Officer; it's so wonderful to see power tempered with compassion.

It wouldn't have been difficult, and it would have saved him the aggravation of getting a ticket.

But he still had a bit of pride, at least. Enough to keep him from using some poor schmuck's death as a way to get out of a stupid traffic ticket that would cost less than he'd spend on an average dinner. "Sorry, no. I'm not going to a funeral. I was just driving too fast."

"Oh." The cop looked conflicted—reward Liam's honesty, or punish his callousness?

And suddenly it was too much. Liam was tired of sitting around waiting for someone else to judge him, tired of being a pawn, a powerless decid*ee* instead of a decid*er*. "I was driving too fast," he repeated, louder this time. "I should get a ticket. You should write me a ticket."

"Well…," the cop said. "Was there—are you in a hurry? Are you heading somewhere important?"

The cop was from North Falls. Liam still had no idea who the guy was, but the reluctance to write the ticket, the hope to find an excuse for Liam's misbehavior? That was North Falls, all the way through. Keep things pleasant, don't stir up trouble, and always, *always* believe the best about Liam Marshall, no matter how much evidence there was to persuade you otherwise.

"No hurry," Liam said. "Nothing important." He felt the old fascination, the almost hypnotic curiosity to see just how far he could push things before someone finally shut him down. "I was just being an asshole. Reckless. Someone could have gotten hurt. I should get a ticket, absolutely. I'll just pay it—won't contest it or anything."

"Well… I don't think I'd call it 'reckless,' really, but—"

"Have you got kids?" Of course the guy would have kids. He was Liam's age, give or take a couple years, and lived in North Falls. He'd have kids. Probably two, maybe three. "What if they'd been in one of those other cars? What if I'd lost control, swerved into them, driven them off the road?"

And finally, the cop was writing. "You sound like you understand how serious it was," he said, his pen working as he spoke, "so I'm going to bump it down a little. But you do need to slow down, Liam.

I'm sure you're a good driver, and it's a really nice car, but this ain't the Autobahn."

"Right," Liam agreed. "I'll slow down." And then, almost absently, he said, "Whose funeral did you think I was going to?"

"Oh, sorry. I guess you might not know him, really. Terry Franks, the guy who owned the antique store? Passed away on Saturday—heart attack. Died at work, with all that stuff he loved so much, so—that's good, right? If he had to go, that's where he'd have wanted to do it."

Terry Franks. Dead. No, he and Liam hadn't been close, but— damn it.

"Liam?" the cop prompted, and he waved the ticket in the air between them. "Sorry about this. But, you know, it's my job…."

"It's fine." Liam took the slip of paper and set it on the passenger seat. "No problem. But—the funeral, for Terry. Do you know what time it was at? Could I still make it?"

The cop checked his watch. "Funeral at two thirty and you've still got an hour of driving. So, no, you'd be too late. But I think they're burying him right after, so you could make it to the graveside, probably."

It made no sense. Terry hadn't really been a friend, and the graveside part of the funeral was generally much more intimate than the church service. Liam had no business even thinking about attending.

But—he'd been heading for North Falls anyway, or at least in that general direction. So he waited for the cop to pull away, then rejoined traffic himself and kept driving.

Terry Franks. He'd had such a small life, as far as Liam knew. No grand adventures, no remarkable achievements. The local paper would carry his obituary, but that would be all. No larger notice would be taken of his passing, just as no larger notice had been taken of his life.

But Liam kept driving, and when he finally made it to the North Falls town sign, instead of turning right and looping back to New York City like he usually did, he continued straight on and then turned left toward the cemetery.

Tall trees just beginning to leaf out. Row upon row of gravestones, all shapes and sizes. And over in the corner, too far away for faces to be distinguishable, a small group in dark clothes, standing next to a hearse.

Liam had the sense, the decency, to keep his ass in the car where it belonged. He wasn't going to push into other people's grief, not when the most he felt was a vague sense of regret, of dismay at wasted potential. Terry could have done so much more with his life, but he hadn't. He'd hidden himself away in North Falls, curated relics from a bygone age rather than creating anything himself, and left any talents he might have to molder, unknown and unappreciated.

No, Liam wasn't really there for Terry. And the one he *was* there for? More than fifteen years ago, he'd told Liam to fuck off and leave him alone. He'd said he never wanted to see Liam again, and Liam had done his best to oblige. It was maybe the one decent thing he'd ever managed to do for Ben, and he wasn't going screw it up now by making a cameo at an acquaintance's funeral.

So he stayed in the car, and he watched as the group stood, clustered, and eventually broke apart. He could recognize Ben even without seeing his face, just in the easy movements, the slight stoop to his shoulders as he spoke to the other mourners, all of whom were at least half a head shorter.

Liam stayed and watched as the crowd wandered back to their cars. Some visited other graves, and a couple glanced over toward the Mercedes. But Liam wasn't interested in any of them, and Ben was walking away, beside an older man—his uncle Calvin, probably, who'd always been close to Terry.

Liam waited until Ben and Calvin were folded into the limo and driving away, taking the back way into town, the way that *didn't* send them past Liam's parked car.

He'd gotten away with his little excursion, and that was his indulgence for the day. For the week or even the month, really. He needed to get back to the city, back to his life—he needed to stop running away and figure out what the hell he was going to do about work, about the humiliation that had just been heaped on him. He needed to *fix* things.

Yeah, that was the plan. But when he pushed the ignition button, nothing happened. What the hell? He ran over it all again: foot on brake, car in Park, hit the button. Nothing. Goddammit, what was the point of having fancy technology if it didn't work?

He pried the cover off the ignition and inserted the stubby little key, turned it, and—nothing. No deep, powerful rumble, just the cheerful birdsong coming from outside his open window.

Another try… and another failure. Nothing was happening.

He got a little desperate, tried all the tricks he could think of, swore quite a bit, and finally slumped back into his seat, defeated. A few deep breaths, and then he pulled out his phone. He was fine. He had this covered. It was a nuisance, not a damn tragedy.

And that was the attitude he needed to have toward the issues at work, he reflected as he leaned against the hood of the car and waited for AAA to show up. Sneaky little Allison Sutcliffe, slipping in and stealing his project? Whatever. Not a big deal. He didn't give a shit, really. She was a blip, a tiny, insignificant bump in the smooth road of his career. He had the record, the contacts, the reputation, and she was just— McTighe had thrown her a bone, that was all. The old man was all about continuity and building talent from within the firm, and of *course* he'd need to start encouraging new people, because there needed to be strong people below Liam when he took his final, inevitable step to the next level.

Okay. That was all fine. He'd overreacted a little, but he'd done it in private, so it was no big deal. And the car was no big deal. Maybe for someone else, someone without his financial stability and resources, this would be an issue. But for him? Just a little blip.

And half an hour later the tow truck showed up, coming down the road from the direction of the highway. Hopefully the driver could take a quick look and do some… some mechanic trick, or something and fix it right then and there. If not, he could tow the vehicle to town, Liam would arrange a rental, and everything would go back to normal.

The truck pulled up behind him, the door opened, and a burly man climbed out. After about three steps toward Liam, he froze and stared. Liam stared right back.

"What the fuck?" the man demanded.

"Seth." *Shit. Shit, shit, shit.* "You're driving a tow truck? I thought—" Well, no, that probably wasn't a conversation they needed to be having. "You weren't at the funeral?" Probably another unnecessary question, but just what the hell was he supposed to be saying?

"I was there," Seth growled. "Had to get changed at the garage and come out here to help some poor stranded motorist. And it turns out to be *you*? You've got some fucking nerve showing your face around here! And today is *not* the fucking day for any of your shit. You need to get back in that car—"

"I'd be happy to," Liam said quickly. "But it won't start. Seriously, I didn't come up to cause trouble. I just—well, that doesn't matter. The point is, I want to get out of here, and *you* want me out of here, so if you can just give me a hand with this, we can both get what we want."

"I should leave you out here to rot."

Okay, that was taking it a bit far. Yeah, Liam had screwed up, but it had been a decade and a half ago. Seth needed to get over it. "Well, obviously I wouldn't just sit down and wait for decomposition to begin. I'd walk into town, probably, and have to hang around for a bit waiting for someone *else* to come deal with the car. I assume you'd agree it would be a good thing if I *didn't* walk into town and didn't hang around?"

"What are you doing up here anyway?"

"Nothing. Absolutely nothing. So I'd like to get home as soon as possible. If you could just take a quick peek at the ignition?"

Seth still looked murderous, but at least he took the last few steps to get to the car. He lifted the key fob out of Liam's hand, careful not to touch any skin, and then slid behind the wheel. A few clicks, a few grunts, and then, "It's broken."

"No shit?"

Seth extracted himself awkwardly from the car. "I can't fix it, not out here. I need to plug it into the computer, run diagnostics—a good old-fashioned car, I could fix on the spot. But this? This car is too *fancy* for that. And the garage is closed until morning."

"So—" Damn, it was a miserable thought, but what were the options? "You can tow me back to the city, right?" Two and a half hours trapped in the cab of a tow truck with the angriest man in the state. Excellent.

Seth didn't look any more enthusiastic about the idea than Liam. "It's already past five. I need to be home for dinner."

"So, somebody else from the garage can do it. Whoever's on the night shift."

"We have one tow truck for the whole town. The whole area. Rissa isn't going to send it off to the city, taking it out of commission for, what, five or six hours, round-trip? And we don't have a damn *night shift*, we just have whatever poor sucker has to haul his ass out of bed to go help people if they get in trouble in the middle of the night. Which he wouldn't be able to do if someone else fucked off to the city with our only tow truck."

"A rental, then. You'll tow the car to town, I'll pick up a rental…." He stopped talking when he saw the expression on Seth's face. And, okay, sure, fifteen years ago there hadn't been anyone renting cars in North Falls, but surely in the intervening years… no. Apparently no one had set up business. He forced himself to smile. "You'll tow me to the closest town that has a car rental company. You can leave me *and* the car there, and I'll take care of things after that."

"There's a 24/7 Hertz outlet in Monticello," Seth admitted almost reluctantly. "I could take you down there." He frowned. "But we're not towing this car. You need a flatbed for this—you should have told the dispatcher to send a flatbed, not a tow truck."

"Do you *have* a flatbed? And why do we need one?"

"Towing's bad for cars. If you have a shitty car, it doesn't matter. But this one? You need a flatbed. And, yeah, we've got one." He shrugged. "It's got Marv Archart's stock car on it, though. In pieces."

"Okay," Liam said, and he raised his hands. Not in surrender, just in dismissal. He could feel the tears threatening again, just as bewildering and foreign as they'd been earlier, and he would absolutely *not* break down crying in front of Seth Gilbert. "Thanks for your time. I'll call for a car to come pick me up, I'll have my garage arrange a flatbed, and everything will be solved. It won't hurt me to spend a few hours in the car waiting. I promise not to walk into town."

Seth's scowl made it clear he wasn't pleased with the plan, but also that he had no better option in mind. "You need to—" he started, but he was distracted by something over Liam's shoulder. "Shit. Shit, shit—"

Liam turned.

Shit.

It was Ben himself, only fifty or sixty feet away, and closing fast.

CHAPTER TWO

BEING A teacher in a small town meant that Ben Harding's life was community property. He'd booked the afternoon off work and now he was going for a run, and even though he'd taken a compassionate leave, not a sick day, he knew that any parents who saw him would notice. Couldn't stay at work with their precious darlings, but had no problem jogging around all over the place. Oh, they wouldn't *say* anything. But they'd notice.

So he'd taken the route out into the country rather than going along the river through town as he usually did. He could relax and enjoy nature without fretting about who was watching.

At least he should have been able to, but as he jogged past the cemetery he saw two vehicles off on the far side of the road. Seth would be driving the tow truck, and, yup, there he was, his bushy red beard clear even at a distance. But the other guy… shit, was he a parent? Damn, nice car, and the guy was kind of—

Ben stopped running so suddenly he almost fell over, too stunned to have properly balanced himself through the deceleration. The other guy. Oh.

He wished he'd kept running. Was it too late? If he just started again, if he powered right past them, ignored them both and apologized to Seth later? Could he do that? Or he could turn around—that was more his style, really. He could turn around and run away, and, yeah, that was pathetic but there was no one on the road right then who didn't already know how pathetic he was.

No, he told himself. *How pathetic you* were. *Totally different. You're older and wiser now.*

He forced himself to walk on, and they stared at him like *they* were the ones freaking out. Okay, good. He could be the calm one for a change.

He should ignore Liam entirely. That'd be the cool thing to do. Say something casual to Seth, something about a new kind of beer or some sport or some other manly topic, and not even acknowledge that Liam existed. That'd be good.

But he was Ben the Chronically Uncool, so before he knew it he'd staggered halfway across the road and was staring at Liam like he was Bigfoot. "What are you doing here?" he demanded.

"I'm sorry," Liam said. The last words Ben had heard from him all those years ago, and the first ones now. "My car broke down. Sorry."

Liam's car had broken down just outside North Falls, not in the city where he and the car belonged. But Ben wasn't ready for a deeper conversation, not when he was still in shock just from looking at Liam. "Okay," he managed. "Okay. I, uh—I've got to go."

"You're sweaty from the run. You don't want to get chilled," Seth said helpfully.

"Right," Ben agreed. He took two steps, then three, and realized he was walking almost sideways, his gaze still locked on Liam's face. Looking for—what?

"You're an asshole," he said. Not planned, but not a lie.

Liam just stood there. Seth nodded in sage agreement with Ben's words.

"And what the *fuck* are you doing here?" Ben demanded, stepping back closer to Liam. "This is—I mean, obviously I don't own the town, but you have no reason to be here, do you? You were so damn happy to leave this place behind, so what are you doing back?"

Liam still didn't answer, and Ben fought the urge to push him, grab him, *shake* him, kick his cheating, lying ass all over the damn road. "Fuck you," he spat.

Liam actually nodded. But, sure, he'd been pretty damn agreeable all those years ago, too, once he got busted. Sneak around and make a fool of Ben behind his back, but to his face? Oh, he was so, so sorry to Ben's face.

"*Fuck* you."

"This is going much better than I expected," Seth said with a happy smile.

That reaction made sense, because Liam had betrayed Seth too. They hadn't been lovers, but they'd been friends, all three of them, and Liam had lied to Seth and destroyed that relationship just as surely as he'd destroyed the one with Ben.

"Nice that he's got a pretty car," Ben told Seth. "Nice that the *things* in his life are valuable."

And Liam turned away.

He'd been quick, but not quick enough, and Ben felt as if all the hot anger that had been running through his body froze. Not all the way to hard, solid ice, but into slush, slippery and useless. Because Liam had been—

"Can you give me a minute?" Ben asked Seth, and he waited as Seth heard the words, absorbed them, questioned them, and didn't care for them.

"You sure?" Seth asked, and when Ben nodded, he reluctantly turned and walked toward the far end of the tow truck.

Ben stepped to the side and Liam turned away again, but there was nowhere for him to look, not with Seth off to the left and Ben angling in from the right. He stood still, then lifted his hands quickly to his face, brushed at his eyes, and muttered, "Sorry. That's—I have no idea what's going on with that. Allergies or something, hopefully. But it's not you. That is, it's not for you to feel bad about."

"Oh, that's really generous of you," Ben sniped, but his heart wasn't in it. Liam had been crying—was *still* crying, because the initial scrubbing had removed the first set of tears but there were more coming now, fat and rounded on his golden skin. "What the fuck, Liam?" Suddenly, Ben realized where they were parked. Liam hadn't—he hadn't known Terry well enough to care about his death, not this deeply. But there were other people buried in the cemetery, obviously, and one of them must have meant something to Liam. "I'm sorry," he said. Then, quickly, "For your loss. Not for thinking you're a fucking asshole. I'm not sorry about that."

Liam took a deep, shaky breath. "Okay. But to be honest—I don't have a loss." Another shaky breath. "Shit, I guess I should have just left that alone, huh? No point dragging you into whatever the hell this is. Sorry. Let's start again. I just—thank you. For your condolences."

Condolences he hadn't needed.

"Dragging me into… what? Seriously, Liam, is there—"

"Everything's fine," Liam said, standing up straighter and talking louder. "Just having a weird—I don't know, let's call it an artistic moment, okay? Just a weird day. Nothing to worry about, and just a bad set of coincidences that you even found out about it."

"Well, it'd be a coincidence if we ran into each other in the city, yeah. But, fuck, Liam, when you drive a couple hours away from your house and park just down the street from mine, you're giving 'coincidence' a pretty big helping hand, aren't you?"

"You never saw me any of the *other* times."

"The other—" Ben needed to sit down. Or have a drink. He probably needed to sit down *and* have a drink. "You've been up here before?" It made no sense. Unless.... "Do you want to talk to Uncle Calvin?" It was a fairly random possibility, but the best he could do. And then, unlikely but not impossible, because Uncle Calvin could play his cards pretty close to his chest when he wanted to, "Have you been talking to him before?"

But Liam shook his head. "No. I haven't come up for any reasons. I just drive sometimes. Jesus, what the hell is going on? Why am I telling you any of this? You don't want to know this."

Well, that was true. Mostly. "Right. So—yeah. You're an asshole, fuck you, and go away." That was all he needed to say. Except… damn it. "But are you okay? Is there something—not me, but *somebody*—is there something somebody should do?"

"No, I'm fine." Even forced, Liam's smile was still a thing of beauty, and Ben had to make himself look away. "Sorry about whatever that was. Just a strange blip. Everything's good with me. I'm doing great."

"Okay." And Ben was suddenly almost dizzy from it all. Liam Marshall. How many hours had he wasted agonizing about this asshole over the past fifteen years? And now he just showed up out of nowhere, totally unexpected. And totally unwelcome. Ben turned and took a few jogging steps away. "So we're back to 'fuck you.'" He took another few steps until he was beside Seth. "See you at Matty's."

"Yup," Seth agreed, and he jerked his head in Liam's direction. "You want me to do anything here, or not do anything? Maybe punching him, in terms of *doing* something, or helping him, in terms of *not* doing something?"

"No. He's—he's nothing. Nobody. Just treat him like any other loser trying to use a fancy car to fill a hole in his pathetic life." Ben instantly felt guilty, remembering Liam's tears, and then angry because how the hell had he let himself get twisted around so quickly, manipulated into feeling actual *guilt* because of a few harsh words, after what Liam had done?

"I need to go," he said quickly, and he took off at a jog that was closer to a sprint, and as he ran he told himself to put it all out of his mind, to let it go, to be glad he'd had a chance at closure and the time to give Liam another "fuck you."

He tried to forget the tears. No, he *did* forget them. He banished them from his memory. He'd just had an unexpected encounter with his first love, and that was mind-blowing enough. He wouldn't let the situation get any stranger, any more complicated.

He'd seen Liam Marshall. What an asshole.

There. That was enough. That was all he'd let himself feel. Liam Marshall was part of the past, and that was where he would damn well stay.

CHAPTER THREE

LIAM DIDN'T want to go to work the next morning. For the past decade he'd been *hungry* to be at the office, showing up before anyone else and usually staying until only a skeleton crew remained. The firm's work space was designed to inspire the architects who spent time in it, and it was open, bright and airy, modern and sophisticated, and Liam had a place there. A place of honor. He'd worked hard, he'd been rewarded, and he belonged.

But now?

Maybe it was partly because of running into Ben. So many unresolved issues—but, no, they'd been resolved. Ben had dumped him. Liam had deserved it. There was nothing unresolved about that, other than Liam's recurrent suspicion that he'd messed up the best relationship he was ever likely to have. But all that had been years ago.

No, he was upset about his job, now. His *career*.

He knew he was being melodramatic. He was healthy, he hadn't been caught embezzling or anything; he was fine. He just hadn't been chosen for a project. There were any number of reasons why that might have happened, and very few of them were anything to worry about. Liam would sit down with Tristan, get an explanation, and move on. Hell, maybe it was actually a *good* thing. Maybe there was an even bigger project, more prestigious, more challenging, right around the corner, and Tristan had wanted to make sure Liam was free to take it on.

But even that optimistic possibility wasn't enough to put a bounce in his step as he approached the front doors of the office. He forced himself to smile, though—he'd be damned if he'd let them see him looking discouraged—and jogged up the stairs from the street. Purposeful, focused—that was the image he wanted to project.

And the first person he saw was Allison Sutcliffe, the bitch—*no, don't use that word, you're not a caveman*—the *asshole* who'd stolen the project from him. Her smile was bright and seemed totally genuine.

"Liam! Good to see you. I'm really looking forward to working together. I set a meeting for the team at ten this morning, but I'd like it if you and I could get together before that to—" She stopped, clearly reacting to the expression on his face. "Oh, shit. Tristan hasn't talked to you yet. I thought he was going to—" She stopped again, and now her smile seemed more forced. "Sorry. I jumped the gun. Never mind."

"Tristan wants us to work together?" Liam asked. It made sense, except that *Allison* had been announced as the project lead. Which would make Liam her fucking assistant? Hell, no, that was asking too much. "I'd better give him a call."

"Yeah, of course. Sorry, you should hear it from him, obviously."

Obviously. Because it was bad news. Essentially a demotion. What the hell was going on? What had Liam done to deserve this?

"Oh, here he is," Allison said, her gaze focused behind Liam, toward the front doors. "Wow, I didn't know he was even capable of being conscious this early."

The last was said in a lower voice, an almost conspiratorial whisper. It was the kind of comment that would have been totally appropriate, totally expected between them prior to the announcement, but now? The familiarity, the implication that they were somehow still on the same team? It made the muscles of Liam's shoulders clench.

Liam shifted so he was looking at Tristan, and the older man glanced from one face to the other before he said, "I see I'm a bit late. Sorry, Liam, I was going to speak to you yesterday but you didn't come back to the office. I thought I'd be able to catch you this morning."

"Timing aside," Liam said, "what's going on?"

And one good thing about Tristan was that he didn't mince words. "I want you to work on the project with Allison. She could use someone with your experience."

Use someone. Liam was just there to be used. He was a tool in the workbox of the true artist. It was unthinkable, unbearable. "Oh. Actually—I was planning to speak to you today as well. About something different." *Hold it together, save face, don't crack.* "Obviously I want to be a team player. I remember the first time I was lead on a project—it was when you were"—*going through that messy divorce, and I stepped in and saved your reputation, do you remember that?*—"preoccupied elsewhere, and I definitely had to scramble a bit. It was a challenge." He found himself relaxing a little.

There was something kind of liberating about this feeling, like he was disconnected from his career, his emotions—his reality. But still able to get some jabs in. "I learned a lot, though, Allison. I think it would be really valuable for you to have that kind of experience, that sink-or-swim opportunity, if you're up for it. As I said, I'm a team player. If you need the help, I'll certainly put my own ideas aside. But for your own sake—oh. Unless Tristan—"

He turned to look at the older man. "Sorry. Possibly this is why you wanted to have the conversation in private. But—if you're not sure Allison's up to it? If you have some doubts?" *Then you shouldn't have put her in charge of the project when you've got someone totally competent standing right beside you!* "Well. Sure, yeah. If help is needed, I can help. The most important thing is the project, obviously. We can't betray a client's faith in us just to manufacture an employee growth opportunity." He smiled benignly.

"I don't think I need the help," Allison said. Her voice was icy now. Good. No more fake friendship, no more casual jokes. "Tristan was trying to find a way to keep you busy, I think."

"Let's not do this," Tristan said firmly. "Liam, you said you had ideas of your own. Anything you're ready to bring to the table?"

And the calm, floating sensation disappeared completely. He'd done a good job of bringing business to the firm in the past, and he was sure he'd bring more in the future, but right then he had nothing more than a few vague hints and jovial, empty expressions of interest. *Shit, shit, shit.* "Actually," he heard himself say, "I was looking at a few personal projects. You know how it is, the collection of smaller jobs that people want you to take on, the things that just get shoved aside and piled up?" The projects he reliably and repeatedly refused to adopt because he didn't want to get bogged down in petty, trivial designs. "I was thinking about taking some time to work through that backlog. A sabbatical, maybe we could call it?"

Tristan's expression was unreadable. "Come into my office," he said. Sure, the humiliation with Allison could be played out in a public space, but now that Liam was trying to reclaim some power—even if he was doing it with totally imaginary projects—they needed to be in private.

But Tristan was the boss, so Liam trailed after him around the reception desk and into the glass-walled space that was the only private office in the whole firm. Tristan shrugged out of his light coat and tossed it casually on the back of the leather sofa, then perched on the stool by his drafting table. He wasn't in the big leather chair behind his desk, so this was supposed to be a casual chat, not a major meeting.

Liam, of course, was left with the sofa, which put him at least a foot lower than Tristan. Supplicant and benefactor. Lovely.

Tristan looked down and smiled gently at Liam. "Do you want to know why I didn't choose you to lead the Taybec Briggs project?"

And suddenly Liam *didn't* want to know. He didn't want to discuss Tristan's view of his failings, didn't want to be analyzed and poked apart. But that wasn't the proper answer, of course. "If there's something you think I should know," he said, "I guess I should hear it."

Tristan was quiet for a moment, then said, "What's your passion, Liam?"

What a peculiar question. "I want to create practical art," he started, but Tristan waved a hand impatiently.

"Not a regurgitation of the firm's promotional materials. I want to know *your* passion. What excites you? What do you *need* in your life?"

Liam stared at him. What was Tristan looking for? Not practical art, apparently, but—

"Let's try it another way," Tristan said. "What excited you about the Taybec Briggs project?"

"My proposal didn't make that clear?" Liam fought through the muddle of his mind. "We were going to create a unique streetscape that would seamlessly combine—"

"No! What *excited* you? What images made you feverish, made you passionate, made you obsessed with the need to create? What drove you to put all the hours you did into the proposal you created? A proposal which, I must say, showed the professionalism and aesthetic sensitivity of all your work. But what's your *passion*?" And he thumped his chest in vaguely the area of his heart.

"My passion." Liam took a deep breath. "Why are we having this conversation, Tristan? You know me. For years, I've done good work for you. I've brought in three times more business than any other associate has, and I've produced the designs the clients want. I could go to any firm in this city, with my portfolio, my client recommendations, and have a job in a second. I could start my own damn firm and have more work than I could handle. I'm not bragging about this—you know it's just the truth. I could do all of that, but I've stayed here, with you."

"You've produced the designs the clients want," Tristan said. He didn't sound like he was arguing, but his eyes were fierce when he said, "What about the designs *you* want? The ones you dream about?"

"*My*…. I'm not the client. If I had hundreds of millions of dollars to spend on major projects, I could build the designs *I* want. But I don't, so I do what they want."

"I agree. But sometimes, for a firm to stay strong, for it to thrive and lead and excel, we have to change the clients' minds about what they want. We have to show them something *better* than what they want, something more exciting, more daring. And that's what I saw from Allison's proposal for this project. And looking at her work made me realize I've *never* seen that from you."

Liam felt numb. "My designs are—"

"Professional. Polished. You bring jobs in on schedule and on budget, and I know that's a rare thing. But where's your passion? Your vision?"

"And you think Allison can do the rest of it? You think this job is *just* about vision? Jesus, Tristan, are you forgetting how much business I bring into this firm? The networking, the PR, the rainmaking, the glowing testimonials and repeat business from clients who *appreciate* me paying attention to the business side of things. You think Allison can do all of that?"

"I don't know. That's why I thought you could work with her, to help her learn that side of things. And, Liam, this is one project. I'm not *firing* you. I know what you bring to the firm, and I value it. You know I do."

"But I don't have vision or passion," Liam said dully. "You value me for my business sense, not as an architect."

"You're a solid architect. An excellent architect. But—"

Liam stood up. Whatever else was happening, whatever was beyond his control, at least he wouldn't sit there like a damn schoolboy being lectured from on high. And being vertical allowed him to pace.

"Without me you'll be laying off half your staff," he managed. Did Tristan not *see* this?

"I'm not firing you," Tristan repeated. Then he sighed. "I'm sixty-eight years old, you know. I'm still healthy and I have no plans to retire—I still love this firm far too much. I still feel *passion* for architecture, and for the work we do. But I'm at the stage of my life when I'm starting to look at my legacy. I want to see what I'm leaving behind. And I want to leave exciting, cutting-edge projects behind. Projects that pushed boundaries. I've made enough money. It's time for me to start making *art*."

Art.

There were other arguments Liam could make, but it was all suddenly too much. This old bastard and his delusions of grandeur, Liam's own powerlessness, the thought of Allison lurking in the office outside, waiting to see what the meeting was about—waiting to gloat? Liam pushed to his feet. "And you don't think I can do that. I'm done, then. I'm gone."

"For the sabbatical you mentioned. A break, a chance to refresh yourself."

"A chance to look for work elsewhere, at a firm where they appreciate my contributions."

This was really happening. His worst imaginings were coming true. There was no bigger, better project that Tristan had been holding in reserve, no misunderstanding or simple remedy or—nothing. There was no solution other than a quick escape. "I'll clear out my station. I assume you'll be contacting my existing clients, but they all have my cell number, and I imagine they'll follow up with me."

"This is unnecessary. You still have a place here. And I still look forward to seeing your proposal for our next project. As you said, our clients have always been more than pleased with your work."

"But not you," Liam said. He immediately wished he could take the words back because they just seemed like they were reopening a discussion that he absolutely, positively wanted to keep closed. He started for the door. "I quit. I hope you and Allison are very happy together."

Tristan let him have the last word, or maybe was just too slow to say anything before Liam was out of range.

He was hyperaware of Allison staring at him as he jerked open the drawers of his desk. There wasn't much that wasn't company property, and he didn't have any boxes or bags, and he'd be damned if he'd take the time to find any. His diplomas and commendations were on the wall, but they were properly anchored and would be tricky to get down. Jesus, why couldn't anything be easy?

He straightened and turned toward Allison's work station. "Tell Tristan to have my stuff packed up," he ordered. "I'll send a courier for it tomorrow."

"Liam—" she started, but he was *not* going to have a conversation with her. Not about this or about anything else.

He strode toward the door, brushed past a couple draftspeople as they entered the building without offering them any greetings, and then he was out on the street, almost gasping for air.

He'd just quit his job. He'd quit. Because—because Tristan had lost his mind, that was why. The whole thing was—it was incomprehensible. Absurd.

His cheeks felt strangely cool, and he reached up and found them wet. He was crying. Again. Walking down the sidewalk of New York City, crying like a stupid baby.

There was something seriously wrong with him. And he had no idea how to fix whatever it was.

CHAPTER FOUR

"WHO NEEDS a brain break?" Ben asked his class of fifth graders. He was gratified to see them pause and actually think about it. It was an extra step in the process—he could have just led the whole class through an exercise, or pulled out the kids he could see were struggling—but he was trying to encourage them along the path to *self*-regulation, and they needed to get better at realizing what they needed and when they needed it. "Let's have the kids who need to rev down over by the flag, and the ones who need to rev up out in the hallway."

As the kids started moving, he could see that they were making the right choices. The ones who needed to calm down a bit were heading for the flag, the ones who'd been dragging were on their way out the door, and the rest of the students were staying right where they'd been, still sorting through their math problems.

It had worked. He'd been picking away at it all year, and this was the most perfect exercise yet, and he should have been elated. Instead? "I'm going to join the flag team," he told the class. "Michelle, can you lead us? And Adeel, you okay being in charge of the hallway crew? You ready to get them pumped up?"

True to character, Michelle looked unsure and Adeel totally confident. Which was fine, because Ben was there to back Michelle up if she needed it. Not that she would—she'd be great. Hell, maybe she'd be good enough to calm him down, to ease the incessant buzzing in his brain, a drone that seemed to focus around images of Liam, emotions related to Liam, speculation and concern and warnings, all related to fucking *Liam*—

Okay, anytime Ben even *thought* the word "fucking" in a fifth-grade classroom, he needed to chill out. He sank onto the floor, cross-legged, and tried to find the right expression of nonpressuring encouragement for Michelle. "What exercise do you think we should try?" he prompted her.

"Uh—" She looked almost wild for a moment, as if she was thinking about sprinting out of the classroom, but then took a deep breath and blurted out, "Colors? Breathing colors?"

Ben nodded, and before he could speak, another student said, "Sounds good."

"We should breathe in blue," Michelle said softly. "Nice, calm, gentle blue. And we'll breathe out orange—being mad and wild all the time."

And Ben followed the drill he'd taught to the children. He visualized the swirling, calm blue in the air before him and breathed it in, deep and full, then held it for a moment before exhaling and visualizing chaotic, angry orange being pushed away from him. Right into the face of poor, sweet Michelle, but the visualization exercises never paid a whole lot of attention to the laws of air currents.

"We'll breathe in red," she said, "but a nice, purple-y red. A strong color, but not a crazy one. And we'll breathe out—that yellowy-green color that's all confused and weird."

Well, Ben wasn't a hundred percent sure that was a visualization that would make sense to most of the students, but it absolutely worked for him. Breathe in strength, breathe out confusion. Hell, yeah, he was down for that.

He could hear the kids in the hallway playing whatever stupid pop song Adeel had selected, and he knew they were having a dance party; he'd known they would as soon as he'd named Adeel as leader. And that was fine. They were kids and Ben had deliberately requested a classroom right next to the gym, where his students could be noisy without disturbing anyone else. Let them dance, let them build up some energy before they came back in to refocus their attention on math.

"Can we do blue and orange again?" a student asked from beside Michelle. "I didn't get rid of all my orange."

"Okay," Michelle agreed. "We'll breathe in blue, and breathe out orange. Is everybody ready?"

Ben breathed along with the students, then stood up when they did and went out to the hall to make sure the dancers were under some level of control.

They were, and they returned to the classroom at least a bit more energized and ready to work.

He took a rare moment of peace to stand still and watch them all. Fifth grade was the end of the simple years; after this, hormones would start gushing and they'd all become irrational, unbearable creatures. But fifth grade? Fifth grade was the breath of cool air on the mountaintop before stepping off a cliff and tumbling ass over teakettle to the valley below.

And he'd been entrusted with guiding these precious creatures through the last sane year of their lives. Jesus, what had the principal been thinking?

Well, he'd do his best and try not to get distracted. He wouldn't think about Liam, not here in this temple of learning. And not at home either, because fuck Liam! Fuck his perfect face and his deep eyes that somehow didn't go red even when he was crying, fuck his soft words and every emotion he stirred up in Ben's soul. Fuck, fuck, fuck… shit. Far too much internal swearing for a classroom.

He tried to breathe in some blue and breathe out some chartreuse, but there was too much activity in the classroom; he couldn't settle into the depth of meditation he'd need to get rid of a disturbance like Liam. He settled for bundling the negative ideas up and stuffing them into an imaginary drawer of his desk. He wasn't getting rid of them, just putting them away for the time being. He needed his full attention for the students, but he'd have to come back to the rest of it eventually.

The technique worked, more or less. Well enough to get him through the day and all the way home, but when he pulled into his driveway and saw Seth sitting there on the front porch, waiting for him, it all came rushing back.

"You're here about Liam," Ben said, forcing a smile as he walked up the path.

Seth nodded and pulled a beer out of the portable cooler by the side of his chair. "How're you doing with it?"

Ben shrugged and took the beer. "I'm fine, I guess." He settled into the wooden chair next to Seth's and kicked his feet up to rest on the porch railing. There were some kids playing a version of baseball on the lawn across the street—very calming. "I mean, it's not a big deal. I ran into some guy I used to know. That's all."

"I've been thinking about it all day—stewing about it—and if it's hitting me like that, it must be five times worse for you. So, no, I don't think he was just 'some guy you used to know.' Your first love—your only love, if we're being at all honest, which we absolutely are—breaks your heart and runs away, then turns up out of the blue. That's some crazy shit, Benny boy."

"It was surprising," Ben admitted cautiously. He pulled his feet back down from the railing. "But it's over with. It was strange, but it's done. I'm fine. It was good, really," he started, but he lost his train of thought. He'd had a theory about why it was good, hadn't he? "Or maybe not good. But everything's fine."

"Okay, you're a genteel guy, well-educated and everything. So tell me… what's the polite way for me to say that you're full of shit?"

"Perhaps you could use nonverbal communication. A raised eyebrow, a sigh or snort, a head shake…. No, not all at once, you just look like you're having a seizure. You're like a big, red, epileptic Wookie."

Seth stilled and they sat quietly for a while. Eventually Seth said, "Uncle Calvin's worried about it all."

"Oh, no, I don't think that's possible, because of course Uncle Calvin doesn't *know* about this. How could he? Liam wouldn't have told him, and I didn't tell him, and of course *you* wouldn't go blabbing all over town about my personal business. So, no, sorry, I don't think Uncle Calvin has any idea about any of this."

"I was worried about you."

"Oh my God, Seth, what did you think I was going to do? What are you, and possibly Uncle Calvin, worried *about*, exactly? 'Ben had a strange run-in with Liam and now I'm worried that Ben might….' What? What dire act do you think I'll engage in if you don't do whatever it is you're doing?"

"Well…." Seth took a swig of his beer. "There was the Kevin incident."

"Kevin wasn't an incident, he was—I don't know. And none of that was actually about Kevin anyway."

"I know. It was about Liam."

"No, that's not right. I was having a little early midlife crisis, and it just happened to coincide with some strange things in a relationship. That was all."

"He loved you and you broke up with him. You broke up with him *because* he loved you. Because you were scared, because of Liam. And your parents, probably, but that's therapy for another day. Today we're talking about your issues related to *Liam*."

"I don't think we are. I think we're talking about—Dinah. How's she doing? Has the morning sickness stopped yet? And is Tamara still excited about being a big sister?" Seth just frowned at him, so Ben added, "No, you're right. There are lots of people who are concerned about Dinah, and even Tamara. But sometimes the father gets forgotten in all this. I'm sorry if I've let that happen. So, tell me, Seth, how are *you*? It's stressful, isn't it? The expectations from society, from yourself, that you be the provider for the family, the protector. But you're bringing a new life into a totally uncertain world. How can you be sure you'll be able to rise to the challenge? Provide and protect for this precious new creature? And for Dinah, while she's preoccupied with being pregnant and looking after the new baby. That's a big job for you, right? Wow. *Stressful*."

Seth held out for a moment, then spoke in a rush. "Okay, obviously I know what you're doing, but yes, it *is* fucking stressful!"

"*So* stressful."

"Babies cost a damn fortune! Not the stuff so much—we've got lots from Tamara still, and everybody shares everything around. But all the extras! Day care and medical stuff and Dinah taking time off work, and she wants a long maternity leave, and of *course* she should be able to do that, she deserves it and our kids deserve it, but she wants me around all the time too, so we can all bond, and I want to bond but I also want to pay the damn bills, and it's kind of hard to do both, and whichever one I do less of you know there are people just lining up to judge me for it, to be *disappointed in my choices*. And then I get stressed about being too stressed, because this is supposed to be a joyful, happy time and I can't even do *that* right, and Dinah's always telling me to relax and enjoy but that's easy for her to say, all she's got to do is gestate, and I have to do everything else, and if she screws up—I mean, she's not going to screw up gestating, the baby is totally healthy and she's doing a great job—but if she did, everyone would feel sorry for her, but if I screw up, everyone's ready to jump all the hell over me!"

"Well. That was actually a bit more than I was hoping for. I was thinking in terms of a little distraction from your invasive questions. And instead—damn. Seriously, Seth, you need to at *least* not worry about *me*. I am just fine. For all the rest of it…. Yikes. Are you guys actually having trouble with money?"

"Not yet. But Dinah's a teacher. She's going to want the kids to have a good education. So that's college to pay for, and—"

"Wait. You're honestly getting this worked up about *college*? No. No, no, no. Tamara isn't even two yet, and the next one is negative three months old! That is too soon to be worried about college. If you expect me to take this panic attack seriously, I'm going to need some more concrete, immediate issues."

"What if something goes wrong with the baby? What if it needs special care or something?"

"*If* that happens, we'll deal with it. But you're still not giving me anything concrete or immediate."

"Well, I'm not sure I accept your criteria for things I should be allowed to panic about."

"No, of course you can panic about anything you want. You just can't expect me to take it seriously."

"I'm panicking because there's a new person on the way, a person I'm going to have to take care of, and I'm really not sure I'm ready for that. I'm—well, I'm still essentially a child myself. Aren't I? I'm too young for all this responsibility."

Ben leaned back in his chair and lifted his feet back up to the railing. "And how old are you, exactly? I know, we're the same age, but—"

"Seventeen," Seth said firmly. "I'm not sure about chronological age—I refuse to be limited by some arbitrary system of dates and measures. My mental age, though? Seventeen."

"You are a horribly boring seventeen-year-old. When you were chronologically seventeen, if you'd looked at this current version of yourself, you'd have been very, very disappointed."

"No Ferrari," Seth agreed morosely.

"Minimal exposure to random hot chicks. I mean, Dinah's lovely, but there's only one of her."

"Job's not bad. I should be spending more time working on race cars, less time changing the oil on family SUVs, but… seventeen-year-old me wouldn't hate my job."

"Leisure time's a bit lame," Ben declared. "No clubbing, no wild adventures on ATVs or speedboats. Just hanging out with—well. With someone you hung out with when you were seventeen. So *that's* got to be all right, surely."

"Nah. When I was—when *we* were—seventeen, we didn't expect you to stick around. Seventeen-year-old me would be pissed that you hadn't gone off on your travel adventures."

"I travel!" Ben protested.

"Going to the Czech Republic for a couple weeks *four years ago* does not count as having travel adventures. And neither does driving down to Florida every other Christmas."

"I'm not sure I accept *your* criteria for what I can count toward my travel adventures."

"When we were seventeen you were going to *live* abroad. You were going to teach in different countries or be a travel writer or—"

Ben didn't want to play this game anymore. "You're a good dad now, with one kid. You'll be a good dad when you have two kids."

But of course that shift was too sudden, and it combined with the unexpectedly kind words to let Seth know Ben wanted the topic changed immediately. But Seth couldn't just let it go. "When we were seventeen," he said slowly, "you were going to live in all different countries and so was Liam. He was going to be an architect and take on international projects, and you were going to travel with him and be versatile and make your career work around his."

"And, freed of that restraint, I've been able to settle down like the routine-loving freak I am."

"It's not too late, you know." Seth looked thoughtful. "Your pathological inability to commit to a long-term relationship has the useful side effect of you not being tied down. Might be time to grab hold of that silver lining and let the cloud—lift you up? Is that at all possible?"

"No. Clouds are collections of water vapor. They are not balloons. And they have no actual linings."

"Pretty crappy metaphor, then, isn't it?"

"To be fair," Ben said, "I think you were stretching it much further than any metaphor deserves to be stretched."

"A bit of stretching is good for things. Push them out of their comfort zone... no, crap, I can't make that work either. I'm just not that great at metaphors."

"Possibly no figurative language is needed. We could just say it straight out. You're dissatisfied with how I'm living my life. My decisions don't meet your expectations. You'd like me to be bolder, more adventurous."

Seth nodded. "It's kind of hard to live vicariously through you when you're not doing anything interesting."

"But it's probably important that I live my life the way that's best for me, rather than the way that's best for you. Wouldn't you say?"

"No, I wouldn't go that far."

They took a little break then, both of them finishing their beers, starting new ones, and watching as the baseball game across the street deteriorated into chaos and mild violence.

Finally Seth said, "If this is the life you chose, and the life you want, then I'm happy for you and I'll do my best to shut up. But if it's the life you just kind of fell into because you were afraid to make different decisions? That's no good."

"My life is the same today as it was the day before yesterday. So why am I getting the big speech now?"

"You know why."

"Because of Liam. But… what about him? Had you actually forgotten he existed or something? You saw him and it just twigged for you? Like, 'Oh, yeah, this guy used to be one of my best friends, and he and my other best friend used to be together, but they broke up. Huh. That puts a whole new spin on things.' Was that what happened?"

"No." Seth picked at the label on his beer bottle for a little, then said, "I miss him. Seeing him—I guess that's what it reminded me of. It made me sad to think how close we all used to be. I mean, the two of us here is good. It's fine. But it used to be the three of us."

"The three of us used to hang out on this porch? Back when the Corrigans lived here? I don't remember that."

"You know what I mean. The three of us used to be friends."

"You and I thought so, at least." But Ben caught himself. "Or—fine, yeah, we were friends. He just didn't—" *Didn't love me. Didn't care enough to be faithful, or at least honest.* He pushed himself to his feet. "Okay. This has been a fun little visit, but I've got dinner to make, marking to do, lessons to plan. And I think you might have some sort of responsibility elsewhere? Some sort of guilt-inducing, soul-crushing burden of love and pain that you need to get back to?"

Seth finished his beer. "Okay. Good talk. I feel like we really resolved a lot, here. We've got a positive action plan, moving forward with focus and determination. Excellent."

"I'm focused and determined to make dinner, do some grading, and plan lessons."

"Uncle Calvin's going to want to talk to you."

"Yeah, thanks for that. Sure is a good thing you didn't keep your damn mouth shut."

"He's Uncle Calvin," Seth said as if he actually thought it was a useful observation.

He left after that, setting off for the short walk to his own house two blocks away, and Ben went inside to his small, functional kitchen. Inside his small, functional house and his small, functional life. He *had* dreamed of a larger world, back when he'd been a kid. He'd craved adventure and excitement.

Now? He was making a chicken breast and brown rice for one, wondering whether he should get crazy and add half a can of mushroom soup to the pot. Ooh, a casserole.

And the biggest excitement in the last... year? More than that, probably. The biggest excitement since Tamara had been born was that his ex-boyfriend had made a brief appearance in town.

And cried.

Liam had *cried*.

What the hell had that been about? Ben had seen tears in the man's eyes only once before, in their final confrontation. And now more tears?

Ben impatiently pushed himself away from the counter. He wasn't going to fall into the trap. Hell no. He'd done his time, torn himself apart trying to figure out what was going on in Liam's head, and he'd gotten nowhere. That was all in the past.

Liam was in the past. He'd popped in and popped out and now he was gone again.

It was a sign of something deeply wrong with Ben that he was actually feeling disappointed with that reality.

CHAPTER FIVE

LIAM KNEW he should be making plans. Either finding his own office space and staff or setting up meetings with other firms that would be interested in hiring him. He definitely needed to get in touch with old clients and give them his spin on the situation. He should be attending to business.

Instead, he got his car back from the shop and started driving again. North again, and then west. Again.

How many times had he made this trip over the years? All the way to the Welcome to North Falls sign, then loop around and drive home, because the sign was a lie and he wasn't "welcome" in North Falls, not by a long shot.

But this time he drove straight past the sign. Down the south hill and over the bridge, and he pulled over for a moment to look down at the park where he and—where all of them used to hang out before they were old enough to have friends with driver's licenses who could take them out to the lake. Wading in the mud by the riverside, dodging goose shit to find places to lie in the grass and gaze up at the sky. Talking without looking at each other and later, finally, *touching*, just hands or feet or other safe parts, still without looking at each other.

Some real Mayberry shit. Except a couple years later, they'd started coming back to the park after dark. All their friends were at the lake, but this thing between them wasn't for public consumption, not yet. Instead, they'd come to the park and found the shadows and they'd touched each other everywhere, hungry and confident. They'd gasped into each other's mouths, strained into each other as if trying to meld their entire bodies together. Ben's face, pale and perfect in the moonlight, his eyes, so deep and trusting—

Yeah, trusting. You asshole. Don't even think about him. You don't deserve to.

Liam put the car back into gear and continued into town. The familiar stores, the bank, the church, the post office. How the hell did he manage to have memories of Ben from every single building? Sure, it was just the post office *steps* they'd spent time on, that summer after seventh grade when they'd all been into skateboarding and the three of them had spent endless hours trying to grind their ways down the metal handrail.

That had ended when Seth broke his collarbone and his and Liam's parents outlawed any sort of stunting. Ben still could have practiced—he'd been living with Uncle Calvin by then, and Calvin, while generally loving, departed from contemporary parenting wisdom in many ways. He'd been almost gleefully willing to let Ben learn by trying things and making mistakes. But it wouldn't have been any fun for Ben to skateboard alone.

And there it was again. Liam was thinking about Ben. Seth too, but Ben, mostly.

He made it through town and up the north hill, turned left, and drove to the end of the dead-end street. A cul-de-sac, his mother had always called it, but Liam really wasn't sure it qualified. Regardless of the precise designation, it had been a quiet street, except for when the big yellow house at the end of it hosted one of its frequent parties.

He pulled up on the shoulder and looked at the house. Did the same people own it, the ones who'd bought it from his parents? They'd been the new medical team, two doctors to take over the clinic and the town GP practice.

Almost twenty years ago now—his parents had stayed in town until he finished high school, then headed off to semiretirement in South Carolina. During college he'd gone to visit them occasionally, always dragging Ben and usually Seth along with him, but for most breaks he'd returned to North Falls and stayed with Ben at Uncle Calvin's, two of them crammed into Ben's old single bed.

Yeah, Ben. Ben, Ben, Ben.

Was there an inch of this town not drenched in memories of Ben?

Maybe for some people, but not for Liam.

He did a quick U-turn and headed back into town.

See them as buildings, he told himself. *Be an architect. Analyze the structure.*

But there was nothing architecturally significant about the buildings, nothing interesting, even. His career had been dedicated to clean, modern design that made a statement. There was none of that here in North Falls.

He should go back to the city. That was where he belonged.

But he pulled over, as he'd known he would, outside the small-engine-repair shop. A two-story building with rented apartments on the second floor and a glass-fronted shop on the first. Lawn mowers and chainsaws and log-splitters on display in the front window, the inside of the building too dark to be visible from outdoors.

Liam sat for a moment and wrestled with his better judgment. Nothing he'd done so far was irreversible. Nobody had seen him; he had plausible deniability. His ignition had betrayed him the other day, but he had no such excuse now.

He got out of the car anyway. It felt as if he wasn't really making any decisions, just being swept along in a current of… fate? No, nothing so purposeful. Momentum, maybe. He'd set something in motion, and it was inclined to stay in motion. Shit, was that momentum, or inertia? Momentum had a better sound to it, but maybe inertia was more accurate, and somehow more fitting considering that he was in North Falls.

And what "something" was he thinking of, anyway, that he'd set in motion?

He pushed the door open, heard the bell chime, and smelled the familiar motor oil, the scent that had been carried home on Calvin's clothes to perfume the little house where he and his nephew had lived. And not much else seemed to have changed either. The same displays of parts and tools, the same battered leather stools, and the same grizzled head poking up from behind the counter. Maybe a little less hair and a few more wrinkles, but the eyes were just as sharp. Just as perceptive.

And they showed absolutely no surprise.

"Liam." Calvin gave him a cordial nod of greeting. "You got a haircut."

Liam felt numb but fought to sound coherent. "I've had quite a few, I guess. But, yeah, my hair is shorter now. In general." There, now that they had that taken care of, he could go back to the city and get on with his life.

"I heard you have a nice car."

It wasn't like Liam's family had ever been short of money, but they'd been a bit less—*a bit less ostentatious?*—a bit less interested in high-performance vehicles. "It's not a Ferrari or anything."

"Still, German engineering. I fought in Germany during the war, you know."

Liam frowned. It was the first he'd heard of any military service, and he really wasn't sure the years matched up. "What war?"

"Vietnam."

"I—wasn't aware there was a lot of fighting in Germany during the Vietnam War."

"Sure. Bar fights never really go out of style."

Liam sighed. What the hell was he doing in North Falls? "Were you even in Germany during the Vietnam War, or did you make that up just for the joke?"

"I was there. I did the standard backpack-around-Europe thing when I was a kid. Saw some pretty nice cars."

Okay, they were back to—well, no, talking about cars hadn't really been the point of the conversation. But it wasn't as if Liam had any idea what the point of the conversation *had* been. Maybe it was time he got a little more direct. "It's good to see you. You look well."

"Thanks. You too. Where are you staying while you're here?"

Staying? Oh, no. No, that wasn't what Liam was doing. Not at all.

But then Calvin said, "This isn't the best place for a real talk. I know, it's not Grand Central Station, but I do have customers coming in and out. We should have a few drinks tonight and get caught up."

And suddenly it sounded like the best possible way to spend an evening. Was it warm enough for a fire in Calvin's fire pit? Probably, if they wore jackets. He and Calvin could sit back there with a bottle of scotch and a couple glasses, staring into the flames, talking when the mood struck them. Maybe Liam would even share the situation at work; Calvin had no patience with mindless authority and lots of respect for people who did their jobs well and without drama, so he'd be outraged on Liam's behalf. That would be nice.

"I guess I could stay. But I don't know where. There's still no hotel, I assume?"

"Connie and Dale Ingram have a bed-and-breakfast. I've never stayed there, obviously, but they're good people. They'd do a good job."

Liam recognized the names, but—a B&B? Possibly his worst nightmare. And he was less than three hours from the city. He could just hang out with Uncle Calvin for a couple hours and drive home afterward.

Drunk.

Shit.

"Do you have their number?"

"Nope. I don't have much patience with those newfangled devices."

"Telephones?"

"Blabber-boxes, if you ask me."

"I've talked on the phone with you lots of times. Not lately, but there isn't much 'newfangled' about—" Liam caught himself. He wasn't going to be dragged into another one of Calvin's nonsensical conversations, at least not until he had a glass of scotch in his hand. "Okay. How can I get in touch with them?"

"Just drive over. River Road, west of Main Street. It's a purple house."

"Purple?"

Calvin shrugged. "It's a nice purple. Almost blue."

"And they're legitimately running a B&B. You're not sending me over to some stranger's house to embarrass myself with weird questions about wanting to sleep in their spare bedroom."

"Damn. That would have been excellent—why didn't you suggest it *before* I sent you to the right place?"

It should have been reassuring, but Uncle Calvin was absolutely devious enough to pull that sort of double-cross, especially if he resented Liam for what had happened with Ben. Which surely he did. "Is there a sign or anything? Something that will tell me I'm in the right place?"

"When you see a purple house, you'll know you've arrived."

"And we can have a drink later? Maybe a fire at your place?"

"Are you coming on to me, Liam? I'm flattered, but…."

Liam was suddenly tired of games. "I'm only staying over because of you. Because I like the idea of talking to you. So if that's not going to happen, there's no point in going through all the rest of it, and I'd appreciate it if you could just tell me that now and save me the trouble of—" He stopped. Calvin was Ben's uncle, his only real family. If Calvin wanted to make Liam jump through some pointless hoops, Liam needed to just shut up and take it. "Sorry. Okay. I'll go see the Ingrams. And if you have some time later—"

"Come for dinner. Six o'clock."

Liam tried to find the trap. "Yeah?"

"You haven't turned vegan or gone gluten-free or anything?"

"No...."

"Good. I'll grill some steaks. Bring a nice red wine."

"Anything else? To go with the steaks?"

"What, are you all city-fancy now? You can't just have a steak and be glad of it?"

"You'll make garlic potatoes," Liam said. He was beginning to remember who he was dealing with. "And something green. You honestly won't worry about it other than that—could be spinach or asparagus or beans or lime Jell-O as long as it's green. And I'm not complaining about that. But you tend to want something sweet as well. Should I pick up dessert somewhere?"

"I prefer homemade."

"Do you like apples?" Liam forced himself away from a *Good Will Hunting* reference he didn't think he could pull off. "Because I'm not currently *at* my home, so if you want anything fancier than apples—"

"Are you saying you have homemade apples? Apples you made in your home, in New York City? Yes, please. Bring me some of those. And the wine. Probably two bottles. At least."

Liam should have engaged more. But how? He could have explained that his apples wouldn't be homegrown, which Calvin clearly knew. What a waste of breath. Why the hell had he thought it would be good to spend more time with this maddening, juvenile pain in the ass?

"Bring some scotch too," Calvin said, and Liam immediately found himself thinking much more favorably about his plans for the evening. "And something warm to wear, so we can sit by the fire. Well, you probably don't have anything like that with you. But I have some of Ben's other castoffs stored away somewhere. I can dig them up for you."

Liam let himself take the hit. Had Ben cast him off? Technically, yes. In the eyes of a doting—well, no, *doting* wasn't the right word— in the eyes of an *affectionate* uncle, had Ben been the one to end their relationship? Yes.

And Liam would accept that. He'd let himself be painted as the victim rather than the villain. Here, in North Falls, he'd let that happen. Nowhere but here.

So he didn't argue with Calvin's "castoffs" comment. What Liam had done to make Ben cast him off? Well, it was nothing he and Uncle Calvin needed to discuss.

"Six o'clock," he confirmed, then left. The B&B, the liquor store, and maybe a bakery or something. He could hit the little department store next to the bank and get a pair of sweatpants to sleep in, maybe some clean underwear.

Hell, he had lots of time. He could drive over to Monticello and do his shopping there, or even find a motel to stay in. B&Bs were unnatural and wrong.

But he found himself reluctant to leave North Falls. It wasn't logical, but he felt like he'd set something—he had no idea what—in motion, and he needed to stick around until it was resolved. Somehow. He'd stumbled into Brigadoon, and if he left now, he'd never be able to find it again.

Yeah, that was some excellent decision making. Very wise of him to not be back in the city putting his life in order; totally logical that he was hanging around in North Falls instead, preparing himself for dinner with Ben's uncle. *Ben's* uncle.

Maybe it was nothing to do with Ben. Maybe... maybe Liam's subconscious was helping him out. New York was a big city, but the architecture world was pretty small. Word of Liam's departure would be circulating by now, creating a stir. Enterprising firms would be recognizing the possibilities.

In a couple days, Liam would be able to make some calls and be greeted with "We were hoping you'd think of us" with no need for awkward explanations.

He was playing hard to get, building up anticipation and demand—something like that. Yeah, it made sense. He was wise to be staying in North Falls for a couple days.

No, wait. For *one* day. Not a couple. *One* day in North Falls. Then back to the city where he belonged.

CHAPTER SIX

BEN SQUINTED at the sheet of paper lying on his desk, covered with barely legible pencil scratches, then turned to look at the boy standing by his elbow. Cole was a great kid and had a good mind, as long as he was able to respond verbally or physically. If he had to actually write something down? Chaos ensued.

"Tell me what's going on here," Ben suggested. "Walk me through it."

But Cole hadn't even started talking when a commotion arose in the far corner of the classroom. An overturned chair, a desk skidding noisily across the floor— "Peyton and Ty," Ben said. Well, possibly he yelled, but only because he needed to be heard, not because he was on his last nerve with these two. "You will *not* start that nonsense again. There is no fighting in this classroom. Not in this whole school. And you both know it."

"He called me a slut!" Peyton responded. Ah, yes, the charming innocence of fifth grade. And Peyton was nice and loud, of course, so every kid could go home and tell their parents about the kind of language Ben allowed in his classroom.

"Totally unacceptable," Ben said firmly. "But you respond with words or you come get me for help. You do *not* get physical." Of course, that wasn't enough. Cole would have to wait to get help with his work. "Both of you. Hallway. *Now*."

They exchanged glares but did as they were told. That was a bit of a victory, at least.

In the hallway, he positioned himself so he could still see the classroom but the classroom couldn't see Peyton or Ty. An audience was never a good thing when working with misbehaving kids. "Ty, did you really call her that?"

"It's just the truth. You know what she—"

"No," Ben said. "That's not any of my business or any of your business so we're not going to talk about it." Although Ben would try to make it his business later, or maybe ask one of his female colleagues to intervene. Hopefully Ty just meant Peyton had held hands with two boys in the same week, but it could be something much more serious. "We don't call people names, Ty. You know that."

"He's been saying that stuff about me all year," Peyton said. She was crying now, not even trying to hide the tears. Damn, what would it be like to show emotion so plainly, so fearlessly? "And my mom said I don't have to take it. She said he can't talk to me like that."

"She's totally right. You don't have to take it." Ben caught himself before he asked the *but did she tell you to start a fight with him in the middle of the classroom* question, because knowing Peyton's mom it was totally possible she had. "But there are different ways of stopping him. Using your words, and if your words don't work, asking for help. You know I wouldn't let him call you that, not if I knew it was happening. Right?"

Peyton glared. "I can handle it myself! I don't need to go running to some teacher for help."

"You can't handle it with violence. Not in my classroom."

"So if someone called you a fag, you'd just take it?" she retorted.

This wasn't going well. Ben could practically hear the mother's words in Peyton's voice; this was a discussion that had been well rehearsed at home. He needed a new strategy. "Ty, go back inside and sit at the desk next to mine. Start writing. Explain to me why it's inappropriate to call classmates names. If you do a good enough job, I'll be able to tell your parents you seem to understand the problem. If you do a bad job, I'll have to tell them you don't have a good grasp of appropriate behavior and will be spending your recesses with me, talking it through, until you do understand."

"You're going to call my parents?"

Good, that was still a consequence that meant something. "I am. What I tell them when I call? Well, some of that is up to you. Get writing."

Ty returned to the classroom, chastened at least temporarily. Ben turned back to Peyton. "If you'd told me he was using that language, he'd be in trouble and you'd be back in the class with your friends. But you *didn't* tell me, and you lost your cool. It's okay to be angry, Peyton, and that language is *absolutely* something worth getting angry about. But as soon as you get physical, as soon as you start a fight, especially with a kid who's about six inches shorter than you are, you lose the moral high ground."

"And if someone called you a fag, what would you do?"

"You're presenting it like it's a hypothetical... *if* someone did that, what would I do. But, Peyton, I've been called that name *lots* of times. And sometimes I get mad when it happens, sure." He leaned into the classroom and announced, "I'm just outside the door. Stay focused on your work, please." Then he looked back at Peyton. "But other people aren't in charge of me. They can't control me like that. They say a word and I *have* to start a fight? No way. I'm in charge of me. Nobody else."

"Like it's so easy."

"You know all the exercises we do in class? You know they have a purpose, right? They're not just a fun way to get out of doing work for a few minutes. They're designed to help us be in charge of ourselves, so our emotions don't take us over. And I don't just make you guys do them. I do them myself. They work for me, and that's why I encourage you guys to try."

"Ty calls me a slut and I'm supposed to do deep breathing?"

"If you can use the deep breathing or anything else to keep yourself under control, fine. If you can't, you tell me and I help you out. But he's saying mean things to get you upset. You know that. So as soon as you get upset, you've given him what he wants. He's won. Do you really want Ty to win this?"

She'd stopped crying, at least, and she was listening. But they'd had similar conversations in the past and she'd seemed to listen to them, too, so Ben wasn't expecting any miracle cures.

"I don't want him to win," she admitted. "But my mom says emotions are good. We're *supposed* to have emotions."

"It's about *controlling* them, not deleting them. You might even say I experience my emotions *more* than some other people because I can recognize them and appreciate them as they occur."

"You can appreciate being mad because someone calls you a—"

"Wait. I let you use the word a few times because it seemed like part of a larger point you were making, but you've used it enough now. It's not a word that's allowed in this school, and you know it."

"My mom says—"

"Let's have a meeting. You, your mom, and me. I'll call her today and see what we can set up." He looked back into the classroom. "I have to get back in there before someone sets fire to the curtains. But this isn't over. This conversation? It's going to keep going. I promise. In the meantime, though, stay cool. It is *not* okay for you to get physical, no matter what words someone uses. Clear?"

"My mom says—"

"I'll hear from your mom when we have our meeting. But this isn't her classroom, it's mine. No violence."

He'd let his student repeat hateful slurs, interrupted her multiple times, and essentially issued a challenge to her mother. Great work. His Teacher of the Year award was probably waiting in his mailbox at home.

Still, the kids calmed down and made it through the rest of the day without anything serious happening. He made his phone calls, got mortification and promises of retribution from Ty's mom and vitriol from Peyton's, and packed up his regular banker's box of journals, workbooks, and miscellaneous projects. He had an exciting weekend of marking and lesson planning ahead of him.

Behind the wheel of his battered Toyota, he headed out toward Main Street. He walked to work whenever he could, but he always seemed to be lugging too much stuff. Maybe he could get some sort of— not a baby stroller, not a wagon, not a damn shopping cart, but some sort of contraption that would let him carry more stuff. That would be good. A good example to the kids too—

He stopped at the Main Street stop sign, looked both ways, then pulled out into the intersection, turning right as the car from the other side of the intersection waited to turn left. The car—the Mercedes sports car—with Liam Marshall behind the wheel.

Liam Marshall.

Liam Marshall.

A horn blared and Ben jerked the wheel, but he was too late. A jolt he felt in his whole body, the screech of metal against metal, and he wasn't sure if his car stopped because he'd slammed on the brakes or because it was hopelessly entangled with the front panel of the—

Oh shit. Entangled with the front panel of the police car he'd just sideswiped.

Everything stood still for a moment, and then Liam—*Liam Marshall!*— appeared at the hood of Ben's car, peering in through the front windshield, eyes wide. "Are you okay?" he yelled.

Ben tried to figure out an answer to the question. He must be fine—he hadn't been going more than ten or fifteen miles an hour, and he was pretty sure the police car had been stationary.

On the other hand, he'd just run into a stationary police car, so "okay" didn't really seem like the right word to describe his state.

"I'm uninjured," he said, but not very loudly.

"What?" Liam yelled back at him.

Liam. Liam Marshall was standing outside Ben's car, yelling at him.

"I may have bumped my head," he said, louder this time. Because it made more sense for all of this to be some sort of hallucination than for Liam to be back in town. Didn't it?

The police officer was out of the car, now. She must have slid across the front seat and exited from the passenger side, since the driver door was still jammed up against Ben's.

Laura Doncaster. Damn. There weren't that many North Falls police officers to choose from, but any of the others would have been better than Laura Doncaster.

"Sir," she said now, as loud and officious as if she were teaching a "how to intimidate civilians" course at the police academy. "Please get out of the car. Now."

Well, that was a reasonable request. But his driver side door was jammed and the passenger seat was piled high with the box of schoolwork, his lunch containers, the snow pants he'd worn on yard duty all winter and was planning to take to the cleaners' when he got around to it, a variety of fabric shopping bags, some of which might have stuff in them—

He hit the button to lower his windows, and miraculously, they worked. "It'll take me a minute," he called through the new opening. And then, because the officer was scowling as if she was about to pull out her gun and fill him with lead, he added, "Sorry, Laura. I'm sure this isn't exactly—"

"Sir. Get out of the car immediately."

"Laura?" Liam said from outside the car. He sounded pleasantly surprised, even charmed. "Laura Doncaster? Wow, it's you!"

"Liam?" she replied. And it became clear that his reaction hadn't been because he was charmed, it had been because he was charming. Laura dimpled like a little girl staring at her first crush. "Holy smokes, Liam, it's really good to see you!"

"You too," he gushed. And behind his back so only Ben could see he made a frantic sort of hand gesture that clearly meant *hurry up and get out of there before I run out of ways to be interested in Laura Doncaster*. "You look great—and you're a police officer! That's fantastic! You always were a leader, so it's a great career for you. Are you enjoying it?"

Ben was temporarily distracted by trying to figure out any way Laura had ever led anything but her little clique of mean girls, but he managed to call himself back to the job of maneuvering around the pile of crap in his front seat. Some of it he jammed into the back, but the banker's box would probably be harder to move than to just slither over—or so he believed until he found himself stuck partway across, his back arched as he braced against the headrest and tried to figure out what his jacket was caught on, how he could get his left foot up and over the gearshift, whether it was too late to reach down and slide the seat back to give himself more room....

Then the passenger door opened, and someone—no, not someone, *Liam*—eased the banker's box out from beneath him, and suddenly everything got five times easier. Still not exactly simple, because Ben was tall and the car was small and he really hadn't planned things out too smoothly, but definitely a lot better than before.

"I have no idea how else to help," Liam said, and it was the amusement in his voice that pushed Ben over the edge.

"You've done enough already," he snapped. "More than enough. What the hell are you even doing here?"

"Have you been drinking, sir?" Laura demanded.

"Oh my God, Laura, enough with the *sir*! We went to school together for *fourteen years*! I used to take piano lessons from your mom and you hit me with a baseball bat in third grade—you knocked out two of my teeth!"

"They were baby teeth. And none of that answers my question about drinking. Sir."

"No, I haven't been drinking! I was at work. Yeah, at the same school you and I spent so much time at together. I teach in the old eighth-grade classroom, the room where you and that blonde girl who was only here for a couple years—what was her name?"

"Stacey Martin?" Liam suggested.

"The room where you and Stacey Martin got caught drinking wine coolers before the spring dance. But, no, *I* don't drink in that classroom. That's not *my* trick."

"Sir," Laura started, and there was enough chill in her voice that Ben knew he needed to stop or he was going to end up in handcuffs. Not because he deserved it, just because he was dealing with Laura Doncaster. Well, also because he'd just sideswiped a police car for no good reason.

Except there *had* been a good reason. Liam Marshall.

Liam fucking Marshall.

"Why are you here?" he demanded of Liam. At least he managed to squirm the rest of the way out of the car as he said it.

"I'm trying to help," Liam said.

"Sir. Please pay attention. I will be administering a field sobriety test—"

"I'm not *drunk*!"

"So you should have no problem with the test. Please look at this pen, sir. I'm going to move the pen and you need to—Ben! Pay attention! You need to follow the pen with your eyes."

Well, at least she'd dropped the "sir," although she picked it up again as she ran him through the other tests. Walking heel-to-toe, standing on one foot—all on Main Street with half the town staring at him. With Liam Marshall staring at him.

Ben tried to do his breathing, tried to bundle up his emotions and store them in an imaginary glove box, tried to turn the stupid sobriety tests into mini meditations, focusing his awareness of the weight of his entire body on one foot, the way it shifted his muscles and changed his balance—

"Sir. Have you consumed any medications or other drugs today?"

"What the hell? I kicked ass on those tests, Laura. Don't even try telling me I failed!"

"People don't usually make that humming sound while performing the one-leg stand test. Not unless they're *high*."

"I was meditating!"

"Were you *meditating* when you ran into my cruiser?"

"No. I was—okay, obviously I messed up. And I don't mean to sound—well, I guess mostly I don't mean to sound drunk or high—but also I don't mean to sound like it wasn't a big deal that I ran into you. But it could have been a lot worse, right? If I'd hit a pedestrian, or an old person—"

"If there had been kids in the car," Liam contributed.

Ben scowled at him. "The point is, considering how bad my mistake was, this is actually a pretty good outcome. Can we try to focus on the positives?"

"The positives."

"I sense you don't want to focus on the positives. Okay, I can understand that. You're the victim here. I got distracted. This is all my fault. Absolutely." Except it wasn't *all* his fault, because he'd been a safe driver his entire life, and the only reason he'd messed up was that *Liam Marshall* had suddenly appeared where he had no damn reason to be. But that was something he'd worry about later. "What's the next step? We're kind of blocking the street." Not that there was much traffic in North Falls, even on Main Street. "Do we need to take photographs or something, or can we just—"

"Sir. Please, let the professionals handle this." Laura glowered at him. "Please step to the side of the thoroughfare and wait. I have already radioed for backup and for the assistance of mechanical operators." She turned to Liam. "And can you stick around as well? We're going to need a witness statement."

"Sure," Liam agreed easily. Of course it was easy for *him*.

Ben followed him grudgingly to the sidewalk, and they turned in unison and sat down on the broad steps of the post office.

"I got a ticket the other day," Liam said.

"Was it for ramming a stationary cop car?"

"Uh, no. I wasn't quite that ambitious. But the cop who pulled me over knew me. I had no idea who he was."

Well, that wasn't too interesting, but it was better than thinking about whatever the hell Laura Doncaster was up to. "You were in town?"

"No, the highway. But I think the guy knew me from here."

"Paul Dixson is a state trooper. Do you remember Paul?"

"Maybe. Shit, yeah, it might have been him."

"He didn't sign the ticket?"

"I guess he might have, but I didn't look."

"So it's not like you actually care who it was. Not like this conversation is of any value to you."

"I was trying to be of value to *you*. I thought it might be good if you were distracted from yelling at Laura Doncaster. *Officer* Doncaster."

"Don't do me any favors." And then, because it was even more surreal and awkward to sit and *not* talk to Liam than it was to sit and talk to him, Ben added, "Why are you here? What's the sudden interest in North Falls these days?"

Liam sighed. "I'm not totally sure. I guess maybe—"

The tow truck arrived and Liam stopped talking. He and Ben watched in silence as Seth climbed out of the truck, stared at the two conjoined cars, and started laughing. Yeah, he recognized Ben's Toyota. Asshole.

Seth looked over at Ben, did a classic double take when he saw Liam, and made a sort of exasperated *WTF?* gesture in his direction, then looked back at the cars and started laughing again.

Ben let himself collapse at the waist and cradled his head in his hands. "Why are you here?" he whined. He wasn't sure if he was addressing the question to Liam or to himself, but regardless, he didn't get an answer.

CHAPTER SEVEN

"HEARD YOU were a witness to the big crime today," Uncle Calvin said as he stood back and let Liam through the front door.

"Not exactly a crime," Liam replied absently. He was distracted by the house, by the familiar and unfamiliar aspects of it. Distracted by how comfortable he was, how instantly he felt at home. "You got a new sofa."

"About ten years ago." Calvin clapped him on the shoulder. "Come on into the kitchen. Pour us some wine and tell me about my desperado nephew."

"He was totally law-abiding," Liam said. "After that one little glitch, he was fine."

"And what about this little glitch? What happened there?"

"I don't know," Liam said. Easier to be ignorant than to try to explain. "Have you talked to him, or just heard about this from everyone else? He'd probably be the best one to tell you what happened."

"I called." Calvin grinned wolfishly as he handed two empty wineglasses over to Liam. "He told me to leave him alone and let him be a complete loser in private. I thought about inviting him over tonight without telling him you were here, just to make his humiliation complete, but... well, I can't say I thought better of it, but I got distracted by something else, and by the time I remembered it was too late."

"And that's the truth? You really didn't invite him over? Because, Calvin, he's made it *completely* clear on both occasions I've seen him that he doesn't want anything to do with me. At all."

"He's made it clear to me too. But, you know—we don't always get what we want."

"I think in this case he should. I mean, I screwed up. I hurt him." Damn, even after all the years, it was still hard to admit to that last bit. Liam distracted himself for a moment with pouring wine, but forced himself to continue. "If he doesn't want to see me, I should absolutely respect that."

"So what the hell are you doing here?" Calvin sounded calm, curious rather than confrontational. "In North Falls, sure, but—at his uncle's house? You think of that as respecting his wishes?"

"Well—I mean—I can respect his wishes without being a total martyr, can't I? You and I used to be pretty close. Coming to a town I used to live in, dropping in on an old friend—that has to be allowed, I think."

Calvin nodded. "Fair enough. You respect his wishes—right up to the point that they get in the way of something you want to do." He lifted the wineglass and took a sip. "Come to think of it, that's kind of what got you in trouble last time, wasn't it? You saw something—someone—you wanted, and you went for it because you wanted it. Didn't worry too much about what Ben wanted."

Liam took a gulp of wine and wished for something stronger. Calvin still sounded calm, but obviously the words were—well. The words were true, and they were exactly what Liam deserved. Except— "Monogamy may not be as important in gay culture as it is in straight culture. You know, we don't have to worry about pregnancy or anything, and we're already challenging one social expectation, so maybe it's not that big of a deal if we challenge another. It's really much more common for gay men to have open relationships—"

"Wait. Are you saying you and Ben had talked about this, and you'd agreed to an open relationship?"

"Well—no. But if we had…."

"If you'd both been goats, it would have been okay for one or both of you to go and fuck another goat. But since neither one of you *is* a goat, the hypothetical doesn't apply. No need to complicate things with a bunch of 'ifs,' is there?" Calvin smiled easily and sprinkled some seasoning onto the steaks in front of him. "You cheated. You hurt him. You can just leave it there, without the justifications."

"So why *am* I here? I don't mean North Falls—although, God, if you can tell me what the hell I'm doing back in this damn town, that'd be great to hear. But I can't really expect you to be able to figure that out when it's got me so totally confused. But why am I in your house? I cheated on someone you love. I hurt him. I did. So why did you invite me over for dinner?"

"It's been fifteen years, boy. You were just a kid. You fucked up, absolutely, but you've paid for that, haven't you? Yes, you hurt Ben, but you hurt yourself too. Don't even try to pretend you didn't. You loved him as much as he loved you. You losing him?" Calvin shook his head. "Damn. That's enough punishment. You don't need to have me adding more on top of it, do you?"

And Jesus Christ, there were the goddamn *tears* again. They were coming faster, Liam was pretty sure. There'd been absolutely no warning this time: he'd been fine, if a little tense, and then? Fuck.

He turned away and took another gulp of wine. He looked up at the ceiling because after the last ridiculous incident he'd googled ways to stop crying and apparently looking upward was supposed to help. Made him feel like he was praying to the second floor of the house, but maybe that wasn't completely inappropriate—he and Ben had definitely come pretty damn close to heaven up there in Ben's narrow little bed.

"You upset?" Calvin asked. "You getting a wittle weepy about your horrible man pain?"

"Okay, you're a man too. I think 'man pain' is really only an insult when it comes from a woman."

"It's not an insult at all. You're a man and you have pain. It's legit."

"And the 'wittle weepy' part?"

"Well, that was a bit much, maybe. But I'm giving you a damn fine dinner. If I want to say some stupid shit while I'm cooking, that's just a cross you'll have to bear." He jerked his head toward the counter. "Grab the wine bottle and those potatoes. It's time for grillin'." He lifted the steaks and started toward the back door. "You can season our meat with your salty tears."

The potatoes were wrapped in tinfoil, and Liam could smell the garlic as soon as he lifted the packet. His mouth watered in anticipation—great, maybe his mouth could steal some of the moisture supply that kept his eyes so ready to spill over—and he wondered why he never made any of these foods for himself. It wasn't like the recipe was tricky. But it was garlic *powder*, he remembered, not fresh garlic.

It wasn't that the recipe was too tricky—it wasn't tricky *enough*. Not fancy enough for his sophisticated life. Gobs of butter, heaps of garlic powder, halved new potatoes, and tinfoil. It was food for peasants, for rural folk, for suburbanites, not for the urban elite like him.

It was going to be so damn tasty.

And whether it was the salivating or the upward-looking, his eyes seemed to have dried up. He handed his precious cargo over to Calvin, who set the tinfoil packet on the preheated grill, and then they both sank down on opposite sides of the battered picnic table.

"This is good," Calvin said, swirling his glass. "Argentinian Malbec, I believe? Nice and earthy—probably a 2012?"

"I saw you reading the bottle."

"I didn't read 'earthy,' though! I made that up myself!"

"It should go well with the steak." And Liam was pretty sure he would have been happy to just keep talking about wine and steak for the whole rest of the night. Just a breather, a rest, a respite from whatever the hell was going on in the rest of his life.

Calvin, of course, wasn't known for letting things rest. "So, what's going on with you? You've been in town two times in three days. Your parents are long gone, and nobody much else has heard from you since—well. Since you did that horrible thing you did. The thing so terrible it cannot be mentioned. The earth-shaking, soul-shattering betrayal of all that humanity values. Since that. So why are you back up here now?"

And just as much as Liam had wanted to keep talking about meaningless things? Now he suddenly wanted to talk about this. Because he was sitting across the table from Uncle Calvin, slightly manic Sage of the Northlands, and it would be a shame to lose the opportunity. "How old do you have to be to have a midlife crisis?"

"Haven't had mine yet, and I'm in my sixties. Try another excuse."

"Vision quest?"

"You're a little old for that, if you're thinking of the Native American ritual. And a little young if you're thinking about the wrestling movie."

Liam sighed, then refilled his wineglass. "I've been up here before. Lots of times. I usually make it to the town sign and turn around. But the other day—I kept going."

Calvin held out his own empty glass for a refill. "Why?"

And Liam told him all of it. No deep analysis, no conclusions. Just the shit with the project, the conversation with Tristan, the overwhelming sense—and if he was honest, it was a sense he'd had before, not just since things started going wrong at work—that he was missing something. That he wasn't doing life *right*.

"Maybe your boss wasn't wrong." Calvin had stood up halfway through Liam's story and put the steaks on the grill, and now he was standing over them, tongs poised and ready. "Pompous and annoying? Yeah, probably. But all the shit about finding your passion... was he wrong about that? Have you really been passionate about what you've been doing?"

Liam wanted to stand up and pace, but he forced himself to stay still. "*You're* saying this? You run a small-engine-repair shop. You think—I mean, where's *your* passion?"

"Small engines," Calvin said as if it was obvious. He turned to face Liam as he said, "I fucking love them. The logic of them, the self-contained genius of it all. I can tear a small engine down and build it back up all with my own two hands. I run my own business, because *that's* self-contained too. Small engines are the ultimate passion for someone who values independence. Hell yeah." He turned back to the grill, lifted the steaks up onto the warming rack, then turned back around. "Now you tell me. What's so cool about architecture? About working for your power-tripping boss and all your Richie Rich clients. Tell me why it's great. But before you do?" Calvin leaned down so their eyes were level. "Pretend you're talking to Ben. Pretend you're talking to someone who sees through your bullshit and your smooth talking, someone who know *you* for who you are. Tell *him* what's so great about your job."

Even without the extra, Liam might have been honest. But thinking about telling it to Ben? Shit. That pushed him over the edge. "Part of it's the prestige," he admitted. "The ego boost. Seeing something I designed getting built? Like, someone spending a hundred million dollars on making something from *my brain* into reality? That's a rush. Absolutely."

"And your name goes on it."

"Well, no. The firm's name. Tristan's name. But that actually proves it's *not* all about ego, right? I mean, the clients probably know who did most of the work, but the rest of the world doesn't. And I'm okay with that, more or less."

"More or less?"

"I'm not saying I don't resent it sometimes. But—no. I'm okay with it, mostly."

"You love your job. You just quit a job you love."

"Are those steaks ready? There's been a lot of buildup for this meal, and I don't want a dried-out steak just because I started babbling about some stupid job bullshit."

"The steaks are resting. Did you just quit a job you love?"

"No," Liam said. As soon as the word was out of his mouth he knew it was the truth. "But lots of people don't love their jobs. I made good money, I met interesting people—"

"*Interesting* people? Or *rich* people?"

"Some of the rich people were interesting. There's no monopoly on character for the working class, you know. Just because someone's got money doesn't automatically mean they're shallow or boring."

"Roughly what percentage of rich people are deep and interesting, would you say?"

"Probably about the same percentage of poor people who are deep and interesting."

"Damn. That few?" Calvin pointed his chin toward a stainless-steel bowl on the table. "Toss that, will you? Salad."

"Green."

"That's right." Calvin was working on the potatoes now, tumbling them out of their greasy, garlicky foil and splitting them evenly between two plates. "This is a well-balanced meal. Now we just need to work on your well-balanced life."

"Yeah, maybe that's part of it," Liam mused as he dished up the salad. "I've been working a *lot*, for a long time. Maybe I just kept coming back up here because when I lived here I didn't work. I mean, being a camp counselor over the summer isn't *working*, right? So maybe I've been drawn to North Falls because it's the last place I really had any leisure time."

"Leisure time. And when you had that leisure time, what were you doing with it?"

Hanging out with Ben, obviously. But Seth had been there too. Lots of people had been there. "We talk about kids today being overscheduled. Maybe I'm an overscheduled adult. It wasn't so much that I was doing exciting things with my leisure time, necessarily, it's just that it was free. I could just lie on the grass and listen to the river flowing by, if I wanted."

"And have you done that yet on this visit? Gone to lie in the grass by the river?"

"No. But maybe I will tomorrow."

"Or maybe you should go see Ben tomorrow." Calvin gave no indication that he'd just dropped a bomb like that. He was still totally casual as he lifted the steaks off the grill and slapped them onto the plates.

Liam, on the other hand, was reeling. "Ben. Go see him. You think— no, we've been through this. I should respect his wishes."

"Has he repeated his wishes lately, or are these just the ones you heard fifteen years ago?"

"There was a lot of 'fuck you' at the cemetery. And I think he told me to go away. He definitely said I was an asshole."

"But that could have just been the shock talking."

"And today he kept muttering, 'Why are you here, why are you here.' It didn't sound like he was all that happy about it."

"Well, he'd just rammed into Laura Doncaster's cruiser. He probably wasn't thinking too clearly."

"Is this real? Do you actually think this would be a good idea, or are you just trying to fuck with both of us?"

"Liam?" Calvin said quietly. "How do you feel right now? Excited, nervous, apprehensive but eager? Maybe even some butterflies?" He found a seat on the other side of the picnic table and casually speared some lettuce onto his fork. "When was the last time you felt this way at your job?"

"So—wait. Was all this stuff about visiting Ben—was it just a test? A trap? You were trying to get me worked up about something so you could prove I'm *not* worked up enough about my career? Or do you actually think I should go see Ben, and you just threw the work stuff into the conversation because you've always got to be clever and talking about two or three different things at the same time?"

"What do you want the answer to be?"

"Aw, fuck you, Yoda, you're not my shrink and I'm not playing your games." He speared a potato and chomped it, and his hostility melted away as the rich, garlicky butter washed over his taste buds. He groaned in pleasure. "Son of a bitch, I missed these potatoes."

"The potatoes missed you too."

"Wait. The *potatoes* missed me?"

"Yeah, that didn't work. I was trying too hard—you got me inspired with the 'Yoda' business, and the thought of *three* different meanings when I'm usually sweating just to have two. I meant—damn it, Liam. Ben loved you. He's gotten past it—it's not like he's been sitting around pining over you, not by a long shot. But he loved you, and he's missed you. You guys were good friends before you were anything else. Maybe it's possible for you to be good friends again. If you have the balls to give it a try."

Liam looked for the trap but he couldn't find it. "Maybe," he finally agreed.

"Okay. That's enough for tonight. Now you can tell me about your glamorous, outrageous life in the big city, with plenty of anecdotes, hopefully including some about celebrities, and I will listen and enjoy without even the hint of a question about whether your life there is as meaningful as it should be."

"And you'll tell me gossip about everyone in town, hopefully with *no* mention of celebrities, and I'll listen without wondering if there's a hidden meaning or moral to your stories."

"Sounds good."

And with only a few glitches they managed to stick to their conversational plans.

Liam strolled back to the B&B shortly before midnight, not drunk but certainly not in any condition to drive, still pleasantly full from the meal, and overall feeling more satisfied, more at peace, than he had in years.

It was probably just the alcohol making him feel that way, but he'd been drunk plenty of times in the past fifteen years. He could give the credit to the steak, but he'd had lots of steak.

Damn. It was the potatoes. The buttery, garlicky wonders.

It wasn't North Falls, wasn't the conversation with Calvin, wasn't the thought that he could go see Ben the next day with a reasonably clear conscience since he was operating with Uncle Calvin's blessing. No, it was the potatoes.

"I'm going to make them for myself," Liam said out loud as he turned up the path to the purple house. "I can have garlic potatoes anytime I want."

But he wasn't sure they'd taste quite the same in the city. Wasn't sure the magic would work outside of North Falls.

"I'll figure something out," he told himself. It was surprisingly optimistic, considering everything that had happened lately. Must have been the potatoes giving him such a good attitude.

CHAPTER EIGHT

BEN'S PHONE rang early that Saturday morning. He squinted at the alarm clock. Oh. Not all that early, really, but he'd tossed and turned all night, restless and fretful, so he *deserved* a bit of a lie-in. But he wasn't going to get it, apparently.

He fumbled his phone off the bedside table, scowled at the call display, then answered the call and lifted the phone to his ear. "What?" he demanded. He'd wanted it to sound like a growl, but it came out more like a whine. Damn it.

"Morning, Sunshine," Seth said cheerfully. When Tamara was a baby, Seth had been assigned the 5:00 a.m. feeding, and it seemed to have permanently transformed him into an early riser. It was really annoying. "What are you doing?"

"I was *sleeping*."

"Oh. Sorry. But you don't want to waste the whole day, do you? It's past nine. We should do something!"

"Are you about to suggest I come over and help you with outside chores?"

"I wasn't, but I appreciate your offer and I gratefully accept! Wear long sleeves because we need to do something with those raspberry bushes."

"Why *did* you call, then?"

"Oh, yeah. Because—okay, I honestly have no idea if I should even mention this. But I'm going to."

"Are you? Sometime soon, maybe?"

"Rissa called me, just now. I'm not working this weekend, but there was a weird situation, and she wanted you to be aware of it but she didn't want to call you herself, so...."

Rissa was Seth's co-owner at the garage. "The car's worse than we thought? Shit, Seth, how much is this going to cost me?"

"Funny you should ask that, actually. Because—maybe nothing."

"Maybe it's going to cost me nothing? What? Like, it's a write-off? If you're trying to put a positive spin on my car being a write-off, you should stop trying. Damn it, what—"

"Not a write-off. But... possibly a concerned citizen has stepped forward and wants to pay for the repairs."

"Possibly... a concerned citizen?"

"Not a citizen of North Falls, necessarily. At least, not anymore."

"Liam wants to pay for my car repairs?"

"Apparently he feels responsible for the accident."

"He *was* responsible for the accident!"

"Really? He was sitting beside you and he reached out and grabbed the wheel and made you run into Laura Doncaster? Because I've pictured this event a lot of times in my mind—and Dinah has pictured it a lot, too, and she is *very* grateful to you for the amusement—but in none of my imaginings was Liam actually in the car with you."

"He wasn't in the car, but—"

"But he jumped out in front of you, causing you to heroically swerve into Laura Doncaster's Chariot of Authority."

"He didn't jump. But he has no damn business being in town, and he caught me by surprise."

"And then you caught Laura Doncaster by surprise."

"Could you please stop talking about Laura Doncaster?"

"But it's okay if we keep talking about Liam?"

"God, better him than Laura!"

"Really. That's a bit of a change, isn't it? I mean—"

"Okay, yeah, I didn't mean it. I don't want to talk about either one of them." Except he kind of did. Well, not about *Laura*. "Liam offered to pay? He went to the garage?" Because he thought Ben was pathetic and needed charity, and because he didn't want the nuisance of talking to Ben again. Whatever the hell Liam was doing in town, it had nothing to do with Ben. This proved that. If he'd wanted to see Ben again, this would have been a great excuse, but he hadn't.

"Rissa said she wouldn't take payment from him without your permission. So I think he may be trying to talk to you to get your permission. Possibly pretty soon."

The doorbell rang.

Ben looked down at himself. Ratty T-shirt, old cutoff sweatpants. He knew his hair was messy, he hadn't shaved, he had morning breath, and he fully expected there were some creases on his face from the pillow because he'd been really, really asleep when the phone rang.

"Is Liam Marshall ringing my doorbell?" he asked in a small voice. "Rissa gave him my address?"

"No, but it's not like he'd have trouble finding someone who would. Everyone knows you, and—well, he's Liam Marshall. People like helping him out."

"This town needs to do some thinking about its priorities. And maybe have a review of privacy legislation." He looked frantically around the room. Should he hide? Was hiding an acceptable response? But if he hid, Liam would go away, and—oh, God, what was he thinking? He wanted Liam to go away. He *needed* to want Liam to go away.

"Are you going to answer the door?" Seth asked. "Damn, I wish I had a video of this. Can we FaceTime?"

"No. Go away."

"Are you going to—" Seth started, but Ben hung up on him.

Liam Marshall was at the door. The door of Ben's house. Their previous meetings had been public, unplanned, rushed, chaotic. This one was... what the hell was this one? Still pretty chaotic, if the churning in Ben's gut was any indication.

Shit. He needed to make a decision. Answer the door or hide under the bed? No, not under the bed. Too dusty. The closet—

And strangely enough, that was what got him moving. He wasn't in the closet. Never had been, never would be. He wouldn't hide who he was, and he wouldn't hide from Liam Marshall.

He resolutely refused to glance into the mirror as he passed the open bathroom door. He didn't care what he looked like. This was going to be a conversation about financial restitution, not fashion.

He yanked the wooden door open and scowled through the screen door out into the bright sunlight. Liam was backlit, the sun forming a fucking halo around his too-perfect face. Because of course that's how it was. Stupid sun. Just one more vote for the sainthood of Liam Marshall.

"What?" Ben said, and this time his voice was much more growly than it had been on the phone.

"I'm sorry—did I wake you?" Liam looked shocked by the possibility. "Is it still early? Shit, I'm sorry. I woke up a long time ago, and the garage was open, and the bakery was open....” He held out a brown paper bag. “I guess I didn't look at the actual time. I brought you cinnamon buns. I don't know if you still like them. I can just leave them, though, and you can go back to sleep. Sorry.”

“You say ‘sorry’ a lot.”

Liam frowned. “I guess I have a lot to apologize for.”

“But ‘sorry’ isn't magic. It doesn't actually change anything.” This was a much deeper conversation than Ben had intended, but now that he'd started it was hard to stop. “It's just—you should stop doing the things you need to apologize for. Shouldn't you? Rather than just doing them and thinking that an apology will make everything better?”

“Right.” Liam stepped backward. “Sor—” He grimaced. “Should I just tell you why I'm here, or would you rather I left and came back later?”

Ben knew better. Of *course* he knew better. But he pushed the screen door open anyway. “I'm awake now. I'll make coffee. Have you already eaten?”

“No.” Liam stepped forward cautiously, clearly looking for a trap, which was a pretty good idea on his part. “But I don't want to intrude.”

For a quick moment, Ben wished he'd had company the night before. Someone really hot, someone casually affectionate—he'd stroll out from the kitchen wearing nothing but boxer briefs, showing off his ripped body and big bulge, and he'd have a mug of coffee for Ben and he'd nuzzle in over his shoulder and kiss Ben's neck and whisper, “Is he staying, or do I get you to myself?” And then—

Well. None of that was going to happen, damn it. “You're not intruding,” Ben said, although it was obviously untrue and he wasn't going to try too hard to pretend otherwise. “Come in.”

As soon as Liam stepped inside, Ben wished he'd suggested they stay out on the porch. It was too strange, too damned intimate having Liam in his house. But Liam strolled in as if everything was totally natural, totally fine, and he glanced around, then smiled. “This place suits you. The colors and everything. It feels like—like *you*.”

“You have no idea what I ‘feel like.’ Not anymore.” Ben turned quickly and headed for the kitchen. What the hell was he doing? If he was going to let Liam into the house, which he'd already done, then he needed to be a better host. Not gracious, maybe, but at least not bitchy. "Sorry," he said, and Liam snorted. Yeah, okay, it *wasn't* a magic word.

"I don't need to be here," Liam said. "If you don't want me here, say so. I went by the garage and asked to pay for the repairs to your car but they wouldn't take my money without your permission. I just wanted to ask you if that was okay. And if it's okay, can you call the garage? Then I can get out of your hair."

And in true preteen angst-monster fashion, Ben hated the idea of letting Liam leave. Letting him walk away again, to be gone for another fifteen years? God, it was unthinkable. "I'll make us coffee," he said, trying to sound calm and less likely to snap Liam's head off. Shit, trying to make himself attractive, acceptable, like a desperate fifties housewife trying to lure her cheating husband back to the nest. Was that what he was doing? Was he *that* pathetic?

"Shit," he said, and he turned to face Liam. "What's going on? I feel like—well, okay, I was just all bitchy about you not knowing, but fuck, Liam, *I* don't know what I feel like, not anymore. Why are you here? I don't mean at the house—no, you can't pay for the car repairs. So if that's all this was, we're done. But if you're going to stay, I want to know why you're in North Falls. You've been away a long damn time, you know. What are you doing here now?"

Liam stared back at him, and it was as if they'd jumped back to who they'd been when they were kids. Ben could read the indecision on Liam's face, the struggle between keeping up his perfect façade or letting himself be open and honest and vulnerable. And just as it had when they were kids, the honest option won. "I have no idea what I'm doing here," he said quietly. "No idea what I'm doing anywhere. I—I don't know."

"Huh." Ben let himself be distracted for a moment by the familiar ritual of measuring coffee grounds and pouring water. But it didn't take long, and while he waited for the coffee to start flowing he looked back toward Liam. "You're okay, though? No terminal illness or big tragedy or anything?"

"I quit my job. But that's not exactly a tragedy. I think—I don't know, the work stuff was the final straw or something. The trigger? But I don't think it's the whole problem."

"Okay." And strangely, it *was* okay. "There's a problem. Something we can analyze and figure out and solve. Right?"

"We?" Liam smiled softly but shook his head. "I can't drag you into whatever this is. After—after what I did—"

"After you cheated on me. Might as well get the words out there." Ben found two mugs, then turned around quickly. "And while we're at it, let's get *all* the words out there. Because you cheated on me a *lot*. Not just the one time you got caught. Right? That wasn't—it wasn't a one-time thing. Not a one-*guy* thing."

"Not a *lot*," Liam protested. He stopped and looked at the floor. "But, yeah. More than one time. More than one guy."

"And I *knew*." There it was. The truth Ben had never shared with anyone, had barely admitted to himself. "I *knew*, and I didn't say anything. Didn't stop you. You just kept getting more and more obvious, like you were fucking *daring* me to bust you. Is that what you were doing? Were you too chickenshit to break up with me like a man so you just kept pushing and pushing? Because you had to know Seth was on his way to your apartment. You could have gotten that guy out of there faster if you'd wanted to. But you didn't want to, did you? You *wanted* to get caught."

"I don't know," Liam whispered. Then in a stronger voice, "What about you? What the hell were you thinking? Why *didn't* you bust me any of the other times? Was it some sort of a game? Did you even fucking *care* that I was doing it?"

They stood there in the kitchen, staring at each other. The coffee was forgotten, the *years* were forgotten, and it was just the two of them again, having the fight they should have had fifteen years earlier. But Ben didn't want to fight anymore. "We were just kids," he said. They'd been in their twenties, but barely, and neither of them had been especially mature for their ages. It felt like an important realization. Like the first step toward forgiveness, not just for Liam but for himself. "We didn't know how to have a relationship. Didn't know we had to *work* at them, didn't know they needed to be cared for and maintained. We thought…."

"We thought love was magic. Thought it was all we needed." Liam shook his head. "No, wait. *I* fucked up. This wasn't—I mean, you not being perfect or not having a clear idea of what was going on is no damned excuse for what I—for me cheating on you."

"No, it's not. But that was a long time ago." Strange how liberating it was to say so. "I can't keep being angry about that. I shouldn't have stayed angry as long as I have." He let the words fill the air, then nodded. "Yeah. That feels right. You fucked up. Absolutely. But we were friends for a long time before we were anything else. I don't want to keep—I don't know, keep denying that, I guess. I don't want to keep ignoring it. We might not have worked as a couple, but we worked as friends, didn't we?"

Liam swallowed hard and looked up at the ceiling as if he thought there might be an answer written on it. "Yeah," he finally said. "We were good friends. At least I think we were. I guess Seth might not agree."

"Seth's a dad now." Possibly not entirely relevant, but maybe it kind of was. "He's got a daughter, and another on the way. He's different. Well, he's still Seth, but he's grown up too."

"Calvin told me about that. The kids, I mean."

"You've seen Uncle Calvin?"

"I stopped by the store yesterday. He invited me over for dinner last night."

"He did? What a liar. He called me yesterday after work and said he had a hot date."

"He was a perfect gentleman all evening."

An awkward pause, then, and Ben tried to ignore it by filling the coffee mugs. "Still just milk?"

"Yeah, thanks."

Ben doctored the coffee and it felt so normal, so cozy, so... so much the way things were *meant* to be. But he couldn't let himself fall into that trap. He'd let go of the past. That was good. But with no past, he and Liam were just two guys, two former friends, having a cup of coffee together before going their separate ways. It was important to remember that.

So it made no sense that Ben turned around, handed the mug to Liam, and said, "You want to come over to Seth's with me? We have to at least deal with his raspberry bushes, and if there's extra help, he'll absolutely have extra work."

"You think Seth would want me there?"

"I think Seth would welcome Saddam Hussein back from hell if he knew the guy was going to help him with the raspberries." Liam didn't object right away so Ben added, "You look pretty citified. I can lend you work clothes if you want. I think we're still both about the same size."

"Citified? I'm wearing jeans."

"Yeah, but I bet they cost a couple hundred dollars, right? At least? And your shirt looks casual, but it's probably woven from the webs of endangered South American fishing spiders or something. You don't want raspberry thorns snagging that fabric. And don't get me started on those shoes."

"I wore one of your jackets last night." Liam looked—not guilty, exactly, but maybe apprehensive? "That green corduroy one you found at the thrift store?"

"You wore—" Ben stopped himself. Was there any reason to continue? Would it be better to just keep his mouth shut?

But while he was dithering, Liam added, "Calvin said he didn't think you'd mind."

And that was too much. "Calvin said that?" One more effort at self-control, but it was no use. "Oh, man. That jacket—I got totally drunk after graduation and puked all over it. I mean, there was puke in the *pockets*. It was everywhere. And I couldn't make myself wear it after that, so Calvin used it for—I don't know, he used it for *everything*. Like, at least one cat has had kittens on that jacket. Blood and feline vaginal fluids soaking right into it. And I'm pretty sure he used it as a big rag sometimes to mop up whatever disgusting crap came along. He—I never knew why he didn't just throw it out. But I guess—" Ben struggled to keep a straight face, but it wasn't easy, not with Liam looking as queasy as he was. "I guess he was saving it for a special occasion."

"Feline vaginal fluid," Liam echoed.

"Don't forget the puke. And you remember Casper? When he got older he couldn't always make it through the night without pissing on himself, and I'm pretty sure Uncle Calvin had him use that jacket as a dog bed."

Liam nodded slowly, processing, then frowned at Ben. "You were never a big drinker. You got so drunk you puked on yourself? After graduation. That was—"

Just after Liam and Ben had broken up. Instead of leaving for their long-planned backpacking trip across Europe, Ben had spent his summer in the magical land of drunken self-pity. Yeah, drowning his sorrows and puking on himself hadn't been a one-time occurrence. "Uncle Calvin put up with a lot from me. Cleaned up a lot of my messes. No idea why he decided to keep the damn jacket, though."

"It wasn't—it wasn't actively disgusting last night. He must have washed it."

"At least hosed it off and hung it out to dry."

"I thought—" Liam shook his head. "He sounded like he'd forgiven me. Like he wasn't mad at me about it all. I thought we were okay, him and me."

And he seemed genuinely hurt to think otherwise. "Liam." Ben waited until Liam looked at him. "He didn't give you the jacket because he was mad at you. Uncle Calvin doesn't mess around with people he doesn't like. It's his weirdass way of showing affection. You know this." Or at least he'd used to know it. "He cut my hair in my sleep *three different times* when I was a teenager. It's not like he was trying to make a point—he didn't care how long my hair was. He was just being a brat. Or remember when we came back from school that first fall and there were those damn birds stalking us? Staring at us through the bedroom window all the time? Uncle Calvin trained *multiple* birds of a variety of species to perch on that windowsill and stare inside. The cranky old coot just has too much time on his hands—it's nothing to do with being mad at you."

Liam eventually nodded. "Sorry. I'm all—I don't even know. I'm a bit of a mess these days. But, yeah, okay, I do know that about Calvin." He sipped his coffee, peered into the mug as if looking for answers to universal questions, then nodded again. "Yeah. If you're sure Seth will be okay with it, I'd like to come help with the raspberry bushes. Or whatever else needs to be done."

"I can safely predict that you and I will handle the raspberries and Seth will do anything else he can think of to avoid going near them. He says it's a redhead thing and his skin is more delicate than normal people's, more vulnerable to scratches. But probably he's just a weenie."

"If you could arrange to fight with him about that, then I could be on his side, and I'd earn some points that way. Any chance of that happening?"

"Me fighting with Seth while I'm doing his raspberry pruning? It's practically guaranteed."

"Okay. If you're sure—"

"It'll be fine. Let me find you something to—oh. I guess myself too." How had Ben managed to ignore his own state of partial dress for so long? How was it still so damn easy to be comfortable with Liam, even after all the crap and all the years? "Let me find both of us something to wear. Guaranteed puke-free."

"Also no feline vaginal fluids, if that can be arranged."

"Trickier, but I'll see what I can do."

Ben took his coffee with him as he retreated to his bedroom. His hand trembled a little as he set the mug on his dresser.

Liam Marshall was in his kitchen. He was drinking coffee, and he was going to go over to Seth's and prune raspberry bushes. This was all real. It was happening.

What if Liam came to the bedroom door just then? If he stepped inside, set his own mug on the dresser, stood in front of Ben, reached for the ragged hem of his shirt, lifted the fabric over his head....

Jesus Christ! None of that was going to happen! And if Liam lost his mind and started it, Ben would absolutely end it. Absolutely.

He yanked a drawer open and pulled out a pair of jeans, then another. Liam wearing his clothes. It was just a practical thing, and Ben couldn't let himself obsess about it. When the day was over, Ben would throw the jeans in the laundry all jumbled up with other clothes, wash it all away, not do anything creepy—

There was a knock on the half-open bedroom door. "Ben?"

Ben's stomach flipped. It was happening. Liam was—

"Do you have clothes for me?"

Right. Clothes. Raspberry bushes and other menial chores. "Yeah, hang on."

And then the devil took over. That was the only excuse—certainly it wasn't *Ben* who stepped out of his shorts and pulled one of the pairs of jeans on, doing the fly up only partway, leaving the button undone. It couldn't be *Ben* who was in charge of pulling off his T-shirt and opening the bedroom door half-naked.

He was about the same size he'd been in college, but everything was tighter, now, the baby fat totally gone. Maybe he wasn't like some model or something Liam might date in the city, but he was in good shape.

And judging by the way Liam froze and then jerked his gaze away, he had the same weakness for Ben's exposed skin as he'd had years ago.

Or else he was shocked and embarrassed on Ben's behalf. Mortified that Ben was debasing himself this way.

Shit. Where was a shirt?

Ben shoved the extra pair of jeans in Liam's general direction. "Here." He reached into the drawer and grabbed the nearest soft fabric his hand found. "And here."

"You—you want me to wear that?"

Ben looked at the shirt. It was canary yellow with green lettering celebrating a race he'd completed a few years earlier. The ugliest item in his wardrobe.

He yanked it back. "No. Possibly feline vaginal fluids on that one." He pulled a plain navy T-shirt out of the drawer and stepped backward, away from the whole scenario. The whole mess. "Pick whatever you want."

Shirt on, he combed his fingers through his hair and then pulled his sock drawer open. "I only have one pair of work boots, but I have running shoes you can borrow."

"Ben, if you don't want me to come, I don't have to."

Shit. Ben took a deep breath, tried to exhale the chaotic rainbow racing through his entire body, then breathed in again. Blue, damn it. Calm, easy, deep blue. "No, it's fine. Sorry. I just—I don't know. It's just really strange that you're here."

"Strange in a bad way?"

"Strange in an unsettling way." An invasive, disorienting, frightening way. "But the Battle of the Raspberry Patch requires all available recruits. Pick a shirt and we'll get going."

Because surely it would be okay if they just got the hell out of the bedroom. Maybe out of the house altogether. Sure, yeah, everything would be fine once they were over at Seth and Dinah's. Tamara would be there, for God's sake, and if there was anything less sexy, less complicated, less confusing than a toddler, Ben couldn't think of what it would be.

"Right," Liam agreed, and he pulled a shirt out of the drawer, seemingly at random.

"Okay. Shoes in the front hall, and then we're ready."

"Yeah… but, Ben?"

Ben turned and raised an eyebrow in question.

"You planning to do up your pants before we go? Or is that how the cool kids are dressing these days?"

"Shit," Ben said. He was close enough to the bedroom door that he could just keep walking as he fumbled with his fly, and hopefully that meant Liam didn't see his flaming cheeks.

It was all so awkward. So silly, so unnatural, so wrong. Well... maybe not unnatural. Maybe not wrong. But it was damn peculiar, that was for sure. It was *strange* to have Liam back in town.

Strange. But bad? Well. Ben would wait and see about that.

CHAPTER NINE

"JESUS CHRIST." Liam stared at the wild jumble of thorny vines in Seth's backyard. "It's apocalyptic. Instead of pruning, should we try napalm?"

"Not unless you want your first meeting with Dinah to go pretty damn poorly," Seth advised from his safe spot on the porch. He had Tamara in his arms, since Dinah was off running errands, and he had already declared that as much as he'd like to help with the raspberries, his childcare duties had to come first. "That's just a year's growth. Well, two years, I guess. The bastards are clever—they grow the cane one year, the berries the next, so you can't kill 'em until after their second year. Not if you want the berries."

"They sell raspberries at the grocery store, don't they?"

"Sacrilege. Those berries aren't as tasty, plus they cost a lot. This is nature's bounty here, buddy. These plants were put on the planet to provide juicy nourishment to my friends and family. They can't be disrespected."

Ben returned from the shed, carrying a set of loppers, a bow rake, and two pairs of heavy leather gloves. "It's a ritual," he told Liam. "Me doing the work, Seth preaching about the sanctity of my labors. Tradition."

"You could think of it as penance," Seth suggested. "If you bring me a few promising canes, I'll whip up a couple crowns of thorns." Then he frowned at Liam. "Or maybe just one."

Liam didn't respond to that dig. Seth had been reasonably courteous and welcoming when Liam had shown up at his front door, but that didn't mean he'd forgotten his totally valid grudge. Liam was on probation, and he'd be stupid to push for more.

"I think we can skip the accessories," Ben said. He handed a pair of gloves to Liam, then said, "I'll start with the loppers and you can be my faithful assistant?"

"Maybe not 'faithful,'" Seth interjected from the porch.

Ben ignored the interruption. "You can use the rake to pull the canes up and away from my face. I'll duck under and cut the old canes close to the ground, and you'll use the rake to pull them free? We can switch after a while."

"Maybe we should pull them all out and plant something else instead," Liam suggested, but he reached out with the rake as directed. "Strawberries don't have thorns, do they? Blueberries? Those are delicious. Goji berries? Really, there are hardly any berries that *do* have thorns. Seems like it'd be easy to avoid this nonsense."

"There are even thornless raspberries," Ben said. He looked up from his crouched position and smiled. "But they don't taste as good."

"The blood of the gardener is good fertilizer?"

"Must be."

They worked quietly for a while, falling into easy, companionable teamwork. After twenty minutes, with only a few fairly shallow scratches to Ben's face, they switched jobs and kept going, then switched back when it seemed fair.

It felt good. Well, no. The job itself felt backbreaking, scratchy, frustrating, and pointless. But working with Ben? *Being* with Ben? It was frighteningly perfect.

Little huffs of frustration followed by rueful laughter when the berry bushes didn't cooperate. Shared triumph when a stubborn cane surrendered. Almost telepathic awareness of each other's plans and actions, anticipation and communication and synergistic intent….

Was it like sex? Well, no, not unless sex with Ben was a lot thornier than Liam remembered it. Maybe it was just like friendship.

"You guys remember you'll have to burn the old stuff, right?" Seth called down from the porch. "You might want to get started on that soonish so you don't have too big of a pile built up."

Yeah, friendship, with all the thorns. "It's a good thing you're holding a child," Liam said, "or you'd be getting some pretty clear suggestions for where you could shove any brambles that need to be stored before burning."

"But I *am* holding a child." Seth lifted Tamara up, *Lion King* style, and displayed her to the backyard. "She is my sword and my shield, my heart and my helm—"

"Your daddy's a bit loopy, Tam," Ben called.

Tamara giggled and stretched her arms out in a better approximation of flying.

Liam stood a little too quickly and felt a raspberry thorn snag at his face. An itchy sting, not even real pain. Only that, in exchange for the privilege of being part of this moment, part of this silly, meaningless, *nothing* piece of time.

But Ben stepped closer and pulled off a glove, then reached up and ran his thumb over Liam's cheek, and the nothingness turned into eternity. The two of them standing together, facing each other, Ben touching Liam, Liam staring back, afraid to move or even breathe in case it broke the spell.

Ben held his thumb up. "You're bleeding," he said gently.

"Fertilizer," Liam managed.

"I don't want to send you back to the city all scratched up. You arrived in pristine condition. You should leave here the same way."

The words were right there. *I don't have to leave.* Or even *I don't want to leave. I could stay here and the scratch would heal and all of this, all of everything, could just fade away as a lesson learned.*

But of course Liam couldn't say that. He *wouldn't* say it, at least. He'd been impulsive before and Ben had gotten hurt; he needed to be more controlled, more careful now. He couldn't give in to some ridiculous berry-induced euphoria. He was an adult, and he had his own life, his own ambitions and dreams, far away from North Falls. Far away from Ben Harding.

And his phone rang as if on cue. It broke the spell, which was probably a good thing, and he stepped away as he fished the device out of his pocket.

It was Marius, Tristan's assistant. There was no reason for him to be calling, surely? The thing with Tristan was done.

But it wouldn't be *truly* done until it was finished in Liam's head, and that wouldn't happen until he was able to take a simple phone call without his chest racing and his stomach churning unpleasantly. He made himself answer.

"Liam," Marius said. He sounded agitated. "We need you here— *Tristan* needs you."

"He needs me for what?"

"He's had a heart attack—well, maybe. He's with the doctors now. We're at the hospital. But he asked me to get hold of you. It only makes sense—he won't be back at work for a while at least, and he needs someone who can hold it all together for him. That's you, right?"

"I don't work for Tristan anymore, Marius. Did the two of you forget that?"

"He's in the *hospital*! He could have *died*! This is no time for pride or stubbornness or whatever it was that got between you two. He needs you now, Liam. Don't let him down."

It was an opportunity. Impossible to deny that.

Liam looked around at the ragged backyard, the half-pruned raspberry patch. Seth and his daughter. Ben.

Ben.

But Liam couldn't live in a magical garden forever. He'd traveled back in time, but it was only for a visit. He wasn't a kid anymore, and his adult life was in the city. It wasn't with Ben. Was it?

"I'll call you back in a couple minutes," he told Marius, then hung up without waiting for a reply.

Ben was watching him, waiting.

"I might have to go back to the city," Liam said.

Ben nodded. "Well, yeah. That's where you live, right?"

"Soon. Like, now. I might need to go back right away. A friend— well, no, not a friend, but my boss—my former boss—is in the hospital."

"I hope it's nothing serious?" Polite concern. That was all.

Of course that was all, because Ben had always been the one with common sense. He'd been the one to keep his feet on the ground and stay connected to reality. He'd humored Liam's flights of fancy, maybe even encouraged them, but he'd never indulged in them himself.

So of course he knew that this visit was something short-term. Of course he knew Liam had to go back to the city.

"They think it may be a heart attack."

"Your car's at my place. You'll have to walk back there and get changed. There's coffee still in the pot, and I have lots of travel mugs— they give them out like popcorn at teachers' conferences. You wouldn't have to worry about returning it or anything."

Wow. Yeah, Ben was more than happy to see him leave.

"What about the raspberry bushes?"

"I'll stay here and finish them off. We've made a good start, but it's already pretty late in the year. Seth should have gotten this done over the winter. I should get them taken care of before they overgrow the house and eat Tamara."

Right. Liam wasn't needed. Ben had it all under control.

Of course he did.

Still, Liam couldn't quite give up. "I can come back," he said. "When I get all this sorted out? I can come back."

Ben looked at him for far too long, and Liam braced himself for what was coming next.

COME BACK. Liam could come back. Liam could tease and tantalize, appearing and disappearing according to whatever important city events he was working around. And Ben could turn himself inside out with anticipation, then crush himself with disappointment when plans fell through. When Liam didn't keep his promises.

Considering how early it was in the day, there was absolutely no excuse for how exhausted Ben suddenly felt. But he supposed he'd gone through more emotional highs and lows that morning than he usually managed in a week, so maybe it made sense. Made sense that he was tired, and made sense that he take steps to avoid any more draining situations.

"Obviously I can't stop you from coming back to North Falls. I still don't really understand what you're looking for, here, but—I hope you find it. Assuming it's actually here. But in terms of coming back to my house? If that's what you meant?" He braced himself and forced a sympathetic smile. Liam was the one with a problem, not Ben. *Liam* should be pitied. "Probably not the best idea, right? It's good that we cleared the air. But that was just wrapping up old business. Now that everything's tidy, we should leave it alone." He turned away for a moment, long enough to snap the loper blades shut around a couple raspberry canes. "Good to see you, though." *Now go. Please, just go, before you notice how my hands are shaking, how I can't look at you, how much of a fucking loser I still am. Please leave me with at least a little dignity this time.*

"Can I—" Liam's phone trilled a notification, and he made a frustrated noise.

Ben took a deep breath, found a bit of strength, and forced a smile onto his face. "Your people need you," he said. Then he raised his voice. "Seth? We're down one knight in the heroic battle against evil. You might need to put some armor on and get out here."

"But who will protect the princess?"

"The princess can help. You're not scared of some stupid raspberry bushes, are you, Tamara?"

"Not scared," Tamara said and began to wriggle out of Seth's arms.

Good. A distraction. "You can come help me make plans while your daddy finds a long-sleeve shirt to shield his tender skin." Ben started toward the porch, but he was still aware of Liam right behind him. Far too aware.

Maybe Ben should have walked faster, but he didn't, so he was close enough to hear Liam say, "So this is…?" And there was something in his voice that made Ben want to turn around. Made him want to take Liam in his arms and comfort him, for Christ's sake. He steeled himself and kept moving.

"Get your sleeves on, Seth," he ordered, then half turned, careful to not make eye contact. "Okay. Good to see you, Liam." Because Liam needed to go. He needed to get the hell out and give Ben some time to do his deep breathing and his visualizations until the bands around his chest loosened and his body stopped vibrating. "Good luck with the work thing."

Liam, thankfully, started to move. Ben plastered on a smile that was too full, too bright. He knew he was making a fool of himself, but it was better to do this than to let Liam see him fall apart entirely.

So frustrating. So damn *enraging*. After all this time, after all the damn work he'd put into learning to control himself, he'd been taken apart so damn effortlessly. *Breathe. Breathe in some nice green from the plants, from the spring air. Breathe out the confusion, the excitement, the fear.* What color was all that? Yellow, maybe. *Breathe out the yellow. Breathe in the rich blue of being around Seth and Tamara. Yeah, Tamara. Breathe in the pure, sweet sound of her laughter, the feel of her chubby arms squeezing around your neck. Breathe out*—Jesus, what color could he breathe out to get rid of the memory of Liam?

Breathe out the swirl of every color, the chaotic blur of too much light, too much movement. Too much everything. Breathe it out, let it float away. Inhale calm, exhale chaos.

"It really was good to see you, Liam. Don't worry about the car—that was my own fault, so I'll pay for it. Drive safe on your way home." He turned and headed back toward the raspberry patch.

Don't turn around. Don't look back. If Liam's still there by the porch? If he's looking after you? You can't see that. Keep walking. It's over. Don't look back.

It's over. It's over.

"Ben!" A male voice from the direction of the porch was enough to make Ben's heart skip a beat, but he knew even before he turned that it wasn't Liam calling to him. It was Seth. "It's too early to offer you a drink, man. But I'm not sure what the healthier option would be. You seem a bit stressed all of a sudden."

Healthier. Well. Ben knew exactly what would be healthy. More of his damn deep breathing, more centering of himself, more calming and meditating and visualizing positive things.

He turned back to the raspberries. Life. So persistent, so determined to survive and thrive and spread. And not only life for the bushes themselves, but life for the birds and animals and humans who took vital sustenance from the delicious fruit. Beautiful. Spiritual, even.

Ben whacked the bushes with the head of the loppers, then dropped that tool and picked up the rake. More length, more satisfaction as the metal head connected with the plants, the teeth snagged and ripped and destroyed. Five blows, then ten, twenty, every muscle in Ben's body straining toward cathartic ruination.

And it did make him feel a little better. By the time he dropped the rake he was still tense, still restlessly angry, but he didn't actually feel as if his whole body was going to explode anymore.

He turned to see Seth and Tamara watching him. "See?" Seth said, loudly enough for Ben to hear it over his own ragged breaths. "People look *silly* when they have temper tantrums. Don't they? Didn't Uncle Ben look silly?"

Tamara frowned in concern. "Why mad?" she called.

Well. Probably a question Ben deserved, but not one he was able to answer. He shook his head. "Just—raspberries."

Tamara nodded sagely. "Prickles," she agreed.

"They taste good, though," Seth said, and he buzzed his lips against his daughter's cheek. "Okay. Come help me find a long-sleeved shirt. By the time we're outside again, Uncle Ben will have that mess tidied up—and *hidden*—and we'll get the rest of the job finished before Mommy gets home. Sound good?"

Tamara agreed with typical enthusiasm and scampered into the house. Seth stayed outside long enough to say, "Is that out of your system, now? If it isn't, you should head out and I'll come find you once Dinah gets back to take Tamara. I get it that you're… agitated? Is that the right word? But Tamara doesn't need to see her favorite buddy going apeshit on the shrubbery. Not twice in one day, at least."

"Right." Shit. Of course Seth was right. Ben needed to get a tighter grip on himself. "Sorry. Yes, I'm fine. Won't happen again."

"It can happen again if you need it to—we can go out in the woods and you can beat the shit out of whatever plants you want. Just not around Tam."

"No, I'm okay."

Okay. Yeah. That's what he was. He was okay. He'd be calm and gentle when Tamara came back outside, and he'd tidy up the battered raspberry fragments like a good boy, and he'd go back to his quiet, tidy, okay life.

And he'd damn well forget about Liam Marshall. Because while Liam was a walking, talking promise of a better, more exciting life, his promises couldn't be trusted. And Ben wouldn't let himself get fooled again.

CHAPTER TEN

LIAM DROVE back to the city in a daze. He had no idea what he'd been doing in North Falls, but now that he was heading away from it, he had no idea why he was leaving.

Well, he knew the practical reasons. Marius had texted and called several more times over the course of the drive, making it clear just how much Liam was needed and just how rich the rewards could be if he complied.

It should have been a dream come true. It shouldn't have felt like stepping back into a gilded cage.

He went straight to the hospital as Marius had requested, waded through the bureaucracy, and found his way to Tristan's room.

He hovered in the hallway outside, strangely reluctant to step over the threshold.

But he'd come all this way. He'd walked away from Ben—well, he'd stood in a sort of daze while Ben practically *shoved* him away—but the net effect was the same. He'd left all that behind in order to come to this meeting. Now he'd damn well follow through.

He knocked gently, then eased the door open.

Tristan was sitting practically upright in the bed, his tablet in front of him, Marius hovering anxiously by his side, and other than a few tubes and a bit too much gray in his complexion, the old guy looked fine. Heart attack? Really?

"You look okay," Liam said, stepping into the room. "How do you feel?"

"Better." Tristan shrugged. "Apparently it was very mild. They're keeping me overnight and running more tests, but I'm thinking of the whole thing as a warning rather than a crisis."

"You thought it was a crisis when it was happening," Marius said firmly. "You were trying to dictate final bequests and instructions for your funeral."

"I'm a dramatic person. I was being dramatic."

"But you're fine now," Liam said. He'd left Ben behind, and this was nothing.

"I'm fine," Tristan agreed. In the face of a glower from Marius, he added, "But, yes, it was a warning. I'm taking it as a warning."

"I see." Liam had left Ben behind. He could have been spending his day with Ben, and instead he was doing this? No, he wasn't playing this game. "Can you clarify—did you *ask* Marius to call me in, or did he do that on his own?"

Marius raised an eyebrow at Tristan, who said, "I asked him to call you."

"And do you regret that now? Is there still something you want to talk about, or should I just wish you a speedy recovery and go order a fruit basket?"

"He's recovering from a heart attack," Marius scolded. "Stop pushing."

"I have it on good authority that he's fine and was just being dramatic."

Tristan pushed himself up a little straighter in the bed. "You're going to make me work for it, are you?"

"Work for it? I'm going to make you at least *say it*. I don't think that's asking too much."

"Fine." Tristan grimaced. "I need you back at the firm. I need to slow down, at least for a while, and I need someone there who can handle things while I'm taking care of myself. That person is you, and we both know it."

"You didn't fire me, you know. I *quit*. So you wanting me back isn't really that big of a deal."

"You quit because I gave the Taybec Briggs project to Allison. But that was only a couple days ago, and we haven't made the announcement public yet. I can take it back. I *will* take it back. You can do it and keep an eye on the company too."

"That's a pretty shitty thing to do to Allison. And a pretty shitty thing to do to Taybec Briggs, too, if you really don't think I'm the best person for the job."

Tristan squinted at him, and for the first time looked a little tired. A little sick. Maybe even a little old. "So what do you want from me? You took your time getting here—I assume you had a good idea what I wanted and thought over your options. Now it's *your* turn to say it. What do you want, Liam?"

It had taken Liam a long time to get to the hospital because he'd been well out of town when he'd gotten the call, but there was no reason to go into it. And the drive back *had* given him time to get his thoughts in order. "I want a piece of the company. We can come up with something in terms of me buying in, but I want my name on the door, I want control over any jobs I bring in, and I want a share of the profits."

"I'm lying in a hospital bed and you're trying to take advantage of the situation like that?"

"I'm not *trying* anything. I'm telling you the terms on which I'm willing to help you out. If you're interested, great. If you're not, that's fine too. Your call. No pressure."

"No pressure." Tristan looked at Marius as if inviting an opinion, but Marius just shrugged.

"It's the weekend," Liam said. "You should have a plan in place for Monday morning in order to keep the gossip from getting out of control, but you don't need to decide anything right away. If you don't want to work with me, you could call Shannon Tate—she's looking for a change, I think, and she's got a good head for business. Lars Pedersen might be able to help out, but you'd have to back up the money truck to get him away from Mikhael. Might be worth it."

"But they won't be familiar with our projects, our staff."

"No, they won't. I'm definitely the best person for the job. Unfortunately for you, I know my value."

Tristan closed his eyes, probably as an expression of disappointment or disgust, but there was enough ambiguity for Liam to say, "You're tired. I should be going."

No one objected, so he left, stopping at the nurse's station on the way to check on regulations for sending flowers or gifts to the patients. Yeah, that'd be smooth, to send a really clean, modern flower arrangement to Tristan—something bold and architectural. That'd be a nice touch.

There should be other details Liam could plan out, other moves in his little power play. He should call up Scarlett and Nolan, architect friends, and see if they were free for dinner, or at least drinks; they were good strategists and would be able to help him brainstorm. Or maybe it was time to get in touch with a few key clients, let them know that he might not be leaving the company and gently manipulate them into contacting Tristan and offering their support.

Yeah, there were lots of things Liam should be doing, but as he stepped out of the bright hospital lobby into the even brighter early afternoon, he didn't want to do any of them. He'd left the car at home and taken a cab to the hospital; now he started walking, hoping the exercise would clear his head.

Strategies. Plans. A real opportunity, right there waiting for him.

He wondered if the raspberry battle had been won and whether there had been casualties. He thought about Ben's car and whether it even made sense to fix something that old or whether it'd be better to send it straight to the junkyard and get something new. Was Ben sentimental about the piece of crap, or was he just cheap? Or, hell, maybe he couldn't afford anything better. Teachers didn't make all that much money, did they?

But maybe Ben really liked the job. He hadn't planned on being a teacher, not back when Liam had known him. Ben had been content to just let things happen and go with the flow. It had worked well, him being so laid-back, because Liam tended to be more driven, and if both of them had been driving at the same time, it could have been pretty messy. No, they'd been a good team. A good couple, until Liam had thrown it all away.

But, no, none of that was what he was supposed to be thinking of. Damn it. There was something important at stake, here. Yeah, partly it was a chance at—not revenge, exactly, but vindication at least. But mostly it was an opportunity. Tristan's firm wasn't huge, but it was prestigious, and being one of two names at a boutique firm was way better than being an anonymous cog in some big architecture machine. Yeah, this was a great chance, a real opportunity.

It would have been nice to talk to Ben about it. He'd always been good at getting excited *for* Liam. Not competitive, not thinking about how something might be of benefit to himself. He'd just be happy because Liam was getting what he wanted.

Would he still be that way? Was he still the same person he'd been before?

Goddammit! That didn't matter. It wasn't what Liam should be thinking about.

He pulled out his phone and poked at the screen, then ended the call before the first ring. He didn't want to talk to Scarlett and Nolan, didn't want to talk to any of his friends or allies, not about this. If it didn't work out? If Tristan decided that Liam wasn't such a prize and decided to go with one of the other options? That was a humiliation Liam would manage on his own; he didn't want an audience for it.

Not an audience of city people, at least.

If he could talk to Ben about it? Not looking for actual practical ideas, just as a sounding board. A support. Yeah, if he could talk to Ben about it, he'd do it. Hell, if he could drive back up to North Falls and talk to Ben and Seth, and even Seth's wife, who was new sometime over the last fifteen years but was probably pretty cool if she'd managed to catch Seth's eye, he'd do it.

He'd talk. He'd share with them.

But he'd blown that years earlier, and Ben had made it clear there was no point in taking a trip any further down memory lane than they'd already gone. Fair enough.

So that left Liam in the city. On his own. Well, that was fine. He'd do just fine without them.

"WHAT DOES he look like?" Dinah asked. She and Seth had been reasonably discreet while Tamara was with them all in the yard, but now that Seth was off supervising Tamara in the bath and Dinah and Ben were relaxing on the back patio with well-earned drinks, the questions were coming out. "I've seen old pictures, obviously, but has he aged well? Sometimes guys like that—I mean, he was so *pretty*, wasn't he? Sometimes they kinda lose it when they fill out. Is he still pretty?"

Yup, there it was again. The same conflict, the same desire to talk about Liam, to obsess over him, fighting with the absolutely commonsense instinct to avoid the topic and work on banishing him from Ben's mind. But Dinah was his hostess and was making pleasant conversation—it would be churlish to shut her down. "He's not so pretty. But he still looks good. Just in a different way."

"Still has the cheekbones, though?"

"Really, Dinah, where would his cheekbones go?"

"They could get buried under fat. That happens. Or just—I don't know. Saggy skin, maybe?"

"We're in our thirties. I don't think we need to worry about saggy skin. Not yet."

She took a sip of her lemonade, then said, "You're still pretty, in case you were wondering. A bit more manly than in the old pictures, but if I compare now-you to then-you, I'd say you're still at least as good-looking. He wouldn't have seen you and been disappointed. In case you were wondering."

"He's spent more time with Uncle Calvin than he has with me. Whatever he was doing in North Falls, it had nothing to do with how good-looking anyone is. And he's gone back to the city now—at least, he was supposed to have—so none of this is important anymore."

"Was it important before? When he was still here?"

"No." But Ben really tried not to lie to his friends so he added, "It might have *felt* important. But it wasn't."

"You're sure?"

"I guess so. I mean—he's gone. We cleared the air, which was good, and he's gone back to the city. Which is also good. He's got a life there."

"A career," she said with a sage nod. "And you know about all that because you've googled him a bunch of times over the years, right? You probably have an alert set up for any mention of his name."

"Lots of people Google-stalk their exes every now and then."

"Yup," she agreed. "And lots of people eventually run into those exes unexpectedly and go through a bit of a—what? Not a crisis, but a period of questioning. They review their lives, play the what-if game, maybe feel a little wistful about all the lives they could have lived if they'd made different choices. Totally normal."

"Really? You do this too?"

"Of course not." She pitched her voice a little louder, giving it enough volume to be sure it would carry through the open bathroom window at the far end of the patio. "Once I met Seth I forgot all other men. How could I ever expect anyone else to compare to his stunning virility?"

"That's right!" Seth called from inside.

In a quieter voice Dinah said, "I only ever dated two other guys, in any serious way. One of them's in the Navy, and I would *not* be a good Navy wife. He's still cute, though, especially in his little uniform."

"The other?"

"He lives down in Atlanta, works for some kind of auto supply place. He has a wife—but I'm way prettier than her."

"You win."

"Hell yeah. Or maybe Seth wins. I'm not sure. But, whatever—the point is, it's fun to look back at old flames. And to talk about that with your friends."

Fun. It wasn't quite how Ben would have described the last few days. "There isn't really that much to say."

"We don't have to limit ourselves to Liam. You've dated *lots* of guys. I mean, even if we leave Kevin out of it, there must be guys you've wondered about. If you hadn't been *quite* so resistant to love's siren song—"

"Wait. Why are we leaving Kevin out if it?"

"Oh. I just thought—you know. Maybe you wouldn't be quite ready to include him in a silly little game."

"Kevin? No, we can play silly games with Kevin. That's fine."

"It's not too soon?"

"Kevin didn't dump me, you know. We broke up—it was mutual. Really, it was more me than him. *I* dumped *him*, really."

"Okay, so—let's play the game. What do you think would have happened if you *hadn't* dumped him?"

"I don't know. I guess… I mean, I'm sure we'd still be together, because there was no way *he* was going to dump *me*. No way."

"Would you be engaged by now?"

Engaged. To Kevin. Sure, it had been Kevin's proposal that had spurred the breakup, so really the only way to have not broken up would have been to get engaged. But—

"Or married, even," Dinah continued. "It's been almost a year, right? If you'd gotten engaged last summer, you might be married by now. Oooh, a spring wedding, lots of pastels—could Tamara have been your flower girl? Seth would have to be the best man, I guess. Sorry about that, but I think it would have been pretty unavoidable. You wouldn't want a church wedding, would you? You're not very church-y. Maybe something in Calvin's backyard? He's got lots of space, and he'd love something like that."

Married. A wedding. Ben, a married man.

Settled down, stable. Kevin was a second-grade teacher in a town about thirty miles down the highway, so maybe they'd have found a house somewhere in the country between their jobs. Kevin had a dog—a good dog, Bob, a fantastic fluffball of shaggy cross-bred love—and maybe they'd have gotten a cat too. "Bob could have been the ring bearer," Ben said. "We could have rigged something up around his neck. And maybe we'd have gotten the cat involved somehow, although probably not. Cats probably don't like weddings."

"What cat?"

"Imaginary cat."

"Oh. Yeah, probably the imaginary cat wouldn't want to be part of it. But what about Calvin? I guess guys probably don't get 'given away' at their weddings, huh? You may be gay, but you're still not repressed by the women-as-property aspect of the patriarchy."

The screen door to the patio slid open then, and Seth stepped outside, a towel-bundled and sleepy Tamara in his arms. "I'm here in time for talking about the patriarchy," he said. "Excellent. Glad I didn't miss it."

"Don't sit," Ben said quickly. "I need another beer."

"You see me carrying this child, don't you?"

Ben turned to Dinah. "Typical man. Thinks carrying a child is all he has to do—no multitasking, no recognition of the generation after generation of women who've *combined* childcare with all the other jobs in their lives. He probably says it's 'babysitting' when he takes care of his own child."

"I'm not sure you can really bug *me* about multitasking, son, not when you were unable to combine the tasks of 'seeing an old boyfriend' and 'avoiding the parked cop car.'"

"Give me Tamara," Ben ordered. "You're holding her wrong—her feet are going to get cold. Then go get us beers."

"Yeah, beers," Dinah said. "Let's talk about *that*. You guys can just sit there swilling alcohol and I'm stuck with stupid lemonade. Where's the justice in that?"

"Well, that's not the patriarchy, hon, that's just reality. If I were able to gestate for you, part-time, I would absolutely give serious thought to maybe babysitting the fetus for up to two weekends per month. But I can't do it, so—" Seth smiled widely as he settled Tamara on Ben's lap. "Beers for me and my man-friend."

He headed for the kitchen, and Ben kissed the top of Tamara's head. "No beers for you and Mommy. Beers are for men."

"For me," she murmured sleepily, and twisted her head to peer up at him. "Juice?"

"Too close to dinner," Ben answered. He knew the drill, and so did Tamara. "Water?"

"Okay."

"Ahem."

She roused herself enough to grin, then obediently said, "Yes, please."

"Garçon?" Ben called. "Your finest clear beverage for Lady Tamara, if you please."

She snuggled back against him, and Ben looked over to find Dinah watching them. "You and Kevin might have been talking about kids," she said softly. "You both like them. You'd be good dads."

"Damn. When you play the what-if game you don't mess around."

"Did you guys ever talk about it?"

"In loose general terms, I guess. But nothing specific, no."

"And your loose general terms were… pro kid?"

"Sure. When you're done with this current one, I'm planning to ask you to be a surrogate for me and my imaginary boyfriend. Sound okay?"

"Your boyfriend doesn't have to be imaginary, though. Not if you don't want him to be." She sipped her lemonade. "I see him pretty often, you know. We're on that primary education panel together. He's still single. I get the feeling he'd be interested, if you gave him a call."

Kevin. She was talking about Kevin, not—not anyone else. "We broke up for good reasons."

"I thought you broke up because you weren't ready to commit."

"That's a good reason."

"Is it?"

"Um—yes? I think so, yes."

"But… is it *really* a good reason?"

"You're annoying when you do that. I know you think you're cute, but actually it's just annoying."

"Is it, though? Is it *really* annoying?"

"Really, really annoying."

"Hey," Seth said, emerging from the house with two beers, a sippy cup, and a bag of potato chips. "Don't call my wife annoying. That's *my* job."

"Insulting your wife is your job, or being annoying is your job?" Ben accepted the beer he was offered and shifted so he could raise it to his lips without disturbing the child on his lap.

"Both. I'm multitasking, being annoying *and* insulting." Seth waited patiently for Tamara to reach for her drink, then found his own spot on the wicker love seat next to Dinah. He smiled at her and leaned over to press a quick kiss to her belly.

It was all pretty perfect. And maybe Dinah was right, maybe Ben should be thinking more seriously about creating his own version of this for himself. Well, his partner wouldn't have a pregnant belly to kiss, but the general sense of domestic tranquility? That could be replicated.

"I don't need a partner of my own," he tried, "because I have you guys."

"We aren't going to put out at the end of the night," Dinah said. Then she waggled her eyebrows at Seth. "At least, not for you."

Yeah, okay, sex was definitely a valuable aspect of being in a relationship. And while Dinah and Seth were good about not making him feel like a third wheel, having his own partner, his own teammate—yeah, that was appealing too. "If I was seriously dating someone I'd have less time to deal with your raspberry apocalypse. You'd miss me."

"I was thinking of it more as having another soldier to help fight the good fight," Seth said.

"What, you're part of this too? I thought it was just your wife, but—you're matchmaking as well?"

"I liked Kevin."

"Of course you did. Everyone liked him. He's very likable."

"But not loveable?" Dinah asked.

"I—" Ben was stymied. Had he loved Kevin? In a way, sure. Just not—damn it. Not the same way he'd loved Liam. But look how *that* had turned out. *Look what happened when you were irrationally, unrealistically in love with someone.* "You're both going to feel pretty awful if you push me into getting in touch with him and he turns me down. Pretty darn awful."

"Nah, I think we'll feel okay." Seth smiled complacently.

"But that's what you think I should do?" It was one more way Ben was being pathetic, really. All the crap, all the anxiety and stupidity with Liam hadn't been enough; now he was begging his friends to run his love life for him. "I should call him? Kevin?"

Seth and Dinah exchanged a look, and damn it, *that* was another great thing about being in a relationship, that wordless communication. "We can't make that decision for you," Dinah said carefully. "But—if you want to be in a couple, and if you don't have anyone better in mind—maybe? Or something else. Maybe you don't actually want to be in a couple at all, and if that's the case, great, never mind any of this, carry on as you are. But if you *do* want to be in a couple, then, well, you need to find someone else to couple up with. If not Kevin, then…?"

Yeah. If not Kevin, then what? Internet dating? Grindr was one thing, but an actual relationship? Much trickier. What were the chances of finding anyone better than Kevin, compared to the chances of Kevin finding someone better and taking himself off the market while Ben was fucking around?

There was the fantasy world, and there was reality. Ben needed to live in reality. He needed to protect himself, control himself, use his head. He needed to set a realistic goal and then find a reasonable strategy that would give him a good chance of meeting that goal.

He needed to call Kevin. And it was too damn bad if the butterflies in his stomach didn't give even a single wing flap in response to the idea.

CHAPTER ELEVEN

TRISTAN CALLED on Sunday evening. He was home from the hospital, planning to take a couple days off and then work part-time for a week or two. And he agreed to Liam's proposal, in principle.

"It's a good solution, really," the old man said. "I'm not interested in the business side of things, and you are. If I have someone on hand to take care of the niggling day-to-day bureaucracy, it'll free up more of my time for my serious projects. My passion."

"That's not quite what I had in mind," Liam said, but he didn't push it too hard. Tristan was saving face, trying to put a positive spin on things for himself and probably for his inner circle. "We can discuss details over the next couple weeks, get the lawyers involved to make sure everything's clear. But in the meantime, I'll go into the office tomorrow and provide some continuity. Do you want to draft up an announcement email for the staff and run it by me before you send it, or do you want me to draft it and run it by you?"

"*Run it by*—Jesus, Liam, I am not going to look for your approval of every communication I have with my staff. If you think this agreement is going to give you that sort of power, you need to think again!"

"No, of course not, just like I won't run every email by you. But something this big, something that involves both of us equally, should be collaborative, right? I assume you wouldn't appreciate it if I sent out an email announcing this to the staff without giving you a voice."

"What are you planning on announcing, exactly? We haven't worked out the details, yet. We may not be able to work out the details, and the whole thing will fall through."

"Yes, that's the sort of finesse we'll need to come up with together. The staff will need to be told *something* in order to explain my presence tomorrow, but we won't want to tell them too much. It'll be a fine balance—do you want to draft up the first version or should I?"

This was what Liam was signing up for? A long future of placating a grumpy invalid who thought Liam was some sort of executive assistant?

No. It was a prestigious firm; it produced important work, and Liam would be part of that. A big part. A *creative* part, not just an administrator. This was a good thing.

He threw himself into the new challenge. Long days all week long, dealing with staff, networking with clients, and even, when he could find some time, working on projects. More idea bouncing than really getting into the details of things, but that was to be expected. And he didn't really mind.

He went home late every night, usually after dinners with clients or colleagues, and fell into bed exhausted.

He was important, he was successful, his career was intense and exciting. It was what he'd always wanted.

And when Calvin phoned on Thursday night, it was the most exciting thing that happened all week.

Not *actively* exciting. More actively bewildering, as was usual with Calvin.

"I was just calling to check whether you were going to be here in time for dinner tomorrow night," the old man said, sounding completely reasonable.

"Uh… what? Dinner?"

"You weren't thinking of driving up Saturday morning, I hope? We need to get started first thing, Liam. I want us on the ground, at work, by eight. Maybe nine at the absolute latest. I think you need to come up the night before. I've got Ben's old room cleared out a bit, enough that you can at least find the bed. You can stay there instead of at the B&B."

"Calvin. What are you talking about?"

"You're not trying to back out, are you? Come on, boy! We need you!"

Liam decided to try another tack. "Can you tell me what I should be bringing? Like… tools?" Because if they were *on the ground* at work, that meant something physical, didn't it?

"I've got all that taken care of. Just bring work clothes, steel-toed boots—you've got a hard hat, right? I wouldn't bother with all that if it was just me, but because this is kind of official, we need to be more careful. Follow all the rules, make sure the insurance guys are happy…."

Calvin stopped talking, clearly expecting more questions, more absurdity, but Liam had been sitting at the computer when Calvin called, and there had been enough clues in the conversation for a quick internet search. The North Falls municipal website had a banner headline advertising their big event.

"Is Community Circle just a Habitat for Humanity rip-off?" Liam asked. "Charities are great, but so's originality."

It didn't take Calvin long to realize Liam was on to him and catch up. "I'll be sure to let the Bindermans—they're the family that's moving in, after hopping from one rental to another for the last eight years—know you think their home is derivative."

"I'm really looking forward to seeing little Julia's face when she gets a look at the backyard," Liam responded, skimming the article in front of him for any more tidbits. "We're building a play structure for her, right?"

"I'm not sure it's in the plans, but maybe there'll be some extra materials... now if only we knew an architect who could draw something up."

Taybec Briggs, eat your heart out. No time for your three-hundred-million-dollar project... I'm designing play structures *now!*

The whole thing was ridiculous. Liam shouldn't give in to Calvin's nonsense, shouldn't even consider making the drive up to North Falls, absolutely couldn't afford to take time off from the firm right then, not even on a weekend. No. It couldn't happen. No way.

"I won't be there until after dinner," he heard himself say. "I might be fairly late. Eleven or so?" That would give him time to take the staff out for a round or two of drinks to celebrate the new management at the firm. He needed to make sure they were all firmly on his side before Tristan came back early next week. *That* was important. This project in the Falls? It wasn't something he could allow to distract him. "And are you sure it's okay for me to sleep at your place? I could call the B&B again, but I didn't really get the impression they were the type to appreciate late arrivals."

"I'll be up. Or if you're *really* late, you can just let yourself in. You know where the room is."

They said goodbye and Liam was left staring at his phone in bemusement. Yeah, he knew where Ben's old room was. He knew the room far too well. It was where he and Ben had spent so much time, through so many stages of their young lives. Innocent childhood games,

Seth often included, and different kinds of games later, ones Seth was definitely *not* part of.

Ben and Liam had snuck in and out of that room through the door, down the hallway right past Calvin's room; or through the window, hanging and dropping or clambering up the wall using the window sills as roosting points. None of it had been necessary—Calvin hadn't been the curfew type and had been more likely to make fun of misbehavior rather than punishing for it, but sneaking had been part of the fun.

Part of it. But being with Ben had been the main draw. And Liam had thrown it all away.

Now he was going back to wallow in it all.

No, he was going back to help build a damn house for a family struggling with poverty.

It made almost less sense, really, but it was what he'd agreed to. Well, what he'd failed to *not* agree to, at least.

Stupid decision. Absolutely the wrong time for it, from Liam's perspective. And from Ben's? Because, of course, that was what this was really all about. It would have been easy to say "no" to Calvin if this had just been one of the old guy's crazy projects. But it was a crazy project *with the likelihood of Ben time*, so weak, stupid Liam had been powerless to resist. Now that he was off the phone, though, now that the first burst of excitement had started to fade, he remembered Ben's distinct lack of enthusiasm at Liam's last visit. There was absolutely no reason to think Ben was looking for a repeat performance.

But Ben hadn't been the one to invite him. Ben might not even *be* at the project. Just because he was Ben the Kind, Ben the Generous, Ben the People Person, Ben who probably *started* the damn Community Circle? None of that meant Ben would be at this particular event. Calvin hadn't mentioned him, Liam hadn't mentioned him, and it wasn't like North Falls wasn't Liam's hometown at least as much as it was Ben's.

Liam was really looking forward to helping out and giving back. He was excited about little—he took a quick peek at the online article—little Julia Bindermans's new home. Nothing to do with Ben. Just being a good guy and helping out.

Liam clicked his laptop lid down and pushed away from the table where he'd been working. He needed to get some sleep, needed to make sure he was well rested. He had a big day ahead of him, and a big weekend after that.

He headed for the bathroom to clean up, then to bed, and he thought about North Falls all the way. The project, and who he might see there, and no, of course, no expectations, but, still, if they were spending time together....

Just harmless daydreams. That was all.

Liam let himself fall asleep with thoughts of Ben and North Falls dancing through his head instead of the work-related ideas that had been occupying him all week, and his sleep was long and peaceful.

BEN HAD always liked building things, and building a home for a student at his school was even more satisfying than regular projects. And, if he was being honest with himself, it was nice to have a distraction from all the thoughts of Liam and all the speculation about what might have been, if things had been only a little bit different. If they'd been more mature, more able to handle a relationship back in college. If Liam hadn't been such a cheating bastard. If—and this one was tougher to think about, but also more intriguing—if Liam hadn't had to leave the week before. If he'd stayed, if he and Ben had talked, if they'd both said all the right things at all the right times? What would have happened?

Maybe nothing. Maybe seeing each other again, clearing the air, and moving on had been the best resolution to it all. But what if... oh, damn, what if....

"You're looking bright and cheerful," Dinah said from the big chair on her front porch. She must have been watching him as he walked down the street and he'd been too involved in his thoughts to even notice. Damn, had he been making faces? He was pretty sure he hadn't actually wrapped his arms around himself and started rubbing while he smooched the air, so things weren't as bad as they could have been.

He pulled himself together enough to respond. "It's a beautiful day, I'm going to be with beautiful people, and we're going to do a beautiful thing. How could I *not* be cheerful?"

"Beautiful people?" she said. "Does that mean Calvin told you? When I heard, I was worried he hadn't."

"Told me what? Heard what?"

"About Liam? Seth just called from the site—I'm surprised he didn't *sleep* over there, he's so wrapped up in all this. If I wasn't pregnant, he probably would have—and he said Calvin showed up with *Liam*. And—you didn't know he was there. He wasn't who you meant by 'beautiful people.'" Dinah clearly saw the confusion on Ben's face and was generous enough to give him a little time to recover. "So you must have meant *me* as the beautiful people! You must have noticed my glow! Yes, some people would say it's just gestational hypertension, but you and I know the truth, right?"

"You always look beautiful," Ben said absently. Then, "Why would *Liam* come to this?"

"I can only imagine," Dinah said, her tone dry.

Ben squinted at her. What was she trying to say? "He's here already? From the city?"

"Came up last night, apparently. Stayed at Calvin's."

Calvin. Of course. After all these years, Ben should have learned. At the first sign of anything confusing or hard to explain, he should just assume Uncle Calvin had caused it and move on with his life. Bermuda Triangle, crop circles, weeping statues—Uncle Calvin's work, all of it. Liam coming back to North Falls? Maybe Uncle Calvin hadn't been responsible for the *first* visit (or for all the unnoticed visits that had apparently come before, if they were even real) but Calvin had definitely been doing everything he could to get Liam back ever since. And he was Uncle Calvin, so he succeeded in causing mischief where a mere mortal would have failed and surrendered the effort.

"He's going to help?" Ben asked. "With the house? That's why he's here?"

"Apparently," Dinah said.

Well, it was pretty hard for Ben to object to a certified architect taking part in a charitable building project. And pretty hard for Ben to withdraw his own participation, considering he was the one who'd brought the Bindermans's plight to the Community Circle's attention. Which meant he'd better start getting his game face on: more Liam time was imminent.

"Seth said he was helpful with the raspberries," Dinah said. She set down the book she'd been reading and pulled herself upright. She and Ben had arranged to walk over to the work site together, but Ben wondered if there was a way he could suggest they drive. He actually wondered if there was a way he could suggest that Dinah stay home with her feet up; she wasn't hugely pregnant yet and she was good with tools, but, really, she was pregnant *enough*, and there were lots of people who'd promised to help out. Was there really any need for Dinah's body to do more work than it already was?

But Dinah was the best judge of that, of course. And Seth would have already brought the topic up, surely. So….

"You ready?" Ben asked.

Dinah held her arms out to her sides as if to display that she was, indeed, prepared, and they started walking.

"Why would he come?" Ben asked.

"Liam?"

Yes, obviously Liam, but possibly Dinah's mind wasn't quite one-track enough to have picked up on Ben's obsession. So he tried to keep his nod polite rather than sarcastic.

"I guess he's just a good guy?" Dinah suggested. Her voice was suspiciously innocent when she added, "Unless you think there's something else going on?"

"Like what? He's got his big important life in the city, after all. No reason for him to be back here, not that I can think of."

"Really? You don't think maybe he's… interested?"

Ben was tempted to push it a little further. Could he keep pretending he didn't know what she was talking about long enough that she gave up? Maybe—she was pretty generous about stuff like that. But he didn't really *want* her to give up. He wanted to talk about this. Not that he had anything at all coherent to say. He made a sort of Wookie noise that he hoped conveyed his frustration, confusion, and ignorance, and waited to see Dinah's reaction.

She raised an eyebrow and didn't seem too impressed with the nonverbal approach. "We never got around to Liam the other day in our what-if game, did we?"

She knew damn well they hadn't. Now, on this sunny morning, on the way to their good deed, a good deed at which Ben would be seeing Liam again… what if?

Was Ben brave enough to even let himself ask that question?

He couldn't get into the mechanics of it, didn't want to think about *how* it might have happened, but... what if he and Liam had stayed together?

But the game didn't work if he didn't think about the "how." "Are we saying he never cheated on me? Or he cheated on me but we got past it, somehow? Oh, God, we'd better not be saying I just kept ignoring it! I didn't just put up with it, did I?"

"*Kept* ignoring it?"

Yeah, of course Dinah would pick up on that. But Ben had wanted to talk about this, hadn't he? He took a deep breath. "We'd better not be saying I stayed that insecure and scared. Better not be saying I was *always* so afraid of losing him that I kept on ignoring the problem instead of dealing with it."

"And suddenly I'm a little less favorably disposed toward Liam Marshall. This was an ongoing thing, and you knew about it, and you thought he'd dump you if you called him on it?"

"I think—I'm pretty sure he *wanted* me to dump him. That way he wouldn't have to do it himself, you know? He wouldn't have to be the one to pull the plug."

"What a weenie."

"Yeah, but I was a weenie too, right? He should have had the guts to dump me, and I should have had the guts to dump him."

"So you weren't really a good couple? The way Seth talks makes it sound like you were meant for each other."

Difficult question. Impossible question, probably. But Ben needed this conversation, so he tried. "We were each other's first and only boyfriends. I know that works for some people—they marry their high school sweethearts and are never even tempted to look at anyone else. But I don't think it would have worked for Liam and me. We both wanted— experiences. Adventures. We wanted to learn things firsthand."

"And you got to learn about broken hearts, firsthand."

"*I* did. I don't know about Liam."

She didn't say anything in reply, which was just as well because they were getting close to the building site and Ben needed a little time to regain his composure. But as they approached the gravel driveway and raised their arms to wave at the people already assembled, Dinah turned to face Ben and said, "Do you want Seth and me to run interference today? Keep him away from you?"

"No. I'm—I was going to say 'fine,' but I think 'okay' might be better. I'm stable. And I don't want to hide from him."

"We could arrange a power-tool accident, if you thought it was justified. I don't think we should kill him, but a nail gun aimed at extremities would probably get him off the site for the day."

Right. *Hiding* wasn't really in Dinah's vocabulary, not if *attacking* was a remotely viable option. "No, it'll be fine."

Ben turned toward the site and saw Liam already standing there beside Uncle Calvin, the two of them intently examining a stack of blueprints stretched out on a makeshift table. Liam was an architect; his dream had come true, and now he was using his hard-won knowledge to help others. He was a good guy. He'd screwed up, sure, but—a good guy, deep down. His extremities should remain unblemished by nail guns; Ben could give him that much.

"Let me know if you change your mind," Dinah said. Then she stomped up the driveway, her work boots a strange complement to her pregnant belly, and Ben followed in her wake.

CHAPTER TWELVE

CALVIN HAD somehow taken control of the job assignments. Liam wasn't sure it made sense; the old man really didn't have any experience in construction *or* management. But nobody seemed to want to argue with him, and since Liam, Ben, and Seth all ended up on the same crew, Liam didn't have any reason to object either.

"Is Dinah going to be pissed she's not with us?" Ben asked Seth.

Liam looked around; he was pretty sure he'd seen a pregnant woman earlier, presumably Seth's wife, but he wasn't sure where she'd gotten off to.

"Nah," Seth said. "She's pretty good at making friends. And really, she knows all the people on her crew anyway."

"But Uncle Calvin assigned Julia Bindermans to the same group," Ben said. "A child. So clearly they'll be doing less demanding work. Aren't you worried Dinah's going to think he's sheltering her because she's pregnant? Like she can't decide for herself what's safe?"

"Why are you trying to make trouble? Why do you want to ruin my marriage?"

"You think that's exactly what Calvin did, and you're glad he did it, because you'd be worried about her otherwise, but you know Dinah won't like it?" The affectionate teasing in Ben's voice made Liam's chest ache. There'd been a time when *he'd* been the one to make Ben sound like that.

"I'm very busy with the tasks I've been assigned," Seth said. "And I'm afraid I just didn't notice anything about Julia Bindermans. I absolutely wasn't monitoring the jobs my wife was assigned, because why would I? She's an adult and can take care of herself and doesn't need me hanging over her shoulder and worrying about her all the time."

"That's good," Ben admitted. "She might actually let you get away with that."

"I've been married for a while. Learned some tricks."

Then they both turned to Liam and seemed ready to get the conversation back to business. "Have you done this before?" Seth asked. "Framing? I know you're an architect, but—hands-on?"

It was tempting to build himself up, but Liam opted for honesty instead. "I've never even supervised this kind of construction. Most of my projects are—well, bigger. Steel and concrete and glass. Not nearly as much wood. I'm an absolute amateur."

"But you can use a hammer," Ben put in. Was Liam imagining it, or did Ben sound almost defensive, as if he didn't want Liam to denigrate himself too much?

"Yeah, I can use a hammer," Liam agreed cautiously. "Haven't for quite a while—the last thing I built was probably that deck for your uncle. But it's not a really sophisticated skill."

"Okay, then," Seth said. "We're on." And he took charge of their little group, apparently able to exercise his tradesman's authority over the white-collar types even when the job at hand had nothing at all to do with his actual trade.

They didn't talk much, not about anything more intense than moving a two-by-four a shade in one direction or the other, but it all felt totally comfortable. When Seth grumbled about the sun being too hot, Ben shot an amused look in Liam's direction and mouthed the words "delicate redhead," and it was like the heat of the day had melted the years away, as if the three of them were back to who they'd been so long ago, when they'd been perfect.

But they weren't perfect anymore, and Liam's shoulders started aching far too early. He worked out regularly, but of course trips to the gym weren't quite the same as actual physical labor. He hadn't even known a muscle *existed* in that particular spot between his shoulder blades and couldn't quite figure out what job it performed or why it was complaining so much about its current exertions, but he managed to work through it.

Still, he wasn't sorry when they took a midmorning break. He and Ben had been doing similar work, and they both ended up stretching their arms and backs in almost exactly the same way when they got a chance. If Liam took the three steps to stand behind Ben, he'd know exactly where to press his thumbs, exactly how to ease them apart and stretch the pain away.

It was an excuse, of course, but it might be one he could get away with. If he was providing a service, touching would be okay, wouldn't it? A friend was in pain. What kind of asshole wouldn't do what he could to ease the discomfort? What kind of loser wouldn't walk over, lean in, let himself feel the sweat-dampened fabric and beneath it the warm, living muscle of a body that used to be so familiar, so treasured—

"Liam!" Seth said, obviously for the second time. "You okay? You kind of zoned out for a minute there."

"Sorry. Uh—work. Just thinking about something at work."

"Everything okay?" Ben asked. He tossed Liam one of the Nalgene water bottles the crew were using instead of disposable plastic and turned to lean against a sawhorse next to the one Liam was leaning on. "You had a crisis or something last weekend. That worked out okay?"

"Yeah. It—well, I was going to say it worked out really well, but my boss had a heart attack, so I guess it'd be pretty insensitive to be too happy about it. But it was a professional opportunity I was able to capitalize on."

"You—you were able to *capitalize* on your boss's heart attack?"

Shit. Liam could have anticipated how that statement would sound to someone like Ben, couldn't he? "Not really my boss, actually, at the time. My ex-boss. And it was kind of an unfriendly end to the business relationship." Was he making this better, or worse? "But when he realized he needed me…."

Yeah, this was making it worse. Making it sound like Liam was taking revenge, gloating over an old man's medical emergency.

"I didn't steal his company away from him or anything." And it had been Tristan's own fault that he hadn't set up a better support system, hadn't trusted Liam earlier. The heart attack hadn't been Liam's fault! He wasn't responsible for Tristan's health or his stress levels or any other damn thing. "We're going to be partners now, that's all. I'm buying into the company. And, yeah, his heart attack was what made him realize he needed a partner, so *that's* how it worked out okay for me, but he could have chosen anyone else to work with. I wasn't blackmailing him or anything!"

"Okay," Ben agreed. "So—congratulations? You're a partner now?"

"Not formally. Not yet. But, yeah, it's in the works. Thanks."

"And you're feeling really good about it," Ben continued. "Not at all conflicted. Not defensive in any way."

"Shut up." But Liam didn't want Ben to shut up. It had been way too long since someone had talked to him like this. Since someone had actually expected him to be a decent human being, and expected him to *care* if he fell a little short of the mark.

Ben grinned at him as if he knew his comments were welcome, and for a moment everything was comfortable and friendly and wonderful. Then—it stopped. The warmth faded from Ben's face, and he looked away suddenly, almost shamefully, as if he'd been caught looking at someone else's secret.

"I'm going to check in with Uncle Calvin," Ben said.

There was no reason for him to do that, not that Liam could think of, but he nodded anyway and sat there as Ben walked away from him.

The moment was over. Liam had to let it go.

STUPID. BEN was so stupid, letting himself get dragged back into the old patterns with Liam.

Sure, he was easy to talk to. Easy to work with, look at, be around. Easy to admire, easy to care about.

Easy for Ben to get his heart broken. Again.

"My back's a bit sore," he told Uncle Calvin. "Maybe there's a different job I could do for the rest of the morning? I don't mean to wimp out—" *I just can't trust myself around Liam Marshall.*

Uncle Calvin, in some sort of modern miracle, nodded. "That's fair," he said. "I can make some changes." He pulled a well-folded sheet of paper out of his back pocket, peered at it, then bellowed, "Seth! Liam! You two and Ben are going to do some painting."

"No," Ben started, but Uncle Calvin steamrolled over him.

"We're painting the trim before we put any of it on," he explained. "Once it's installed we'll just touch up the nail holes and be done with it. And it's all white, so that's easy too. You can set up over there, by the shed."

"No," Ben started again, but by then Liam and Seth had both joined them.

"No more framing?" Seth asked. "I thought we were really getting into the rhythm of things."

"Little Benny's back is hurting him," Uncle Calvin explained.

Seth nodded. "It's been a while since Little Benny has done any real work."

"He did okay with your raspberry bushes," Liam said. Then he added, "And, honestly, my back's sore too. I know, I'm just another spoiled office drone, right?" He turned to Ben. "Right between your shoulder blades? Feels like someone's cutting you with a razor blade every time you move your arms?"

Well, yes, damn it, that was exactly what it felt like, but the idea had been to get further away from Liam, not to have the man stick up for him and commiserate about their shared pain.

"Maybe we should just fight through it," Ben suggested. Not that it really mattered—going back to work on the framing with Liam would be just as intolerable, just as irresistible, as shifting over to work on painting, still with Liam.

"Take a break, stretch out, come back to it later," Uncle Calvin advised. "This is a weekend-long marathon. Can't have you falling apart the first morning."

Falling apart. A melodramatic way to refer to a sore back, but strangely apt as a description of Ben's actual issue. He felt like he was dissolving—well, no, not *all* of him dissolving, just the outer parts. The barriers he needed in order to protect himself from Liam were crumbling. Ben was left exposed and vulnerable. And he didn't like it.

Or at least he *shouldn't* like it. But when Liam grinned at him and wondered out loud when they'd turned into old men, it was impossible not to grin back. And having started grinning, so very difficult to stop, or to persuade himself he should feel bad for not stopping.

They got back to work, and after a while, Ben gave up on trying to resist. The whole day started to feel like it existed inside a bubble. A bubble full of hard work, sure, but also sunshine and friendship and butterflies dancing around the weeds at the edge of the building lot *and* the insides of Ben's stomach every time he spoke to Liam or looked at Liam or thought about Liam....

It was horrible and wonderful and terrifying and comforting. Ben couldn't stand it for another second but never wanted it to end.

He knew exactly what was happening, of course, although he wasn't sure what to call it. *Falling in love* made it sound like something new, and there was nothing new about this feeling. It would have been easier to dismiss it if he'd never felt it before, never felt it *for Liam* before. He could have called it infatuation or said he had a crush, or had fallen in lust. But none of that was right.

His love for Liam had never gone away, he realized. He'd rejected it, done his best to crush and ignore it, but it hadn't died. It had smoldered away, hidden under all the layers of crap he'd—no, *they'd*—thrown on top of it. But now the embers were being exposed to oxygen, were being fanned back to life, were bursting into beautiful, warming flames.

He was so screwed.

Chapter Thirteen

THERE SHOULD have been some sort of festivities that night. Liam wasn't sure exactly who would have had time to plan anything, or energy to take part, but even sitting around the building site with a few cases of beer and ordering some pizzas would have been *something*. Instead, the teams just sort of dissolved around dinnertime, dragging tired bodies home for some well-deserved rest. But no beer or pizza, at least not with everyone all together.

Ben didn't even say goodbye. Well, he waved, but the wave was for *everyone*, with nothing special for Liam.

Because you're nothing special, he told himself. *Because you're just some guy he used to know, some idiot who keeps driving up from the city for weird reasons. There's no cause for him to pay any more attention to you than he does to anyone else.*

Except… as Ben and Seth and the pregnant woman who must be Seth's wife reached the corner and were about to turn, Ben *did* look back, and it really seemed like he was looking right at Liam. But when Liam raised his hand and waved, Ben turned away as if he hadn't seen the gesture.

So Liam climbed into the passenger seat of Calvin's pickup truck and sat quietly as they drove through the still-sunny evening.

"I'm not getting any younger," Calvin said. He sounded—well, he sounded sincere. But that didn't mean too much, not with Calvin.

Still, Liam tried to be sympathetic. "None of us are. I'm going to be creaky as hell tomorrow."

"You did good work today, though."

It had to be a trap, didn't it? Liam waited for the punch line, but it never came.

Neither of them said anything for the rest of the short drive, and they stayed quiet as they pulled into the driveway of Calvin's house and slid stiffly out of the truck.

"I worry about Ben sometimes," Calvin said. Liam stood frozen on his side of the truck, and Calvin leaned his forearms against the hood and looked across at him. "His parents are—well. My sister was always a flake, and she sure picked a hell of a guy to have a kid with. They're both useless, obviously, or Ben would never have come to live with me. When I'm gone, Ben will be all alone."

That didn't sound right. "You'll be around for a long time, still. And he's got good friends, and a place in the community."

"Right." Calvin stayed still for another breath, then pushed away from the truck. "Right. He'll be fine, and it's a hell of a long way away anyhow." But there was something strange in Calvin's voice, an unfamiliar emptiness that Liam didn't like at all.

"Why did you invite me up here this weekend?" A bit of a jump in the conversation, but if anyone could handle that, it'd be Calvin.

Calvin turned and started slowly toward the house. No answer? No rambling, nonsensical explanation from Calvin the Verbose?

And he was walking like an old man. Liam had never given much thought to Calvin's age—when they'd first encountered each other Liam had been a snot-nosed kid who thought any adult was hopelessly over-the-hill, and after that there'd never been much reason to think about it. Calvin was just *Calvin*. But now?

"Are you okay?" Liam took a few long steps and caught up to Calvin before he made it to the front door. "Did you overdo it today, or is this something more serious?"

"I'm fine," Calvin grumbled. He shoved the front door open—of course it hadn't been locked—and stepped inside. At least, he tried to step, but he stumbled over the low rise, and Liam reached forward to steady him. Calvin shook himself free from Liam's grip. "Mind your own business."

"That's pretty rich, coming from you." Liam kept his hands half-outstretched, ready to reach forward and grab Calvin again if necessary. A bruised ego was better than a broken hip.

Calvin shuffled off without a reply, which was just one more sign that things weren't quite right. Resisting the urge to verbally spar? That wasn't the Calvin he knew.

The Calvin he *had known*, at least. But maybe things had changed. Maybe this was all normal, now. But if it *wasn't* normal, Liam had to do something about it. He wasn't sure exactly what that "do something" would look like, but he'd figure it out when the time came. *If* the time came. If all this wasn't just what Calvin was like these days.

Well, it wasn't a question Liam could answer for himself.

And it wasn't just an excuse. It wasn't another weird reason for contacting Ben. It was totally legitimate to be worried about the health of a friend, especially if that friend was elderly. Did sixty count as elderly? Sure, it was close enough.

Liam let himself make the phone call. The pleasant fluttering in his stomach? That was probably just relief at the idea of getting some help. Everything was fine. He was just being a good friend.

BEN FELT unsettled. The day had gone well enough. Certainly from a practical standpoint, they'd gotten a lot done. And there'd been nothing unpleasant, nothing painful between him and Liam.

No, it had all been a bit *too* pleasant, really, and that was probably what he was reacting to. He just needed some time alone to center himself. Maybe he'd meditate, or do his breathing exercises—they'd have the same effect, he was sure.

But maybe he didn't *want* that effect. Maybe he didn't want to get rid of the unsettled feeling, the sensation that something was about to happen, something wonderful and terrifying and important. Maybe he wanted to savor it, feed it, let it grow and expand—

His phone rang from the front hall, and he scolded himself as he went to answer it. Of course he didn't want drama, didn't want to encourage himself to wallow in whatever nonsensical emotions he was coming up with. He was a mature adult, and he would behave in a rational manner.

His call display showed Uncle Calvin's number, and Ben schooled himself against remembering who was staying at the house. If Calvin was inviting Ben over for dinner—dinner with Liam Marshall—how would Ben respond? He knew exactly what he *should* say, but—

"Hi," he said as he tucked the phone between his cheek and shoulder. "What's up?"

"Ben? It's Liam."

Ben was temporarily speechless. Liam. On the phone. Calling Ben. As if that was just something they did whenever they felt like it.

But Liam continued with, "I'm sorry to bug you, but I'm a bit worried about Calvin. Obviously it's a bit hard to be sure of anything with him, but he seems—not right. Maybe he's just tired? But he's acting kind of dazed. Stumbling around—shit, I think I just heard him knock something over. He's in his bedroom."

In his bedroom? When he had a guest to entertain and/or torture? "How long's he been in there for?"

"Not long. I could be making a big deal about nothing. But you know, all the stuff about getting treatment for strokes as soon as possible—not that I'm saying he's having a stroke! Seriously, he might just be tired."

"I'll be there in five minutes."

"He'll be pissed if he thinks you're checking up on him."

"Let him be. He doesn't get to invite himself into every aspect of my life and then expect privacy in return."

"I was worrying more about him being pissed at *me* for calling you."

"You're tough, you can handle it." Ben managed to bite his tongue before pointing out that Liam had quite a bit of history with pissing off members of his family. Why drag up ancient history when Liam was trying to help Uncle Calvin?

So he ended the call, grabbed a few beers out of the fridge, and jogged out to the car. By the time he was at Calvin's he was regretting the beers—he'd thought they'd be a good cover, a way to pretend he was just stopping by for a little visit, but maybe he shouldn't be creating a cover. Maybe this was his opportunity to make it clear to Uncle Calvin that they were a family *in both directions*, and Ben was just as entitled to interfere in Calvin's life as the reverse.

But that would be a fight, probably, and if Uncle Calvin actually was sick, Ben shouldn't be fighting with him. And even if he was fine, it wasn't too gracious to start a family brawl with Liam as an audience. Although Liam might actually be a good ally in the argument; he cared about Uncle Calvin enough to want to—

Shit. No. No, no, no.

Ben grabbed the beers from the back seat. Liam wasn't a damn ally, he was a temporary visitor with unclear motivations. He'd had his chance to become part of the family fifteen years earlier, and he'd blown it.

Still, it was hard to remember that when Liam stepped out onto the front porch and waited, clearly impatiently, for Ben to come up the walk. The poor guy was worried.

"I think I heard him throw up," Liam said as soon as Ben was close enough to hear his near whisper. "But I'm not positive." He scrubbed his hand over the back of his head. "Sorry. I'm not much use for any of this."

"You called me. That was useful." But Ben wouldn't let himself be sidetracked into trying to comfort *Liam*, of all people. "Where is he?"

"Still in the bathroom. I knocked and he told me to go away, so I went away."

Of course he had. Why stay and fight when you could just disappear?

Ben shoved the beers into Liam's hands with a little more force than was probably necessary. "Put these in the fridge. I'll go deal with Uncle Calvin."

Of course, dealing with Uncle Calvin was easier said than done. Ben knocked on the bathroom door, and the pause before a response was long enough to make him edgy. Finally, though, Calvin barked, "Go away! I'm fine."

"Yeah, you're great," Ben agreed. "Stuck in the bathroom while you have a guest downstairs. Totally normal for you."

"Ben? What are you doing here?" Uncle Calvin's voice sounded thin and tentative. Damn it, there *was* something wrong with him.

"I came over for a beer." And the proof was downstairs in the fridge. "Liam said you'd been up here for a while, so I decided to check on you. What's going on?"

"You came over for a beer? With Liam?" And even through the weakness, Ben could hear a trace of interest.

"Can we focus on you for right now? What's wrong with you? Do you need to see a doctor?"

"No."

Of course, Uncle Calvin's arm could be sliced off at the shoulder and the stubborn old goat would still insist he was fine.

"So you're going to come down for a beer?"

"In a while."

"You want me to start something for dinner? Or we could order in?"

There was a distinctive retching sound from the other side of the door, the noise that came from a stomach that had already thoroughly emptied and was now trying to eject itself from its host body.

"You're pretty sick." Ben wasn't sure if Uncle Calvin was in any condition to reply—probably easiest if he wasn't. "And it came on pretty fast, which is kind of scary. I have no idea what symptoms we should be looking for to be sure it's not something serious, but that's okay, because we happen to live in a community with a significant number of experts on that topic. We call them doctors." Another gagging sound. "I'm going to call over to the clinic and ask for some advice. You're okay with that, right?"

And Ben left before giving Uncle Calvin a chance to pull himself together and reply. He had his phone out on the way down the stairs and had already dialed before he made it to the kitchen where Liam was waiting, concern clear on his face.

It was amazing how the usual rounds of bureaucracy seemed to melt away once Ben mentioned he was calling on Calvin's behalf, and within a minute or two he'd been assured that Calvin's regular doctor would call back as soon as possible, even though it was a weekend. Ben sipped the beer he was holding and—wait. How the hell was he holding a beer?

He looked over and saw a matching bottle in Liam's hand. Liam had opened beers for both of them, given one to Ben—and Ben hadn't even noticed? Maybe he was too caught up in worrying about Uncle Calvin, but maybe Liam was just that damn smooth.

Or maybe the two of them were just comfortable together, just that natural. But Ben couldn't let his thoughts wander in that direction.

"Kurt Mason's going to call." And just because they had to talk about something, he added, "He was a couple years behind us at school. Do you remember him? Small kid, red hair? Weird to think he's a *doctor* now."

"I like my doctors in their forties. Old enough to know what's going on, young enough to still be on top of things."

"Uncle Calvin likes his doctors younger than him so he can boss them around."

"From what I remember of Kurt Mason, I'm not sure he'd be all that easy to boss."

"Yeah, Uncle Calvin's plan kind of backfired on that one." Ben grinned and sipped his beer. "I'm not sure what we should be doing in the meantime. Should I be up there sitting outside the bathroom door, listening to him puke in case he asks for help? Or should I give the poor man a little privacy?"

"No idea." Liam made it sound like commiseration rather than dismissal. "If it was me, I think I'd want the privacy... but not if I was having a heart attack or something."

"Do heart attacks make you puke?"

"I have no idea about that either." Liam pulled out his phone, obviously ready for some research, and Ben managed to resist the urge to peer over Liam's shoulder, calling up a browser on his own phone instead.

They'd only been searching for a couple minutes when there was a knock on the front door and a male voice called out, "Hello? It's Kurt Mason. Calvin? Ben? Can I come in?"

"Kurt!" Ben strode out to the front hall, vaguely aware of Liam trailing behind him. "I expected a call, but not a *house* call."

"I was on the way home from the golf course." Kurt gestured down at his clothes. "I may not look too professional, but I've got my bag with me, and—holy shit. Liam? Liam Marshall?"

And there it was. The familiar admiration that came far too close to hero worship. As if Liam was something special, something more important than other people in his surroundings. Kurt was a *doctor.* He saved lives. And he was excited that some stupid architect was back in town?

But it wasn't professional admiration, and Ben knew it. Knew it because he'd felt it himself for too damn long. Liam was magnetic, charismatic—beautiful. It wasn't sexual—or at least, not *only* sexual. It was just pure charisma, and it was all the more effective because he didn't seem to use it to his advantage. At least not most of the time.

"Uncle Calvin's upstairs in the bathroom," Ben said. They needed to keep things moving in the right direction. "I can take you up there."

Kurt nodded, clearly called back to his official capacity, but he grinned at Liam as he passed and reached out to clap him on the shoulder. "Good to see you," Kurt said, and he made it sound like this casual interaction had made his damn week.

It wasn't that Ben was jealous, exactly. He was just—well, he had no idea what he was. And he shouldn't be getting distracted by any of that anyway.

So he stood and listened while Kurt tried sweet-talking Uncle Calvin into opening the bathroom door and then resorted to threats to call the fire department to have them break it down, and wouldn't that be embarrassing and no, there'd be no financial compensation for the repairs. Finally, there was a click, and Kurt was able to turn the doorknob.

"Wait downstairs, okay?" he told Ben. "Close enough that you can hear me if I call, but far enough away that Calvin can have some privacy."

"The backyard," Uncle Calvin croaked. "Wait in the backyard."

"Downstairs is fine," Kurt said firmly. Then he slipped into the bathroom and closed the door behind him.

Ben obediently headed downstairs, where he found Liam waiting for him with two bottles of beer, one in each hand. He wordlessly handed Ben's to him and said, "We just wait?"

And that was what they did. They stood there at the bottom of the stairs like two anxious fathers awaiting news from the same delivery room, and at some point they finished their beers and Liam got them new ones, and muted voices filtered down to them from above, loud enough to hear that Kurt was doing most of the talking, but too quiet to be sure just what he was saying.

Finally, the doctor came down the stairs and smiled at—at *Liam*, for fuck's sake! "Calvin wants me to tell you he was right," Kurt said. "He *did* get sick because he had chicken instead of steak last night."

"What?" Ben demanded. Was Kurt being charmed by Liam *and* by Calvin?

"Food poisoning," Kurt said. "Salmonella in chicken legs. I took a culture and I'll get it analyzed to be sure, but I'm pretty confident. There's a national recall, but it hasn't gotten as much publicity as I'd have liked."

"He'll be okay?" Ben asked.

"I'll keep an eye on him to make sure he doesn't get dehydrated— I'll come by again tomorrow, if that works for everyone? But, yeah, he should be fine. He's in great shape, especially for his age—he wanted me to be sure I told you *that* too. He wasn't as enthusiastic about me telling you to pick up some Pedialyte, but it wouldn't hurt. If he'll drink it. Otherwise, water is good. No coffee, no alcohol. No spicy foods."

"But he's going to be okay." Ben needed to hear it just once more.

And Kurt seemed to understand. He reached up and clapped Ben on the shoulder, then looked him in the eyes. "He'll be okay," he said firmly.

And Ben believed him. Mostly. But he still took a long swig of his beer and wished it was something stronger.

He and Liam showed the doctor out and then were left in the front hall together.

"I'm sleeping in your bed," Liam said.

Ben stared at him.

"Upstairs. Calvin turned your old room into a guest room. That's where I slept last night. I just thought I should mention it, because if you wanted to stay over, you'd probably want to sleep in there. And I could move, of course. To the couch, I guess?" Liam peered skeptically into the living room, clearly measuring the couch and realizing it was too short for a grown man to stretch out on.

"What's wrong with the regular guest room?"

"What?"

"There are three bedrooms, Liam. There always have been. Did you never notice that?"

"I guess he's using it for something else?"

"He wasn't a couple weeks ago." Ben frowned and started up the stairs, then down the hall without even a quick inquiry as he stormed past the bathroom.

Was this another one of Calvin's games? The sickness seemed genuine enough, but before that, back when he'd been healthy, there was no damn reason to put Liam in Ben's bed. The bed the two of them had shared so many times. No reason other than game playing by an annoying, interfering—

He pushed the door to the guest room open and stopped short.

The room was jam-packed with boxes. Ben nudged one with his foot, and it moved enough to show that its contents weren't heavy, but too little for it to be empty.

"Is Calvin a hoarder now?" Liam asked from too close behind Ben. "That's new."

"He's not a hoarder." Ben crouched and read a few labels. Party supply stores, baby shops—everything he'd need for the baby shower he'd decided to throw for Dinah and Seth. Being stored in a totally logical place. In Calvin's home, where he could do whatever the hell he wanted, without any need to ask for Ben's permission.

He straightened up. "Okay. Yeah, this room is out of service. And I would like to stay over, just to keep an eye on him. But you don't need to take the couch—I can."

"That's stupid. You're two inches taller than I am."

"But you got here first. And you're the invited guest."

"It's your room. There's nothing more 'first' than it being your room."

"That hasn't been my full-time room for almost two decades. And maybe I don't need to stay, anyway. It's not like I live that far away."

"You'll just worry if you go home. You won't get any sleep. I'd like to say you can trust me to look after him, but we both know he's going to be even more of a pain in the ass with me than he would be with you. And assuming Calvin's well enough to be left alone, you've got a big day of building ahead of you tomorrow." Liam looked down at the beer he was holding, then shrugged. "I can still drive. There's a B&B I've stayed at before. I can give them a call."

"They're hosting the building team—the pros who were babysitting us all day? They're from out of town. There's no room at that inn."

"So I'll have some *more* beers and sleep outside. Is that hammock still up?"

"You could stay at my place," Ben said. It was too much, too damn intimate, but it was a hell of a lot better than offering to share the bed at Uncle Calvin's. And if they didn't solve this issue soon, Ben knew that was the exact offer he was going to make. He'd have some rationale about it being totally platonic, just a matter of convenience, but he knew he'd blow through that at the first hint of a suggestion that Liam might be interested in more. And as devastating as it would be to have a one-night stand with Liam, it would be even worse if Liam didn't show that tiny hint of interest to set it all off.

There was no winning that scenario. Having Liam stay at his house while Ben took his old room at Uncle Calvin's? Awkward and weird, but not disastrous. "I have a guest room. Minimal boxes. Clean sheets."

"Sounds like paradise, but are you sure?"

"Absolutely." Absolutely better to have Liam as far away as possible. That was the only way Ben had a prayer of getting through this night.

CHAPTER FOURTEEN

LIAM DIDN'T sleep well. He kept wanting to get up and look around. Not snoop, exactly, but—well. Something close to it.

He managed to resist, but the mental effort made it hard to relax. Knowing he was in Ben's house, only feet away from Ben's bed? Yeah, that made it hard to relax, even if Ben wasn't actually *in* the bed.

It made for a fitful, restless night before he walked to the job site. Ben was there, since Seth's wife had volunteered to look after Calvin, but he was back to cool, remote, frustrating Ben. Liam wanted to grab him, drag him behind a stack of lumber, and pin him against it and kiss him until he stopped being mad, until they both forgot their history, their mistakes, forgot their damn names, let go of everything that got between them—

Liam carried sheets of drywall instead. He cut and fit and taped and worked and pushed all other thoughts out of his mind.

At lunch, Seth fell into the food line behind him and followed him over to a spot under a shade tree. They settled, took a few bites of food, and then Seth said, "You having fun?" in a tone that made it clear he knew it was a stupid question.

"I shouldn't be here." It was so clear, really. It had been just as clear the day before, of course, but Liam hadn't been as tired then, and it had been easier to keep his spirits up. "Ben doesn't want me here, and I have a lot going on back in the city. What the hell am I thinking, wasting my time like this?"

"If Ben *did* want you here, would it still be wasted time?" Seth sounded like he was picking his words carefully, but Liam wasn't sure he appreciated the effort.

"Hypotheticals are just one more way to waste time. I can't afford to be messing around with all this."

Seth shrugged. "We've gotten a lot done—we're ahead of schedule, even with Calvin sick. And you were an extra anyway. If you can't be here, we'll be fine without you."

It wasn't said in a mean way. Seth was trying to help, not to hurt, and Liam knew it. Still. *We'll be fine without you.* He wasn't needed. He was just an extra. There was a community here, a damn family, but he wasn't part of it. He'd blown his chances at that years and years ago.

The sandwich was too dry. He took a slug from his can of pop to wash down the bite in his mouth, then forced himself to take another and swallow it before saying, "I'm not going to quit. I said I'd do it and I'll do it. And I'll stop bitching about it. Sorry."

Seth shrugged easily. "It's fine. I invited the bitching, and you've been working hard. It's not like you were moping around, not getting anything done. Really, you're a better worker when you're a bit mad—I wonder if there's some way for us to harness that. We could team you up with somebody really annoying, and you could work out your frustration with amazing feats of building-related strength."

"You sound too much like Calvin, with his schemes and manipulations."

"He's the master. I'm a mere apprentice." Seth frowned. "Actually, I think Dinah might be his real apprentice. I'm kind of worried about her spending the whole day with him today. She'll come home even more Machiavellian than she was this morning."

"A day spent looking after a sick old man is going to make your wife sinister? That seems like the reverse of what I'd expect."

"Expectations do tend to reverse themselves once Calvin's involved." But Seth really didn't sound too worried.

"You guys are pretty happy together, huh? Things have worked out well for you."

Seth's smile was sweet and genuine. "I'm the luckiest man alive. Wife, daughter, life—everything's fantastic."

"Damn. Are you auditioning to be the annoying guy who makes me work harder?"

Seth's smile widened. "I have to *audition*. Damn, I don't know—is it really that much of a treat to be the guy hanging out with you?"

Well, Ben would clearly say it wasn't, but Liam didn't let himself point that out. He asked polite questions about Seth's family and actually found himself enjoying the answers and the conversation that flowed from them. Seth *was* a lucky man, and it was hard to resent him when he acknowledged it so openly.

Ben stayed remote for the rest of the afternoon, and when it all wrapped up around four, he kept himself conspicuously distant from

Liam as everyone exchanged sweaty, satisfied hugs of congratulation for a job well done.

Liam's hands were blistered, with bandages wrinkled and grimy from work; his neck was sunburned despite repeated applications of sunscreen; every muscle in his body was complaining, with a special scream coming from those bastards between his shoulder blades; he was grimy, smelly, and he had a three-hour drive home before he could do anything about either of those issues.

And he still would have been perfectly satisfied with his life if only Ben would smile at him. A little wave, maybe, a suggestion that he knew Liam was alive. That he *cared* Liam was alive.

But Liam didn't get what he wanted. Seth and most of the rest of the team were friendly and happy with him, but Ben? He left earlier than anyone else, saying he had to get home to Calvin, but clearly more interested in getting the hell away from Liam.

So Liam drove home, lonely and smelly, got disgustingly delicious drive-through burgers for dinner halfway home, made embarrassed excuses to the neighbors he met in his building's elevator, showered, pulled on clean clothes, and tried not to sulk.

But it was deeper than a sulk, wasn't it?

He was legitimately disappointed. He'd hoped for something, and it hadn't worked out.

But that wasn't the end of the damn world. He needed to keep himself together. He hadn't started crying, at least, so that was a small victory.

And it was Sunday night, which meant he had a phone call to make. Not that it was likely to be interesting enough to distract him from his misery, but it was probably important that he keep to his routine. He found his phone, ignored his aching muscles, and made the call.

"Liam!" his mother gushed. "We just got in the door. We had an early dinner over at Charles and Martha's. They have a *lovely* new pool—well, more than that, a sort of pool *area*—an 'outdoor room,' they called it, with the pool and a cabana and a patio and some beautiful plants, although those are still a little small. But they'll grow, of course! And your father is—it's Liam, dear. Go get on the other line."

"Sounds like a nice evening," Liam managed. He'd hear about his father's golf games and his mother's dinners and he'd give them a watered-down version of the situation at work. He wouldn't mention any peculiar building activities at all—and it would just be a typical Sunday-evening parental check-in.

Or so he thought, until his father got on the phone and said, "Liam. I'm glad you called, son. We were going to get in touch with you later this evening." And there was something unnaturally grave in his tone.

Cancer. Heart disease. Bankruptcy? Suddenly Liam's own complaints seemed petty. "What's going on?"

"Well, it probably won't affect you much, really. But we wanted to let you know before we made it public."

"Okay…."

His mother broke in. "Your father and I are getting a divorce. We've been talking about it for a while, and we just… well. It's time."

"A—what?" He took a moment, trying to make the words make sense, but it did no good. "I—I've never even seen you guys have a fight! What the hell are you talking about? You're in your sixties, you're living your perfect lives on the beach with all the golf and whatever—why the hell would you get a divorce?" He waited a moment, then demanded, "Is this a joke?"

"Of course it's not a joke," his dad said. "It's something we've been thinking about for quite a while."

"You've been thinking about getting a divorce? Why? You guys have always been solid."

"But is that all there is to life?" his mother asked. "Being 'solid'?"

"I swear to God, if you start talking about the importance of *passion*, I'm going to hang up."

"What? Why? What do you have against passion?"

"I don't have anything against it, I just—" But his trials at work didn't seem like something that would add to the conversation. "Never mind. But you guys don't need to get a divorce! That's really drastic." Yeah, this was good. He'd be a problem solver, a mentor. "Why not do a trial separation or something? Take a trip without each other? Just test this out without diving into it."

"We've already done those things," his father said. "We aren't stupid, Liam. And we aren't asking for your permission on this. We're just telling you what's going on."

"You've already—what do you mean, you've already done a trial separation? When? What the hell? You didn't mention that to me?"

"Well, there was no real point." His mother sounded completely placid and content with the entire situation. "We didn't want to upset you for nothing, if we decided not to go through with it. And before you suggest it, we've done counseling too. That was actually what made us realize we don't need to be married anymore."

"You went to marriage counseling, and it made you realize you should get a divorce? I think you should ask for your money back."

"Not at all," his father said. "It helped us realize that our marriage hasn't *failed.* It did what it was supposed to do. It gave us a stable family for raising our child, it gave a framework for us to merge our social and financial lives... it worked. But our needs have changed now, and the marriage won't work for our new needs."

"What the hell kind of counselor were you going to? You're in South Carolina, not California—this 'conscious uncoupling' bullshit doesn't make sense for you!"

"Conscious uncoupling," his mother mused. "I like that!"

"Me too," his father said.

"Of course you both like it—you share the same brain! You've agreed on every single thing I've ever heard you discuss for my entire life! Why on earth would you walk away from that?"

"Why do we need it?" his father asked. "Are we so weak that we need an exact twin to echo our thoughts on every matter? We can't handle a little dissent, a little disagreement? We can't let ourselves be excited by new ideas and new experiences, with new people?"

"Yeah, but—" But what? Liam needed to get a grip on this conversation. "Couldn't you just join a different golf club or something? Find a new group of ladies to have lunch with? Hell, you could make bigger changes than that—start volunteering somewhere, or maybe even start a little business or get a part-time job. There are lots of changes you can make and still stay together."

"We want to date other people," his mother said. "We want to have relationships—*sexual* relationships—with other people."

Liam fought the urge to drop the phone. "Okay, I'm not really ready to discuss your sex lives with you—"

"And we're not inviting you to." His father's voice was firm. "This isn't actually something that requires your opinion or your input, and it certainly doesn't need your approval. We've made our decision, and we'll be letting people know about it starting tomorrow. We're both planning to stay in South Carolina, at least for the immediate future, so if you come to visit, we'll both be happy to see you. Your mother's staying in the house for now, but we may end up selling it. I've got an apartment—I'll email you the address and phone number."

"Wait—you guys are okay for money, right?" They'd always been comfortable and had helped Liam quite a bit when he'd moved to New York. But maybe they'd overextended themselves, contributing to his flashy life? "You wouldn't be selling the house because you *need* to?"

"We're fine," his mother said reassuringly. "But the house was too big for two of us, really, so I can't imagine it won't be too big for one."

"Jesus," Liam managed.

"Think of it like a retirement," his father said. "It's an ending, yes, but it's also a new beginning. It's a good time to look back and celebrate, as well, and we're planning on doing that. We'll be sending you an invitation in a couple weeks—we're hoping you'll be able to come down for a party we're planning."

"You're having a divorce party? Like, both of you, together?"

"It's going to be lovely." His mother sounded just as enthusiastic about this as about any of her other events. "We'll have the catering set up by the house, but a fire down on the beach, and I found some absolutely darling candle holders with little tinted glass globes to go over the flame and keep the wind off, so we can light the path through the dunes with those instead of the floodlights. The floods really aren't very festive, are they? And not flattering either. I think the candles will be romantic."

"And we're thinking of having our favorite foods from all the places we've lived together. Or at least something *inspired* by those foods—like on one of the cooking contests on television."

"We met when we were going to school in Vermont, so we'll have something with maple syrup. Maybe some variation on kielbasa for our time in North Falls. You know how much we loved Dan Stuart's kielbasa."

But Liam really wasn't ready to help his parents plan the menu for their Happy Divorce party. "This is—" He stopped himself. These were his parents, and they'd made their decision. Decisions, plural, he supposed, and that was going to take some getting used to. But they both seemed fine with the situation. Pretty damn chipper, really. "Okay. I mean—okay. You're right. This is your decision. I—okay." Was there anything more to say? "Let me know if you need anything, I guess?"

"Just your handsome, smiling face at the party!"

"And maybe some kielbasa," his father said. "It'd be nicely authentic if we imported the food from the actual places we lived. We can check on the internet first—if Dan Stuart isn't in business anymore there's no point, or maybe he has some way to ship food from his shop. But if that didn't work out, maybe we'd be able to persuade you to take a trip up to North Falls at some point?"

"Maybe," Liam agreed faintly.

They finished the call with a few of the inane niceties Liam had been expecting in the first place—good to know that the impending dissolution of his forty-year marriage hadn't affected his father's golf game at all—and then Liam stood in his apartment, staring at the wall.

His parents weren't upset. He knew them well enough to know that neither one was much for putting a false face on; if they felt something, they showed it, and in this case they just weren't feeling all that much. They were fine.

He certainly had no right to be upset on their behalf, and he didn't think he *was* upset, not really. But he was… unsettled, maybe?

Something that he'd thought was permanent had turned out to be just as temporary as everything else in the damn world.

He left the apartment without a real plan for where he was going, but maybe it was time he stopped fooling himself about that. If he was just going for a wander, he'd walk. When he left home and climbed into his car with no real destination in mind? Well, he had a damn destination in mind.

He rolled into North Falls a few hours later, windshield wipers sluicing a gentle rhythm as he drove. He'd blown right past the Welcome To sign without even thinking about turning around. That was either progress or deterioration, he supposed.

And he didn't mess around with his tour-around-the-town nonsense this time either. He drove straight to Ben's house, then parked on the street in front of it. He climbed out of the car, made it halfway up the walk, and at that point his nerve deserted him.

He stood there in the rain, wondering what the hell he was doing. He wanted to see Ben, yeah. He wanted—he wasn't even sure he had words for all the things he wanted from Ben. But that was his problem, not Ben's, and showing up at—he looked down at his watch—a little past midnight on a day when Ben needed to wake up the next morning for work? When Ben had made it crystal damn clear that he wanted nothing to do with Liam?

There wasn't a light on in the house and Liam was going to go knock on the door. That was a dick move. He and Ben had made some sort of peace and that needed to be the end of it.

Still—he couldn't quite make himself turn around and leave.

So he stood there in the rain, staring at the house.

And that was when a voice, unexpected but oh so familiar, reached him from the dark corner of the porch. "You going to stay out there?" Ben asked. "Or do you want to come inside and get warm?"

Chapter Fifteen

It was dreamlike, maybe because Ben really should have been in bed and actually dreaming. But he hadn't been able to sleep, so he'd bundled up, gotten himself a glass of scotch, and gone out on the porch to watch the spring rain.

And to wait.

Yeah, it had really felt like he was waiting.

Like he'd somehow known Liam was on his way, and maybe even known Liam would pull back, would stop himself from coming all the way up on the porch and knocking on the door. Maybe Ben had known Liam wouldn't make the final move without encouragement.

And of course Ben shouldn't give that encouragement. He knew better. But he'd used up all his powers of resistance, and now? Now it was just fate. Inevitable.

He stood up slowly, still dreamily, and waited at the top of the porch steps. Liam approached with caution, came halfway up the stairs, and said, "It's okay that I'm here?"

Ben reached for him, brought his hand to Liam's cheek, and curled his fingers just enough to draw Liam up the rest of the way onto the porch. He ghosted his thumb over the scratch from the raspberry bushes, just a ghostly line now, and the freckles across the tops of Liam's cheeks that hadn't been there at the start of the weekend. They shifted in under the roof, eyes locked on each other, and somehow it was okay that Liam was there. Where else would he be?

Their kiss felt just as natural, just as predestined, as all the rest of it. No urgency, just want that turned to need, rain dripping off Liam's forehead onto Ben's overheated skin, cold fingers finding warm ones and interlacing.

Liam pulled away. Not far, and clearly he had to make an effort to do it, but why the hell was he bothering? He licked his lips and said, "Scotch. How much have you had?"

"I'm not drunk." Ben tugged at Liam's hand. "Come inside."

"Are you sure?"

Ben just tugged again, and this time Liam let himself be moved, guided, through the front door and down the short hallway to Ben's bedroom.

Liam's shirt was wet, and when Ben slid his hands under the hem and up over Liam's abs, everything was chilly. He kept going, rucking the shirt up and over Liam's head, exposing glorious skin as he went. Ben bent his head to nip, to kiss, to taste, and he felt the shudder run through Liam's body.

"Is this okay?" Liam asked again.

No, it wasn't. It was either wonderful or terrible or somehow both at once, but it was definitely something extreme, something a lifetime away from "okay," in one direction or another. If they stopped to talk about this, if Ben stopped to *think* about this, it would all be too real, and being with Liam wasn't something Ben could afford to want, in reality.

So instead of answering the question with words, Ben raised his lips to Liam's and kissed him, long and deep, and Liam stopped asking unanswerable questions.

There were no more hesitations after that. Ben pulled his own shirt off, and they had skin on skin. Ben fumbled with the fly of Liam's jeans, trying to somehow give his hands space to work without breaking the contact between their chests, their bellies. He *needed* more, but he couldn't bring himself to accept the tiny bit of *less* that would allow the more to happen.

Until Liam took charge. He shuffled them toward the bed, and when they got there he just kept pressing, easing Ben back so he was sitting on the mattress, freeing up his legs to wrap around Liam's ass and pull him in closer. They surged together, hardness meeting hardness, and even through layers of clothing Ben could feel the heat. A rhythm, then, waves flowing from one body to another, like when they'd been kids, too shy to take their clothes off and too desperate to stay still.

Well, Ben wasn't shy anymore, or at least this night he wasn't. He put a hand on Liam's chest—skin so warm and smooth, so soft over the hard muscles beneath—and pushed him away. Just a little. Kept him within the warm circle of Ben's legs, but made room for getting his jeans undone. Liam, bless him, took care of the rest, shimmying out of the rain-damp denim and tugging his boxer briefs down at the same time.

He stumbled, almost fell, and laughed breathlessly. "Shit. Gotta get my shoes off."

Ben should have laughed in return, should have said something kind, but he didn't want this to be comfortable. He couldn't let himself think it was something he was going to get used to. He waited silently as Liam dealt with his clothes, then moved fast, kicking one of his own bare feet up to brace against Liam's chest and hold him away for a moment.

If this was going to be the only time—the last time—he saw Liam like this, he wanted to be sure he had time to appreciate the view.

Liam was still for a breath or two, then slid his hands up Ben's legs, inside his sweatpants. He got a good grip on the fabric and tugged, and Ben lifted his ass and helped with his hands, and the pants were off and they were naked together. Perfectly, terrifyingly naked.

Liam fell forward, wedged a knee between Ben's, braced his elbows on either side of Ben's face, and they kissed. If the sensations had been intense before, when they were half-dressed, they were almost unbearable now. Every inch of Ben's body was electrified, magnetized, needing and wanting and straining. His breath came in gasps and moans that would have been mortifying if he hadn't heard their echoes in Liam's mouth.

It would be too easy to come just like this, but Ben wanted more. "Fuck me," he gasped, and Liam moaned in return, then rolled them, shifted them, got them close enough to the bedside table that he could reach it and fumble in the drawer without taking his lips away from Ben's body.

Ben let himself float. Not away—he wanted to be absolutely present for every moment of this. But he didn't need to be in control. For this one night, he could let go and just feel, just be. He could *trust*. The stretch, the pressure, the fullness, the friction. The perfection, with Liam hovering above him, skin flushed and eyes intense, whole body tensing and relaxing in time with his thrusts. And Ben's own body responding without any thought or effort, rising to meet the pleasure, then letting him fall away before inevitably rising again.

Ben could feel his orgasm building and tried to push it away. He didn't want to come; he just wanted to stay like this, with Liam like this, forever.

His body had different ideas, though, and it seemed like Liam's did too. They moved together, both of them caught up in the same primitive, desperate dance, and they came together, shuddering their mutual release.

A moment of frozen time, or maybe *layered* time, as if this was them as they were but also them as they'd been so many times before. Them as they always should—but Ben got control of himself before that traitorous thought was able to leave his subconscious.

It had only been now, and it *could* only be now, and he damn well needed to remember that.

"You okay?" Liam asked, shifting himself only halfway off Ben's body so their legs were still entwined, their torsos still connected.

Again, the word was wrong, so Ben just smiled and let his fingers play through Liam's hair, now damp with sweat as well as rain. It was only now, so he had to savor it all.

They were quiet for a while, both of them awake, Ben staring at the ceiling, Liam—well. Liam staring at Ben, it seemed. Eventually Liam said, "Do you ever hear from your parents?"

It took Ben a while to shift his train of thought to the new topic. "Sometimes. My dad called a couple years ago—wanted money. My mom's doing a bit better, I think. She was out in Colorado last I heard."

"Is it different, now? You're an adult. You don't need them anymore, right?"

"I never needed them. If Uncle Calvin hadn't stepped in, I would have been in trouble, but getting to move in with him? He's a pain in the ass, but he's ten times the parent either of them ever was."

Liam kissed Ben's shoulder. A simple gesture, not one that should have made Ben want to cry, or to push himself out of bed and run away.

They were quiet again for a while. Eventually Liam shifted over so he was lying on his back, staring at the ceiling along with Ben, and said, "My parents are getting a divorce."

On one level it was shocking news. Liam's parents had always seemed absolutely, placidly content with each other. But Ben hadn't had any contact with them for fifteen years, so that was lots of time for things to change. And really, hearing Liam say it made a lot of other things make sense.

Like what the hell Liam had been doing in North Falls over the past couple weeks. "That must be really unsettling," Ben said carefully. It must have made Liam question a lot of things, trying to track them back and see where they'd gone wrong. Maybe coming to North Falls had been his attempt—or part of his attempt—to understand his parents.

Sex with Ben? Well, a little comfort, a little distraction, falling into an old habit—no need for there to be only one reason for it, obviously.

And no need for Ben to spend too much time reviewing his own motivations either.

"I think it'll be okay," Liam said, and it took Ben a moment to realize they were still talking about Liam's parents. "I mean, it's not really my business, is it? And they seem fine with it."

"That's good." Ben probably should have had something more profound to say, but he didn't.

"Yeah. And there's—there's stuff at work that I kind of wanted to talk to you about, but I'm tired, and you have to get up tomorrow morning, and God knows I have to get up tomorrow morning—I need to be back in the city first thing."

Okay, Ben could do this. He could be practical and helpful, the cool and mature one-night stand. "Do you have an alarm on your phone? You could set it for a few hours from now—enough time for you to have a little snooze, but still good to get back to the city."

"You don't mind?"

Ben wondered what would happen if he said yeah, he did mind. Nothing good, he was sure—not that Liam would be a total jerk, but it would make things awkward. And there was no need for that. "No problem," he said, and he leaned off the side of the bed and found Liam's jeans, with his phone in the pocket.

"Thanks," Liam said as he took the phone. "This—I'm not sure what we just did. I mean, I'm not sure what it means."

It doesn't mean anything. It can't. But Ben just said, "Shhh. You're thinking too much. Set your alarm and go to sleep."

And Liam did as he was told, snuggling in against Ben like a tired puppy.

Ben, on the other hand, stayed awake, staring at the damn ceiling, until Liam's alarm went off and the brief, peaceful daze came to an end. They were both awake now. Both back to reality.

CHAPTER SIXTEEN

LIAM DIDN'T want to leave. Not right then and possibly not ever. But he had responsibilities, opportunities… he had somewhere to be.

And Ben wasn't exactly begging him to stay. More like hustling him out the door, really. For the second time that weekend, and it was getting a bit old. Still, how to object without sounding whiney?

"Should I make you coffee?" Ben asked. He seemed far too chipper and cheerful for a middle-of-the-night conversation and leave taking. "I have lots of travel mugs, remember?"

"No, it's fine. Stay in bed—sorry I woke you."

"I wasn't sleeping." Ben shifted to the side of the bed, keeping the sheet carefully tucked around his waist as he groped for his pants. They were being modest around each other now?

Liam pulled his own jeans on, grimacing as the still-damp fabric slid over his skin. Damn, he wished he'd had the sense to hang them up so they'd have had a chance to dry. But, no, he guessed he *didn't* really wish that, because if he'd been calm enough to think of something so practical, it would have meant he wasn't all that into what he was doing. And he had been pretty damn into it.

He turned quickly, found Ben by the side of the bed, sweatpants on, and took the one step to bring their bodies back close together, back where they should be. "I can come back tonight," he said, reaching for Ben's hand.

But Ben pulled away. "Oh. No, I don't think so. I actually—I have plans tonight."

"Oh." Yeah, okay, that made sense. Ben had a life, after all. "So—when? Tomorrow? Because whatever we're doing here, I want to keep doing it. We should talk it through, I guess. I get that. But when? You must have some time before the weekend, right? Maybe I can hire a car to drive me, and I can sleep in the back seat or something."

"No." And Ben stepped even farther back, as far as he could go without climbing right up on the bedside table. "Actually—I'm seeing someone. I mean, I was seeing him, and then we took a bit of a break, but we're having dinner tomorrow—well, today, now—and I'm pretty sure we're getting back together. So, you know. This, with you? This was good. It was a good way to wrap things up, right? Leave it all on a positive note?" He smiled, and Liam realized that all the chipper cheerfulness was just an act, a candy coating on a bitter pill.

It shouldn't have felt so wrong. He and Ben hadn't been together for *fifteen years*. All of Liam's adult life, really, because he'd just been a kid the last time. So this was—it was nothing big. It was a return to the status quo. The aching pit in his gut was imaginary.

"He's... this other guy... you're sure? What if it doesn't work out?" Liam tried to find his own smile and was pretty sure it looked just as fake and desperate as Ben's. "I don't mean to wish bad luck on it or anything. But if it doesn't work, or if you have dinner with him and realize he's not quite what you're looking for...."

Ben was quiet for a moment, then looked up and said, "If it doesn't work out with him, I'll find someone else for it to work out with. Not—not you."

"What? Why? I mean, this—" Liam gestured at the bed, as if that was somehow enough of an illustration of what he was trying to say. "This was good, wasn't it?" But that wasn't the important part. There were lots of people he could have sex with; there was only one Ben. "We can—we were good, before. We could try it again."

"We weren't good. If we'd been good, you wouldn't have slept around and I wouldn't have let you. And this, tonight? Sure. Sex. But there's a hell of a lot more to it than just sex." He shook his head. "No. This was a nice goodbye. It was a good end to something that dragged out way longer than it should have."

He started moving, cautiously edging past Liam, who was too stunned to do anything to stop him. "I'll make you some coffee for the road. And I have some muffins. I'll give you one of those, and a couple pieces of fruit." He was heading for the kitchen now, his voice fading as he moved away. "It'll be like a little car picnic!"

A car picnic. Liam found the rest of his clothes and pulled them on. He had been dismissed. Again. This had been—he had no idea what it had been. He had no idea why he'd come to North Falls, why he'd gotten in contact with Ben, why he'd *slept* with Ben, or why he felt so damn shitty about leaving Ben. But he was absolutely damn certain he didn't want Ben's car picnic. So he pulled his shoes on, found his keys, and walked.

He didn't sneak; Ben must have heard him coming down the hall, and he must have heard him bypassing the kitchen and heading for the front door. But Ben didn't turn around, didn't say anything, and neither did Liam. He just left.

It was over.

It had been dormant, it had started to regrow, and it had been killed. And he didn't even know what "it" was, exactly.

Didn't matter, he told himself as he climbed into the car.

The street was still dark and deserted, and he let himself drive a little too fast as he headed out of town.

He was going back to the city, back to reality. Back to his career and his ambitions.

That was where he belonged.

Ben was right. It had been a nice goodbye. Liam had been an idiot to think it could be more than that.

BEN WAS an idiot. He'd known it all along. When he'd stood up on the porch and called Liam to him, he'd known what would happen, and he'd known it would hurt, and he'd done it anyway. Nothing to blame Liam for, not this time. Just his own stupidity.

He went back out on the porch, this time without the blanket that had kept him warm earlier in the evening, and stared into the night. Liam was gone. Ben had *told* him to go.

Because you had to. Because you can't have that kind of instability in your life. You need peace, you need calm, you need... Kevin?

Well, that didn't feel quite right, but there was no denying that Kevin was the path to stability. *Kevin* wouldn't show up on Ben's front walk past midnight on a school night, not unless he'd been invited and plans had been made for how to ensure that everyone still got enough sleep.

Kevin wouldn't *keep* Ben up even after they'd parted, fretting and freezing, sitting out on the damn porch without a jacket or a blanket, trying to figure out how to feel about whatever the hell was going on. No, Kevin wouldn't pull that shit.

Kevin wouldn't have some weirdass crisis over his parents' divorce—Kevin's parents were already divorced, so that was handy—and start digging into old relationships that should have stayed buried. Kevin wouldn't hang out with Uncle Calvin—well, sure he would, but not without Ben! He wouldn't sneak around like that.

Kevin wouldn't cheat.

He wouldn't leave Ben with a gaping, aching hole in his chest that couldn't be filled with all the alcohol and casual sex and deep breathing in the whole damn world. Kevin wouldn't do that.

Liam was the past, Kevin was the future. Or someone else, someone Kevinesque. Kevin was a symbol, not necessarily a man.

No, asshole, he's a man. With feelings and worries of his own. You can't drag him through all this if you don't have a positive attitude.

Right. Okay. Yeah. Ben needed to make sure he was being honest with Kevin about all this. But he had absolutely no idea what being honest would look like.

The cold eventually drove him in from the porch, and he curled up in bed and dozed for at least a couple hours. A massive coffee injection got him as far as midday at work, but by early afternoon he found himself staring at the children in a sort of daze, not really hearing anything they said, and not really caring either.

Unacceptable. He had a sacred responsibility to be at his best for his students, and he had not met his obligation. Not by a long shot. More coffee in the staff room, a vague semblance of attention for the rest of the day, and then home. He probably wouldn't have even *noticed* if he'd sideswiped another police car as he drove through town, but there were no flashing lights behind him as he pulled up at the house, so that had to count for something.

He stumbled inside and into bed. He'd take a short nap and be up and ready to go. No problem.

Except the next time he opened his eyes the light was different, the sun almost down, and there was a noise somewhere. Oh. There was someone knocking at the front door. Liam? Come back?

Oh, shit. Not Liam. It was likely *Kevin*. Because Ben had called him, and crawled a little, and suggested they get together, and Kevin had actually agreed to give it a try.

Ben fumbled for his phone, but it wasn't in his pocket. A moment of panic, but he'd probably just left it in the car. Or at school. Or possibly he'd tossed it in the trash at some point and put a piece of garbage in his pocket, but he'd treat that as the worst-case scenario.

He rolled to his feet and stumbled to the front door. And there Kevin was on the porch, looking sweet and cute and stable. And a little concerned.

"Are you okay?" he asked. "You weren't at the restaurant, and I tried to call but you didn't answer."

"Jesus, what time is it? How—I'm sorry. I—" *I stayed up all last night worrying about a guy and then fucking him and then worrying some more.* No, that probably wasn't the way to go. "I have no idea what's going on. I'm just really tired."

Kevin took a half step back. "Are you coming down with something? I just—I have a really busy week. I can't really catch anything right now."

Well, that was an easy out. But, damn it, Ben wasn't supposed to be looking for outs. He *wanted* this. "No, I don't think I'm getting sick. I just didn't sleep well last night." For reasons that did not need to be discussed. "How late am I? I don't know where my phone is, and I don't have any clocks."

"It's almost six thirty. With some people, I wouldn't have worried, but you're not someone who leaves people waiting. Not usually."

Right. *You're not* usually *an asshole.* "Sorry. I, uh—what do you want to do? If you give me five minutes I can get organized and we can go back down to the inn." It wasn't like they needed reservations, not on a Monday night this early in the season. "Or I can cook for us here. Or if you want to call it off, I totally understand." *But I do* not *hope for that result. No, I do* not.

"No, I don't want to call it off. I—sure. I can wait five minutes. We can go downtown and start again."

Start again. Yeah. That was what this night was about. "Great," Ben said. "Thanks. And sorry again. I—this was a one-time thing, I promise."

"No problem. Okay if I sit out here while I'm waiting? I missed this porch."

He missed the porch? Strange, but— "Sure, yeah."

Ben hustled to the bathroom and splashed some water on his face, brushed his teeth, and looked at himself in the mirror. Kevin. Yay, Kevin!

No butterflies. It wouldn't have mattered if Kevin had turned around and walked away for good—Ben would have just come back inside, done some grading, and gotten a good night's sleep.

That was a positive. He was being Zen about this; he was calm and had himself under control. He was a pebble in the stream, or a leaf on the wind, or—whatever. He was good.

And he stayed that way all evening. His cell *was* in the car, so that was easy. They had a nice dinner at the Welland Arms, getting caught up on what each of them had been up to, with a few strategic exclusions on Ben's part. And, hell, maybe on Kevin's part too. That was fine; it was none of Ben's business. Then Kevin drove them back to Ben's porch and, after satisfying himself that Ben was absolutely not coming down with something, there was a good-night kiss. A nice kiss, one that Ben knew from experience could turn into nice sex. But neither of them pushed for that.

"We're going to do better this time," Kevin said. "We won't panic, won't run away from things."

Well, that was fucking patronizing, considering that it had been *Ben* who'd "panicked" and "run away" the last time. But he just smiled. He didn't say, *We won't push for more than the other person wants to give this time*, because there was no point to it. They were looking forward, not back.

Another sweet kiss before Ben went inside and closed the door firmly behind him. He checked his cell to be sure there hadn't been any messages, and he got ready for bed.

And as he lay there in the dark, he forced himself to think about Kevin. Or his students, or Seth and Dinah and the new baby, or the situation in the Middle East—he could think about almost anything, really. Just not about Liam. Liam was the past. Liam was gone.

He turned it into a sort of chant. *Let go of the past, embrace the future. Let go of the past, embrace the future.* It wasn't perfect, but it was boring enough that he eventually drifted off. And where his dreams took him? Well, he couldn't be held responsible for his damn dreams.

CHAPTER SEVENTEEN

"YOU'VE GOT him where you want him," Nolan crowed. He lifted his glass of champagne, and Scarlett mirrored the gesture. They were having post-dinner drinks, Liam had told them what was going on at the office, and they seemed genuinely excited for him. Secretly strategizing and figuring out ways to turn the situation to their advantage? Probably. They'd worked together at the same firm fresh out of school and had always been competitive with each other. But they were excited as well.

"Don't get ahead of yourselves," Liam warned. "I wouldn't even have told you if I thought anyone at the office would be able to keep it a secret."

"Anna sounded thrilled," Scarlett said with a warm smile. Anna had worked at Scarlett's firm before moving over to Tristan's, and the two women had stayed friends. Mostly. "She said she was really worried when you left—thought the well was going to dry right up. *And* she likes you, of course. She's looking forward to having a boss who isn't staring at her ass all the time."

"Do *not* make me start worrying about sexual harassment lawsuits. I'm supposed to be celebrating."

"Ah, the burden of command." Nolan lifted the champagne bottle out of the ice bucket and refilled their glasses. "You gonna pull Allison off the Taybec Briggs project?"

Liam didn't remember having discussed the Taybec Briggs project with Nolan or Scarlett. Well, maybe while he'd been working on the proposal—shit, yeah, while he'd been working on the proposal. They knew he'd wanted it, knew he hadn't gotten it…. "No," he said. "I won't really have time to give it the attention it deserves. And I can still have input, obviously—Allison has a lot to learn, and I can mentor her through this."

"You've just got it all put together, don't you?" Scarlett raised her refilled glass. "To Liam—first of us to claw his way to the top."

"Make room, though," Nolan said, "because we're right behind you."

They drank that toast, and a few more, and Liam tried to relax and enjoy the moment. This was something special. He'd worked for it. Sure, he'd also capitalized on an old man's heart attack, but—well, opportunity had knocked. He'd just answered the door.

Of course, that wasn't exactly how Ben would see it. Ben's moral compass had always spun a little less freely than Liam's, and he'd never really been too ambitious. Would he even be proud of Liam's current accomplishments?

And why the hell did Liam care?

He drained his glass and stood up. "Thanks for this," he told the others. "I really appreciate it. But I've got to get home now—lots of work to do tomorrow."

"Yup, that's the future," Nolan said sagely. "You think you were working a lot of hours *before* this? Just wait. Tristan's gonna expect even more from you now. And you'll be more in demand for social stuff, promo opportunities—damn. We'd better say goodbye now, because we may never see you again!"

Just like Ben might never see him again. But at least Nolan was kind enough to look sorry about it.

Ben hadn't cared at all.

Liam pasted a smile on his face, got his kiss from Scarlett and back slap from Nolan, and made his way out onto the street. He was far enough from home that he could easily justify a cab, but he started walking anyway.

Everything had worked out. The people at the office had seemed genuinely excited by the change, and things were going smoothly. Allison had been satisfyingly unsure of herself before he'd pulled her aside and offered a little reassurance. He'd been vindicated, and he'd celebrated with his friends. It was good. Everything was good.

And his goddamn face was wet again. Crying? Seriously?

"No," he muttered, and he brushed impatiently at his eyes. He needed to make a doctor's appointment or something—maybe his tear ducts were blocked, or overproducing—he didn't really know how tears worked. Because he'd damn well never had to know, because he didn't cry!

"Everything's good," he told himself, and he walked a little faster. If his cheeks got wet again, he refused to acknowledge it. Everything was fine. Better than fine. He was incredibly lucky. He was absolutely not crying.

BEN MADE it through the week. Two more dinner dates with Kevin both ended with kisses and thinly veiled preaching about not rushing into anything or making anyone nervous. The dinners themselves were fairly pleasant, and it wasn't as if Kevin didn't have a pretty good reason to be cautious of Ben's level of commitment, so Ben tried to put up with the irritation at the end of the night.

And he tried not to think about how things had been different with Liam. Petty irritation? Hell no. Ben would have told Liam to stop being such a prissy pain in the ass, Liam would have told Ben it took one to know one, and they would have had a quick fight followed by scorching makeup sex.

Well, that's how they would have done it when they were kids. But, Ben reminded himself again, the way they'd done it when they were kids hadn't worked. Liam had cheated. Ben had—well, Ben still wasn't quite sure how to classify his own behavior, but it certainly hadn't been mature. It certainly wasn't the way he wanted to behave *now*.

And it wasn't really that important for him to understand the details of it because it was all in the past, and he was focused on the future. Yup, the future. He was spending time with Kevin, not thinking about Liam—well, hardly thinking about him at all—well, yeah, he was working through some issues, possibly, that were somewhat related to Liam, but—

It wasn't a good sign that when his phone rang on Friday afternoon, his first thought was that it must be Liam calling. There was absolutely no reason for it to be Liam. Liam was gone, he was done. But when the display showed an unfamiliar number with a Manhattan area code, there was no surprise. It all felt fated, somehow.

Ben answered calmly, and the jolt through his belly when he heard Liam's voice? It would have been nice to pretend that it was surprise, but Ben wasn't *quite* that good at self-deception. Or at least not that quick.

Still he managed to keep his cool as he said, "Why are you calling, Liam? I thought we agreed that we wouldn't be seeing each other."

"Agreed?" Liam snorted. "If that's what you want to call it. But actually that *is* why I'm calling."

Ben braced himself. He needed to be strong. Whatever Liam was about to say, Ben would just be cool and controlled and deal with it. "What do you mean?"

"Calvin called me. Thanked me for my nursing care, so I think he must have been pretty delirious while he was sick. But whatever, he sounds back to normal and I guess he's having a baby shower for Seth and his wife tomorrow? He invited me to come. I said I didn't think it would be a good idea since you and I aren't—well, I think I said something lame, like that we aren't on great terms or something like that. Anyway, he said he was sure you'd be fine with it. But Calvin isn't known for his tight relationship with either reality or the truth, so I thought I should give you a call and make sure. You know, because of the 'wouldn't be seeing each other' thing."

Uncle Calvin. Was it possible for the man to be Ben's savior *and* his nemesis? "Why would you want to drive all the way from the city just for some baby shower?"

Liam was still polite but several degrees cooler. "I don't think my motivations are actually any of your business, are they? I mean, unless they involve you, which they don't."

"But you're asking my permission to attend?"

"'Permission' is probably a little strong. But I don't want you to throw a scene at Seth's big day, so I thought I'd better check in. If you're not going to be able to control yourself—I don't know what the baby-shower equivalent of ramming a cop car would be, maybe passing out and falling on the cake or something—then I guess I'll have to stay away. But if you *can* control yourself? If you've moved on with your new-old guy and are totally over me in every way? Then there shouldn't be a problem with me coming to the party. Right?"

Ben found himself suddenly yearning for Kevin's little tidbits of cattiness. So much more subtle, so much easier to ignore. "What's Seth's wife's name, Liam? What about his current kid? Name would be nice, but do you even know gender? Age? Are you honestly pretending you give a shit about Seth? Really?"

"We spent some time together at the building site, remember? And Seth and I were friends before either of us knew who the hell the geeky little kid with all the books even was. I let that friendship get messed up—let my shit with you affect how he and I got along—but that was a mistake. I'd like to see what I can do about fixing it. Although, again, none of that is any of your damn business."

"You seriously don't think you're taking this stroll down memory lane a little too far? Your parents are getting divorced. I guess you're finding that traumatic. But you know you can't actually transport yourself into the past, right? You can't travel back to a magical, simple time when everyone's parents still—"

"What are you even talking about? My parents? I was—surprised, I think. That's the best word. It shook me up a little, for, like, four hours, and then I was over it. None of this—My parents? Seriously? How the hell are you connecting this to my parents?"

"Four hours? You came up here the day of Terry's funeral, you were upset at the graveyard, you hung around for days, came back for the build, you were thinking about them the night we—you know. Sunday night. How is that four hours?"

There was a pause before Liam said, "I only found out about my parents on Sunday. The earlier stuff—why did you think my parents were involved?"

Ben fought to bring order to his thoughts. "I—well, why *else* would you have been up here?" Then he remembered Liam's words on that first day. *You never saw me any of the other times.* How many other times had there been? And why had Liam made the trip, ever?

"Hey, Ben?" Liam asked, his voice soft. It stayed gentle—*deceptively* gentle—as he said, "You're not interested in me, remember? We wrapped things up, left it all on a positive note. Right?"

Ben wanted to rage, to scream, to hurl insults or challenges or demands. But he was an adult now. He was mature and had self-control. At the very least he wouldn't let Liam's little trap do its job. He swallowed hard, then said, "You're right. This is none of my business. And it's none of my business if you want to go to Seth's baby shower. His wife's name is Dinah and their daughter is Tamara. They're both pretty wonderful. I think you'll really like them."

And those final few words were enough to bring him back to a calmer place, at least temporarily. "Thanks for calling to check on this—I guess I wouldn't have had the right to object even if I'd wanted to, but I appreciate the chance to avoid the surprise. I think the cake would have been safe, but you can never be sure."

"Okay. I guess I'll see you tomorrow."

And that was all.

Or at least it should have been. But instead of settling down to get some grading done as he'd been planning, Ben changed into running clothes and set out along the river. He tried to find peace in the flowing of the water, the singing of the birds. He gave up on that and tried to fall into the rhythm of his strides, the slap of his footfalls along the path. He had no thoughts, no emotions. He was a machine. A running machine, working effectively, efficiently, mindlessly.

Liam? There was no Liam. There was only the pounding of his feet, and of his heart. The burning in his legs, the sweat soaking his shirt. He was physical, not mental. He was at peace.

At least temporarily.

CHAPTER EIGHTEEN

LIAM BROUGHT a Sleep Sheep to the baby shower. He'd bought it the night before on the recommendation of a couple mothers at work, gotten it gift wrapped at the store, and written something carefully neutral on the card. That night, after tossing and turning for several hours, struggling to get some rest, trying not to think about who he was going to see the next day and how it all would go, he'd ripped through the paper, yanked the damn sheep out of its box, and cycled through the sounds. The heartbeat and whales were creepy, the surf made him restless, but the rain? Hell, yeah. That rain hit the spot.

Which meant, of course, that he had to make another run to the baby store in order to pick up a new Sleep Sheep the next morning. He was helped by the same clerk as the day before, and he had to resist the urge to make up excuses for why he was becoming some sort of Sleep Sheep shepherd. His shopping decisions were none of the clerk's business.

Just like Ben's life was none of Liam's.

Just like it hasn't been for the last fifteen years, he reminded himself. *No reason to start getting worked up about it now*. After all, he'd been the one to try to convince Calvin about the different mores of gay relationships. He knew perfectly well, in theory and in practice, that it was possible to have sex, *good* sex, with someone you didn't really care about. So why the hell was he acting as if he and Ben had made some sort of commitment to each other just because they'd fucked?

He drove into North Falls without being able to answer that question. The closest he could get was "wishful thinking." He'd wanted it to mean more. He'd wanted—well, he wasn't completely sure what he'd wanted. But he definitely hadn't been dreaming of a day when he'd walk into a damn baby shower and see Ben with his new boyfriend. Old boyfriend. Whatever. Except—what the fuck? That asshole got a second chance, but Liam didn't?

Possibly that asshole hadn't cheated on Ben and then waited a decade and a half to try to make amends.

He'd found parking well down the block from Calvin's house. Considering that many of the guests probably lived in town and would have walked, the number of cars suggested a serious shindig. Not that Liam would expect anything less from Calvin, but his limited experience with baby showers suggested that they tended to be more intimate affairs.

He was glad he'd gotten a gift receipt for the damn Sleep Sheep, because with this many guests there were bound to be some duplicate presents.

Yeah, that's what he was going to worry about. That would be his dominant thought walking into this party.

Damn, I sure hope nobody else bought a Sleep Sheep. Or at least I hope my sheep is the first one to get opened so I'm not the loser who has to sit there and watch them open a present somebody else already gave them. Yeah, this Sleep Sheep thing is a real issue. I am really, really concerned about the Sleep Sheep. Nothing else. Just the sheep.

"Liam!" a jovial voice called as he approached the house. Calvin was in the doorway wearing a long, flowing shirt with some sort of characters embroidered around the hem. Ragged jeans underneath, but the shirt was festive enough to count as dressed up, at least for Uncle Calvin. And he seemed genuinely pleased to see Liam, although of course that could all be an act. Pleased that mayhem was about to erupt at his event, possibly.

Still, Liam's smile felt pretty natural. He held up his gift box. "Have you seen anything else this size and shape? If you have, I think we need to hide the others until after mine is unwrapped. That's totally normal, right?"

"You're the third person who's asked," Calvin agreed seriously. He squinted at the box. "Football?" he guessed.

"Do babies enjoy football, generally?"

"Babies don't give a shit. Well, no, let me correct myself—that's about *all* babies do. So you might as well get them something that'll be useful down the line." He stood back from the door and gestured Liam inside. "I bought it a little cask of scotch. Seth and Dinah can stash it away somewhere—if they don't get desperate and drink it themselves—and the kid can crack it open when he or she turns sixteen."

"Uh, twenty-one, technically."

"Technically," Calvin agreed.

"Wait. Did you honestly buy the baby a cask of scotch?"

"Scotch doesn't age in the bottle, so it had to be a cask for there to be any meaning to the gift."

"You're focusing on the 'cask' part. I admit, I was distracted by the 'scotch.' For a baby." Liam shook his head. "I can't decide if that's the best baby gift I've ever heard of or the worst."

"That was just the effect I was trying for." They were in the kitchen then, and Calvin waved an arm in roughly the direction of the fridge. "Beer in there. Wine and hard stuff out on the deck. Snacks out there too."

Liam peeked through the kitchen window and almost recoiled at the sight. The yard was jam-packed with people. There were yellow and white ribbons and sashes and huge paper flowers hanging from every tree, several oversized, inflatable animals that might have been Disney, might have been knockoffs.... "You went all out," he managed.

"Seth's family's been in the area since settler days, and Dinah's a teacher—everyone loves teachers, as long as they're cute and sweet, which Dinah is. This party is the social event of the season."

Cute and sweet. Sure, Liam loved cute, sweet teachers. Surly, emotionally withdrawn teachers? Were they popular with everyone too, or was Liam special that way?

He reached into the fridge and pulled out a beer, then looked over at Calvin and got the nod that made him grab another. He twisted the lids off, held one of the bottles out to his host, and said, "I called Ben and asked if it was okay that I came."

Calvin nodded. "He told me. You're a spoilsport for ruining the surprise. I didn't get to see the cop car incident—I was hoping to get *some* fun out of this."

Which was kind of why Liam had brought the topic up. "If you're just looking for entertainment? If I'm only here because you want to torture Ben? I know you don't owe me anything, but we both care about Ben, so for his sake—"

"Kevin!" Calvin said brightly, looking somewhere over Liam's shoulder. "Excellent timing! I don't think you've met Liam, have you? He and Seth and Ben all grew up together. Liam, this is Kevin—he's Ben's date."

Liam turned reluctantly and found himself staring at an empty doorway. "Where'd he—" he started, but one look at Calvin made it clear there had never been anyone to be introduced to. "I guess it's too much to hope that Kevin is imaginary *all* the time? Like, Ben's not actually dating anyone?"

"That would be too much to hope for, would it? That would be something really special for you?" Calvin reached up and gripped Liam's shoulder and steered him toward the back door. They paused on the threshold, looking out at the crowd, and Calvin jerked his chin toward the big maple tree. Ben was standing underneath its branches, talking to some guy. Some guy who was smiling at Ben in a way that made Liam want to march across the yard and punch the guy in the face. And Ben was smiling back.

"Kevin," Calvin said calmly. "He exists. And, honestly, he's pretty nice. Unbelievably boring, but so is Ben these days. Which means they're a good couple, I guess."

Liam closed his eyes, but when he opened them the guy was still there, still smiling. But now Ben was looking over toward the house and had clearly seen Liam, judging by the way his expression had darkened.

So. There it was. The other guy—Kevin—made Ben smile. Liam made Ben frown. Hard to get much clearer than that.

Liam knew with a sick twist in his gut that he shouldn't have come. Yeah, he wanted to rebuild the relationship with Seth, but there would be other opportunities for that. Times that wouldn't be as painful. He'd only accepted Calvin's invitation because he'd wanted to see Ben. Because he'd been a fool. Again.

Calvin clapped him on the back and said, "Put the present over on that table—we're not going to sit around and watch them get opened. Too boring. And make sure you sign the onesie—we're doing that instead of a guest book."

Then he raised his voice and addressed the crowd. "Now! It's time for the games! I warned you all that these aren't optional... but not everyone will be taking part in every event. We need an audience of rabid fans, obviously. And don't forget to write down your guesses for the games in the living room—guess the number of jelly beans, match the baby photos to the adult guest photos, and all the rest of that stuff. Out here, though, we're going to be starting with the pregnant-man shoe-tie event! So, let me set up the first contestants! Only men wearing shoes that lace up are eligible!"

Liam faded back out of sight and counted himself lucky to be escaping. Keep it casual, drop off the gift, sign the damn onesie, and get the hell out of—

"Careful," a female voice came from too close behind him. He'd almost backed into her. He turned and saw a pregnant woman smiling back at him, her hand cradled protectively over her belly. The same pregnant woman who'd been with Seth at the house site. "I'm walking for two, you know. Can't dodge as quickly as I should."

Oh, shit. "Did I just almost crush the guest of honor?"

She beamed at him and held out her hand. "I've seen you, but we've never really met. I'm Dinah, you're Liam, and we should have a drink."

"Are you allowed to drink? Not that it's my job to police your alcohol consumption. Or anything else. Sorry. Your body is not public property."

She smiled. "You've been well indoctrinated. Excellent. And of course I can drink. Not *alcohol*, but… liquids. You can get me a glass of the pink punch in that beehive cooler. I watched Calvin make it and put the lid on, so I know he didn't sneak any booze into it. Then come sit with me on the porch. I'll save you a seat."

That wasn't the quick escape Liam had been planning, but he wasn't quite churlish enough to snub a woman at her own baby shower, so he did as he was told.

When he returned from the buffet table with a Solo cup full of punch, Dinah was perched on one side of the porch swing. She patted the seat next to her. "I'm not used to weighing this much. Come sit down so I don't have to keep worrying that the whole thing is going to tip up like a see-saw."

"That can't really happen," Liam said. "The design of the swing—"
She raised her eyebrows. Oh. She wanted him to sit down, not give her a lecture on physics and structural mechanics.

He handed her the cup and took a seat, and for a moment they sat quietly, watching the men taking their shoes off and stuff huge balloons under their shirts.

"I'm pretty sure this is going to end with at least one injury," Dinah said. She didn't sound too concerned about it.

"I expect Calvin's planned for it."

"Hell yeah, he has. He invited both of the town's doctors and *all* the nurses, plus quite a few paramedics and firefighters. If they're not on duty, they're here. This party is ready for anything short of thermonuclear war."

"No cops, though?"

"Calvin doesn't particularly care for law enforcement."

No, he didn't. Strange to have this woman, this stranger, remind him of that, though. "How long have you known Calvin?"

"I knew *of* him since a couple weeks after I moved to town, probably." She grinned. "He's a bit hard to miss. But I didn't really *know* him until Seth and I got together. It's been about eight years now."

"Eight years," Liam echoed. Seth had been involved with this woman for almost a decade, and Liam had never heard of her until the last couple weeks. Was he fooling himself, thinking there was any friendship left to reclaim?

He'd apparently been wrong about any lasting feelings from Ben, so was there any reason he'd meet a better reception from Seth?

They were quiet again, watching as the men raced across the lawn to their discarded shoes and contorted themselves, trying to get the shoes on and tied without popping their balloons.

Again, Dinah was the first to break the silence. "He missed you, you know."

Ben? No. There was no reason for Liam to believe that, and no reason for Dinah to be talking about him. Seth. "He did? I mean, does he still, do you think? Or has a couple weeks of renewed contact taken the luster off?"

"I think you're as lustrous as ever," she said, and there was a light in her eyes, a curve to her lips that made him hope, stupidly, desperately, that maybe she really *was* talking about Ben. "You hurt him, though. You hurt both of them."

Liam nodded. He couldn't say he was enthusiastic about taking a scolding from this stranger, but she was Seth's wife and this was her party.

But she surprised him with a Calvinesque shrug. "Oh well. They survived."

"That's it?"

Another shrug. "I could come up with something more if you wanted, but I'm not sure I'd really be able to sell it, you know? The outrage or whatever. Honestly, it was a hell of a long time ago."

"And everything's faded. It's all… done."

"Not all, maybe."

Before he could ask her what that meant, beg her for an explanation or a benediction or whatever other deep pregnant-lady wisdom she could come up with, a balloon popped out on the lawn, and then another.

"Kevin's out," she said, and he hoped he heard a little satisfaction in her tone. "Oh, and Dr. Miller. That's too bad—my money was on him."

"Not literally? You aren't actually *betting* on this?"

"Calvin's got a book made for every event. Jesus, I can't drink—I need to have fun somehow!"

Liam might have pushed a bit harder on that, maybe tried to figure out which events Calvin had signed him up for and what his odds for success were, but he was distracted by watching Kevin, shaking his head in defeat, returning to find comfort by Ben's side.

Ben threw a defiant look in Liam's general direction before he took Kevin's hand and kissed his temple.

Dinah snorted. "You do something new to piss him off, or is he just being a brat?"

"Something new?" Did sleeping with him count as something new? "Not that I know of. But I guess it'd be easier for him if I wasn't here."

"Easier. Yeah, it probably would be."

He was imagining the—the *tone* in her tone. Wasn't he? He was imagining the slightest hint of a sneer, to suggestion that "easier" wasn't a worthwhile goal for someone like Ben. She wasn't really suggesting that Ben could do better? Better than Kevin?

Fuck. Even if she was, that didn't mean she meant Liam.

He slumped against the back of the porch swing and drank the last of his beer.

"Good," she said. "Now, one more. I've bet on you, so I want you warmed up, but not drunk. And not too full. And possibly I should tell you now—Seth and I have already made up the spare bedroom for you to sleep in. There's absolutely no way you're driving home after you've competed in all the games Calvin has you signed up for."

"Games? Like—*drinking* games? At a baby shower?"

"At a *Calvin* baby shower." She smiled happily. "It's going to be a hell of a party."

Chapter Nineteen

"I'M REALLY not sure it's a good idea," Kevin said.

Ben tried not to frown at him. Of *course* it wasn't a good idea. Did Kevin really need to point out something so obvious? Ben rolled his shoulders and tried to focus on the task at hand.

"And not really appropriate," Kevin added. "Why on earth are there fraternity party games at a *baby shower?*"

"*Frat* party," Ben said. Damn, he'd sounded mad. He forced a smile and said, "I don't think anyone uses the whole 'fraternity' when they're combining it with the word 'party.' Maybe college disciplinary committees. But nobody else."

"I actually sat on my college disciplinary committee."

Of course he had. Ben smiled again. "I'd like to hear more about that—it must have been really challenging, but rewarding at the same time. But right now, I need to focus on the baby pong."

"Beer baby," Uncle Calvin said from somewhere far too close. "It doesn't make sense to cut out the 'beer'… we're still going to drink beer. It's the 'pong' that's gone."

Yes, the pong *was* gone, because instead of tossing ping pong balls at the other team's cups they were tossing little plastic babies. It was either the best baby shower Ben had ever been to or the worst.

He rolled his shoulders again and put on his game face to glare down the long table at the opposition. Seth. Good aim but easily distracted. And Liam. What the hell had Calvin been thinking when he came up with these teams? Seth and Liam, Ben and Calvin himself. Kevin excluded, because—because Kevin wasn't really part of this. This set of old friends. Old enemies.

Old. That was the part to remember. Calvin had set up a little trip down memory lane, but it was just a quick visit to the past. Ben was living in the present. With *Kevin.*

Who had drawn his lips up into a positively prissy little moue of disapproval.

Ben could fix that later. *After* he and Calvin destroyed Liam and Seth at baby pong. Beer baby. Whatever.

"Visitors go first," Calvin said, and he tossed a baggie of plastic babies to the other end of the table.

Liam nodded seriously, pulled a plastic baby out, and bounced it on the table. "Totally erratic," he told Seth after several bounces. "Unpredictable. We need to go for the direct throw."

Seth had been tossing his own plastic baby from hand to hand, and now he nodded. "Roger. Direct throw."

Yeah, beer baby was *on.*

Seth had the first toss. A direct hit, beer splashing up out of the plastic cup. Then Liam. Damn it, another hit.

"That means we go again!" Seth crowed, and he and Liam did a ridiculous little high-five dance. Well, wasn't it nice to see them getting along so well? Wasn't it just *lovely*?

Ben downed his beer and braced himself, but both Seth and Liam missed on their second chances. Now it was Ben's turn. Oh, no, apparently it was Calvin's, because the old guy was lining up, working out a sort of modified overhand toss—and, splash, right into a cup. Hell yeah.

"Pressure's on now," Liam said. He was watching Ben with— damn it, with a completely inappropriate level of intensity. Sure, it was just because of the game, but the eye contact, the slightly open mouth, the way he was leaning forward, anticipating, waiting for Ben to—to toss a damn plastic baby into a cup full of beer. That was all. He needed to keep his focus.

He threw and the stupid baby bounced an inch to the side of the target.

"It's okay, partner," Calvin said. "We're still fine. We're in this."

Yeah, they were in it. They were in it to *win* it. To teach Liam that he couldn't just swan back into town for no damn reason and think everyone was just *waiting* for him, like the last fifteen years hadn't happened, like the *cheating* hadn't happened, like everyone had been in a cryogenic holding chamber and had only been thawed out when he'd shown his face, like—

Plop. And then immediately after, another *plop*. No!

"Death cup!" Liam and Seth yelled triumphantly. Ben didn't want to know which of them had thrown first and which of them had the killer instinct to throw second, into exactly the same cup. He'd thought Uncle Calvin was his nemesis, but what if it was really Seth? Or Liam?

Well, actually, Liam made a lot of sense. Liam was almost certainly his nemesis.

"Now we drink that cup plus two more?" Calvin asked innocently, as if this were just a happy little game at a happy little—oh. Yeah. A baby shower. Ben needed to dial it back a little. Possibly there was no need to have a nemesis in beer baby.

Ben lifted his cup and glanced over at Kevin, who was still looking decidedly unimpressed with the entire situation. A raise of the cup in salute, but Kevin just shook his head in response. Oh well. Chug, chug, chug. Encouraging cheers from the crowd—from Seth and Liam, even— but not from Kevin.

There was a third cup. Ben had drunk one, Calvin had drunk one, and there was a third. There was no reason for Ben to drink it. No reason for him to be part of this game at all. Sure, Calvin would be disappointed if he walked away. Seth wouldn't think much of it. But they'd both forgive him. And Kevin would be impressed. Kevin would think Ben was mature, ready for a real relationship, ready for commitment, maybe even for….

Ben reached for the third cup, lifted it to his lips, and downed the contents in four swallows.

"That's my boy," Calvin said. "Now, free your mind. Let yourself *be* the baby. You're the baby, and you're so thirsty. You just want a little beer. No, wait, you want to *swim* in the beer! Swimming is fun for babies. Swimming in beer? Yeah, sure, that'd be fun for anyone. You're a little baby, and you want to go swimming in the—"

"That's not helpful." Ben straightened, the plastic baby gripped securely but lightly in his hand. He looked down the table. Seth, making some truly ridiculous faces, and Liam, so calm, so cool, so fucking *perfect* all the time.

Ben took a deep breath, stared Liam straight in the eyes, and tossed the baby. He didn't even smile as he heard the *plop*.

Seth was quick, though, pulling up the cup and starting to drink before Calvin had a chance to even try for a death cup.

And Liam was still looking at Ben. Ben was still looking back. It wasn't uncomfortable, exactly. At least, it wouldn't have been if they hadn't had an audience.

The *click* of Calvin's baby hitting the table barely registered.

But it was impossible to tune out Calvin's overly dramatic groan, the way he clutched Ben's arm in despair and slumped toward the ground....

"We're going to need to work out a signal for if you ever have an actual heart attack," Ben told him. "Especially after last weekend. Otherwise you'll be gasping in real pain and I'll just ignore you."

"I *have* real pain! Did you see how close that shot was?"

By the time Ben looked back at Liam, the moment was over, and Liam didn't make eye contact again for the rest of the game. Which he and Seth won easily.

There was a brief stretch of peace after that while Calvin marshaled a round of pin-the-fetus-on-the-uterus, and Ben took advantage of the chance to go to the bathroom. After he peed out at least some of the beer, he washed his hands and splashed water on his face. He did a few of his deep breaths, trying to get rid of the orange-pink-yellow swirl of Liam and replace it with some nice, calming blue, but someone banged on the door partway through and the whole exercise fell apart.

There was another event, players racing to be the fastest to drink a beer from a baby bottle without using their hands, and Liam was at his competitive best, throwing himself down on the ground and holding the bottle with his feet without any apparent self-consciousness. Ben went back into the house and made his guesses for all the stupid games in there, trying not to think about how flexible Liam still was, how he frowned in exactly the same way he used to when he was concentrating on something, working toward something... sucking on something....

Ben pulled another beer out of the fridge and rubbed the cool glass over his face before opening the bottle. He didn't really need more alcohol, but he was going to have some anyway.

He was in the yard talking to the mayor, Mack Cleese, having trouble with the conversation because, as usual, all he could think was *don't call him Mayor McCheese to his face, don't call him Mayor McCheese to his face*, when he heard Calvin calling his name.

"Stroller race is about to start! You should come see this!"

Ben wasn't sure why he was being singled out for a special invitation, not until he got closer to the starting line and saw the teams. Fairly innocuous for the most part, but Liam was at the end of one line,

Kevin at the other. They were both anchors for their teams; they'd be going head-to-head for the win.

What the hell had Calvin been thinking when he set all this up? Maybe he really *was* Ben's nemesis.

Ben found his way to Kevin's side while Calvin explained the rules with typical glee. Each participant had to get the stroller through the obstacle course without touching the unstrapped-in baby doll or letting it fall out. They were only allowed to touch the stroller on the handle, not grab hold of the two ends and carry it. Not sophisticated, but clear enough. Then Calvin added, "And you have to chug a beverage at the far end before you race back and hand off the stroller."

Kevin frowned and looked toward Ben as if—what? Asking permission? Ben was pretty sure he didn't grant it, but Kevin turned around anyway and said, "I'm not comfortable with that part of the race. I don't think it's a good idea to encourage alcohol consumption as if it's some sort of sport."

And Ben agreed with him, mostly.

Calvin just looked confused. "A *beverage*," he said. "There's an assortment down there. Beer, soft drinks, fizzy water—I made them all carbonated, to be fair. But I'm not sure why you'd jump to the conclusion that they're all alcoholic."

It had been a trap, obviously. Calvin had set Kevin up with the beer baby and baby-bottle race, made it seem like the same pattern was repeating, and acted innocent when Kevin made the logical assumption. Typical Calvin. But why was he doing it?

Not that Calvin ever really needed a "why" for his shenanigans. Personal entertainment was always reason enough. But with the whole party to plan, the guests to fuss over, the games—the *real* games, not his twisted extras—why would he bother with Kevin now?

And why had he invited Liam?

It was hard to believe that the two decisions weren't connected, but what on earth was Calvin trying to prove? What decision was he trying to make on Ben's behalf? And why the hell did he think it was his place to do… whatever the hell he was doing?

Ben reached for Kevin's hand and laced their fingers together. "Thanks for asking about that," he said, loud enough for everyone to hear. "You're right—drinking alcohol like it's a sport is pretty unhealthy and immature."

Kevin's surprise was clear enough to make Ben feel guilty. Apparently his date—his boyfriend—hadn't expected any support. But he'd still had the courage to speak up and express his opinion. An opinion that Ben agreed with. Mostly.

"You're a good guy," Ben said, more quietly this time, so only Kevin could hear. "A really decent human being."

Kevin smiled. "I try to be," he agreed.

It should have been a sweet moment. It shouldn't have made Ben want to grit his teeth and yank his hand back from Kevin's grip. Shouldn't have made him feel like he was trapped.

"First racers, on your mark...," Calvin said, and Kevin let go of Ben's hand as if he'd forgotten they'd even been in contact. He edged forward, all his attention focused on the race.

Apparently Kevin was taking the stroller obstacles pretty seriously.

And so was Liam, Ben discovered as he drew back into the crowd of onlookers. All the participants were fully engaged, yelling advice and encouragement, and otherwise acting as if they were in the finals at the Olympic Games. Calvin had chosen extremely competitive people for this event.

Made sense that Liam was acting that way—he'd always been driven and intense. But Kevin?

The first three contestants made it through the course without injury, although one runner from each team spilled the doll out of the stroller and had to race back to the top of the course to restart the run. Liam and Kevin started out neck and neck. Liam had a good initial sprint but took the first corner too fast and almost lost the doll, then had to waste precious seconds trying to get it flipped all the way back into the stroller. Kevin took a more balanced approach.

Calvin was commentating on the action like a demented sports announcer, and almost everyone at the party was gathered and cheering for one team or the other or both. The racers reached the far end almost in unison and grabbed their beverages—beer for Liam, a can of ginger ale for Kevin—and that was where Kevin lost his edge. Liam chugged his bottle like a frat boy while Kevin took a gulp, winced, took a sip, looked pained, took another sip, made another face, took a sip—and Liam was off. His team roaring, the crowd electrified, all eyes on him as Kevin took one more sip, then set his can down on the messy, liquid-strewn table, on its side.

The base of the can was turned toward the crowd, and there was so much activity, so much commotion as Kevin grabbed his own buggy and took off after Liam, only a stride or two behind. Ben couldn't really see, not for sure, that there was liquid spilling out of the can.

And Kevin didn't waste any time worrying about it. He made up time as he and Liam weaved their way through the bags of disposable diapers, and he had almost caught up when they hit the final turn, charging around the huge stuffed elephant Calvin had said would belong to Tamara when the party was over.

They were close, but Liam was ahead, and there was no reason he wouldn't stay that way. He stretched out almost horizontally, the stroller keeping him upright as he sprinted for the finish line, his entire body driven and focused on its goal, its destination, its home—

And Kevin collapsed to the ground with a yelp of pain. He was clutching his ankle as Liam blazed across the finish line and was absorbed into the arms of his jubilant teammates. Kevin looked up, caught Ben's gaze, and looked down at his ankle, shaking his head.

Ben did his duty, but he didn't rush. He edged through the crowd, made his way down the lawn, and crouched next to Kevin. "Twisted it?" he asked as neutrally as he could manage.

"I guess, yeah. There was a hole—not a hole, I guess, but an unexpected dip." He forced a smile. "It's not like we can expect Calvin's backyard to be equipped for Olympic sprinting."

"Olympic stroller racing," Ben corrected absentmindedly. "Oh well. You gave it a good try. Want to get up and walk it off?"

"I'm not sure I can just walk it off." Kevin poked gingerly at his ankle. "I wouldn't have stopped running if it was just something minor, you know."

Ben thought of the ginger ale can—it'd be empty by now, certainly. And it didn't matter anyway. So what if Kevin hadn't totally finished the drink? So what if he'd taken a fall and was faking an injury in order to cover up his loss? Ben couldn't be sure any of that was true, and even if it was… so what?

"What do you want to do?" Ben shifted around so he could sit on the grass next to Kevin. "Do you need to go to the hospital? Or just ice it? Do we need to leave?"

That was when he noticed the shadow falling over their legs and looked up to see Liam peering down at them. "Everything okay?" he asked. His face was gently flushed, his hair tousled, and Ben had to force himself to turn away. He couldn't see Liam like that, not without—well. He just wouldn't look at him, and that made everything simpler.

"I'll be okay," Kevin said. "It's too bad it happened—I think I had you."

"You think so?" Liam didn't sound angry, or even frustrated. The patronizing bastard sounded amused. "We'll have to have a rematch someday." Then something changed, shifted in the air, and Ben knew without looking that Liam's attention had turned to him. "Calvin wants you, Ben. Apparently you're surprisingly good at the boring games inside. Even though I've won a lot of events out here, Calvin says you made up enough points on the other stuff that we're tied. He's got some sort of head-to-head—"

"No." Far too much emotion in that word, and Ben took a deep breath before saying, "I don't know what Uncle Calvin's up to, but—no. I'm done."

"Done… at the shower? Like, Kevin needs you to go nurse him back to health?"

"No. Done with the games."

Liam knew what Ben was saying—Liam always knew. But he pretended otherwise. "That's not cool, man. Calvin's put a lot of time into all this. I know it's kind of surreal, but there's just one more game, you might as well—"

"There's never just 'one more game' with Calvin." Ben knew it too well. "He'll always keep pushing, testing, until somebody says 'no.'"

Still, Liam played stupid. "I think he means it this time—he's got the trophy all ready to present. There are quite a few trophies, actually, with all kinds of different titles. He's put a lot of work into this, Ben. Be cool, okay?"

"Cool?" Too loud, and it all got worse when Ben pushed himself to his feet and glared at Liam. Adorably, sexily disheveled Liam. But Ben wouldn't think about that. "There's nothing *cool* about this! About him inviting you, you being here, him setting up all these contests— pressuring poor Kevin into this stupid race! And now Kevin's hurt, and you're still *here*, and—"

"Keep your voice down," Liam said. A suggestion, calm and pleasant. "Kevin's not really hurt—you know that. And the rest of it? What did you tell me about that disgusting coat he loaned me? Messing around with people is Calvin's weirdass way of showing affection. That's all this is. Don't build it into something bigger."

"Do *not* tell me how to handle my uncle!"

"Ben." For the first time, Liam let a little emotion into his voice. "You're losing it. If you don't want to do the last game, fine. I'll—" He cast a derisive look in Kevin's direction. "I'll tell him I pulled a muscle or something, okay? Fake injuries for everyone. Just chill out. This has been a really nice party for a lot of people you care about. Don't mess it up."

It was exactly right. Exactly what Ben needed to hear, and said in a way that let him really see what he was doing and how destructive it could be.

And that rightness—that fucking *perfection*—made it all so much worse.

"Oh, you're the hero?" Ben growled. "You're the golden boy who cares about everybody else and just tries to make it all work out, and *I'm* the asshole who wrecks it? Is that how you see things?"

"If you're talking about fifteen years ago, then, no, I was the asshole. Everyone agrees on that. But if you're talking about right now? Hey." Liam stepped back and raised his hands in surrender. "If you're so damn determined to wreck things? Okay, yeah. Right now, *you're* the asshole."

"You push and push, and when I finally say 'no'—"

"How the hell am I pushing? I *asked* if I could come to this, and you said fine. You *said* you were past it all and none of it mattered. You remember that conversation? You said you wouldn't have had a right to say 'no' even if you wanted to. And the other night? You said it was all over. So what the hell's your problem now?"

"You *know* what my problem is!"

Not only too loud this time—also too damn honest. Liam stared at him for a long moment, then took a half step forward. "If I know what the problem is, I know what the solution is too. Jesus, Ben, there are no guarantees in life. I can't—I can't promise that everything will be perfect forever. But I really think we're worth taking a chance on. Don't you? You said the other night that this was over, but if it really was, it wouldn't be an issue for you to see me."

Ben stepped closer too, and his voice came out low and growly. "It was *done* fifteen damn years ago when you fucked—I was going to say when you fucked your Art History TA, but really I guess it was over when you fucked *half the campus*."

"So I guess I *don't* know what your problem is." Liam's gaze was still steady and level, too intense to be anything but intimate. "And I'm not really sure what *my* problem is, either, except—" He looked away, then back. "Except I miss you. I can't really understand what's wrong with my life in general, but the one thing that's totally clear to me is that *you're not with me*, and you should be. That's—"

"Excuse me," Kevin said, his voice almost trembling as he rose to his feet. "This is outrageous. Ben has made his feelings on this matter *crystal clear*. It's unfortunate that you're struggling with something in your life, but to impose on *Ben* this way, to make him feel as if it's somehow his fault or his problem?"

He stepped between Ben and Liam, and it was as if he broke a vacuum seal, neutralized a magnetic bond—did *something* that brought Ben back to reality, back to Uncle Calvin's backyard with half the town staring at him as he listened to ravings—absolutely surreal *lunacy*—from Liam.

"It's been fifteen years," Ben said. "It's over." It had to be over.

"And there's absolutely nothing left?" Liam said it wistfully, almost sweetly, but there was something else, something extra that Ben couldn't quite figure out.

Still, he knew the answer he needed to give. "There's nothing left," he said firmly.

And Liam was ready. "So there's no problem with us doing the final event, right? No reason you can't play one more stupid game in order to make your uncle happy?" He glanced dismissively at Kevin. "Your date seems to have recovered from his horrible injury, and I think he's still got about half a can of ginger ale he could be drinking while he waits for us to play. So what's holding you up? Let's go."

A dare. That's what it was. Sure, Ben and Liam had turned into something else, but at the heart of their relationship they'd always been friends. The two of them and Seth, endless summer days, almost-as-endless winter adventures after school or on weekends—they'd been kids together. And the inability to walk away from a dare was a bone-deep instinct in any kid.

And there was a part of Ben, a sweet, adventurous, *joyful* part of him that wanted to respond the same way now. Of course he'd take the dare, and play one final game, and spend more time with Liam. And his resistance was already so weak, his self-control so challenged, that a bit more time was all it would take before he crumbled. Kevin was nothing, Liam was everything; Ben would take Liam home, or hell, maybe just upstairs, and they'd be together in the way they always *should* be together, and it would be perfect and golden and glowing.

But not permanent. Liam would leave, and Ben would be left behind, empty and alone. And he just wasn't strong enough for that to happen again.

"I'm leaving," he said quietly. Kevin immediately put his arm around Ben as if offering support, and Ben resisted the urge to tear himself free. "I'm done."

He knew they still had an audience, and he forced a smile onto his face for the benefit of the crowd. "We need to get some ice for Kevin," he announced. "He'll be fine, but there's no point messing around."

And Kevin supportively added a bit of a limp to his step, although Ben was pretty sure he was favoring the wrong leg.

"You guys are made for each other," Liam said as Ben made his way past. "You're both quitters."

The words rose to Ben's lips, the accusations and rebuttals. Maybe Kevin and Ben were quitters, but at least they weren't *cheaters*. Except for the unfortunate ginger ale incident. And remembering that was enough to keep Ben's mouth shut.

He made his apologies to Calvin, trying not to wonder if the disappointment in the old man's face was solely because the playoff game was cancelled, and threw the jauntiest wave he could manage in Seth and Dinah's direction. They waved back, Dinah making a face of slightly overdone sympathy in Kevin's direction.

They were halfway down the front walk when Ben heard a cheer from the backyard. "They gave Liam the trophy," he said.

"Liam," Kevin said. "He's—well." They walked a few more steps; Kevin wasn't even trying to limp anymore. He stopped at the sidewalk and turned to Ben. "I'm going home."

"Oh. Okay. Is your ankle hurting?"

"No. But—I need to take some time. By myself." He paused, maybe a bit more dramatically than necessary. "To think about whether it makes sense to continue this relationship."

Oh.

It was clear that Kevin was waiting for a reaction. Begging, maybe, or at least reassurances. But Ben didn't have them to give, and Kevin didn't deserve to be lied to. "I guess that's a good idea. I mean—Liam is not a threat. Not an issue. But I can see how this would all be a little unsettling for you."

"Not an issue," Kevin echoed. "Well. That's—" He stopped and shook his head. "Maybe we can talk later in the week."

"Sure," Ben agreed. And then Kevin left, and Ben was alone. Standing pathetically in the street as his current maybe boyfriend walked away from him while his ancient definitely boyfriend received kudos and applause at the booze-soaked baby shower of Ben's best friend. That was his life. That was what he'd managed to achieve for himself.

Damn it. He needed—maybe regular meditation wasn't going to be enough. Maybe he needed some sort of retreat, some intensive intervention.

Maybe he needed a damn lobotomy.

If there was a surgery to remove just the Liam-related memories, a sci-fi storyline so he could travel back in time and—and what?

What would he change, exactly?

His own behavior, he supposed. When he'd first suspected that Liam was cheating, had it already been too late? Could he have fixed things if he'd spoken up, if he'd been brave enough to have the fight instead of hoping it would all just go away?

Could everything have been different?

He took a deep breath and started walking. There was no surgery, no time travel. He had only one life, only one chance. He needed to be smart and not waste time on daydreams.

He needed a drink. That, at least, seemed like an achievable goal, even if he'd be meeting it alone.

CHAPTER TWENTY

LIAM WENT home with Seth and Dinah as they'd planned and helped Dinah sort and unwrap her gifts while Seth drove the babysitter home. He made sure his Sleep Sheep was opened early, which was about the only real victory he'd managed that day.

Sure, there was the trophy. The man on top of it was bowling, and the plaque on the base was Magic Marker on masking tape, but, still, technically—but, no. Liam hadn't even won that, not really, because stupid Ben had refused to play the final game.

They were about a third of the way through the massive pile of gifts before Dinah said, "So. Ben was pretty mad today."

Tempting to deny or divert, but there was also appeal in talking about it. "I guess he was."

"At you."

"Seems like."

"For a reason?"

Well, Liam knew better than to get into that. But knowing better didn't seem to have too much of an influence on his actions these days. "I shouldn't have been there. He and I are over and done, and he doesn't want me hanging around."

"Wow. That's—" She pulled a boxed leather football out of the gift wrap and smiled. "I knew it was going to be a football. Katie's been talking to Calvin."

Liam had no idea who Katie was, but he was suddenly almost overwhelmed with *wanting* to know. This Katie, this woman who took Calvin's insane ideas and ran with them, who brought a smile to Dinah's face, who was somehow part of this warm, weird, alcohol-drenched little community—Liam wanted to know her. He wanted to be invited to her house, and yes, damn it, he wanted the invitation to be for two people and he wanted Ben to be his companion. He wanted—

"Write it down," Dinah prompted, pointing to the pad of paper on Liam's lap. "You said you'd be the secretary, so secretary up. *Katie—*

football. I probably won't need to be reminded of that one, but you still need to write it down."

He did as he was told.

Dinah took a sip of her punch before she asked, "Do you think you *are* over and done? You and him?"

"I guess. I mean—if he says we are, we are. Right?"

"But you wish you weren't?"

"Yeah." It didn't even hurt to say it.

"Why?"

The question came quietly and was simple enough, but it wasn't easy to answer. Not with the depth Dinah probably wanted and definitely deserved. "Maybe I'm just chasing the past," Liam admitted. "I think that's what Ben thinks—he had some crazy theory about this being because my parents are getting divorced, but that's not it. But yeah, maybe I'm just trying to go back to the last time my life was really *good*, you know? Maybe."

"And what's so not good about your life now?"

"I don't know. I mean, it's good, right? Good job—great job, really, as of a couple weeks ago. Nice lifestyle—good apartment, fancy parties with all the movers and shakers and artistic types. Yeah, I'm there as one of the—I don't know, the supplicants? The ones kissing up, not the ones getting kissed up to. But still."

"Friends?" she asked as she reached for another gift. "Romance?"

"Friends," he agreed. Not great friends, maybe, but good enough. And romance? "I get laid all I want." Which was probably a bit crude, but if this woman was married to Seth, surely she could handle it.

And she didn't seem at all fazed. "But that's not all there is to romance. I mean, Ben gets laid all *he* wants, too, as far as I know."

That wasn't something Liam really wanted to think about. Except— "Wait. Are you saying Ben isn't totally satisfied, romancewise? Like, there's room for growth there?"

She didn't answer, just took a sip from her glass of lemonade, then began opening the present on her lap. As she worked she said, "So what's missing from your life? What are you looking for, really?"

He sighed. Seth, bless his heart, had provided not only a glass of scotch but also the bottle in case refills were necessary. If this conversation continued, they definitely would be. "I think I got distracted by all the shiny things. Like, the things I've been chasing after—money, famous people, making a damn name for myself—I think they're all surface-level. Does that make sense? And then after I chase them down? I'm like a dog chasing after soap bubbles—they look fascinating, and it's fun to *try* to catch them, but when I do finally grab hold, they disappear and I'm just left with a bad taste in my mouth."

"Nice analogy," she said.

And then she waited. Damn her, she waited.

Into the silence Liam said, "I think I worry that *I'm* just a shiny thing. Just a soap bubble. No depth, nothing beneath the surface. Easy to pop if I ever slow down, stop dodging and floating."

"Bunny onesie," Dinah said.

Liam stared at her, and she jabbed her finger at the pad of paper. "Bunny onesie. Margie Kane. Write it down."

He did as he was told, then looked up. She grinned at him. "Bought myself a little time to think. Pretty clever, huh?"

"Brilliant."

"And now you get the benefit." She reached for another gift. "Do you think shiny things are always empty? I was going to go with, 'Why do you think you're a shiny thing' but I decided against it. Because, honestly, yeah, you're pretty damn shiny. You're good-looking and successful and funny and sweet. You're shiny, sure." She looked at the gift she was holding. "If I controlled the universe, this present would be deeply significant. It would be something shiny, obviously... a baby rattle? One of those silver ones from Tiffany's or something? And then—I don't know. I'd expand things out from there." She squeezed the present and shook her head. "But it's a onesie. Guaranteed. And I don't think anyone's buying me shiny onesies. So—you're a shiny thing. Fine. But that doesn't mean you're empty."

"For sure?"

"For sure," she said firmly. "I don't know you too well, but I know Ben and Seth and Calvin, and they were close to you for a long time. I'm not saying you didn't screw up back then, but I don't think one screwup is enough to neutralize all the affection they had for you for so long. I trust their judgment—Seth had the excellent taste to fall for *me*, for example—so I know there must be something to you. Something more than the shiny surface."

And it was happening again. The tears, not yet falling but threatening, and all because this woman, this virtual stranger, was willing to believe he wasn't totally useless. Awards and publicity and kudos from all directions had left him dry-eyed and calm, but this? Apparently this was too much for his tender emotions to handle.

Dinah was kind enough to turn her attention to the gift for a moment, unwrapping a polka-dotted onesie with a matching hat, and Liam dutifully recorded the details. When he looked up from the page, Dinah was squinting at him.

"Is there something we could do with polka dots?" she asked.

"Something we could *do*?"

"As an analogy. Your soap bubbles got me inspired." Oh, she was still on that track. He tried to catch up to her, but she was racing ahead. "Something about the dots all being different colors but still coordinating nicely—that's true, and it'd be a good analogy for *some* life issue, I'm sure, but I can't think of a way to really fit it to the current conversation. Maybe something about how the onesie is cute but also useful? And soft? Oh, and this is a *good* onesie, because the soft is on the right side! Sometimes there'll be outfits that are super-soft on the outside, the part adults touch, but then weirdly scratchy on the inside, the part that's right against the baby's skin. Those suck. They're for looks only. But good clothes, like this, are soft on the inside, pretty on the outside...." She stopped, scrunched up her nose, and shrugged. "I don't know. That's not an all-time classic, I admit. But for now— you're a good onesie, Liam. Pretty on the outside and warm and soft on the inside. Sound okay?"

"You're very kind. A little strange, and you're almost certainly spending too much time with Calvin, but—kind."

She grinned and took a sip of her punch. "I spend a lot of time with Ben too. Seth and I—possibly mostly me, but Seth didn't think it was a bad idea—we kinda prodded him to give Kevin a call and see if there was something left in that relationship."

Ridiculous that it felt like a betrayal. "So why am I here? It's kind of you to host me, but if you think Ben should be with Kevin—"

"Oh, I don't think he should be with Kevin."

"What? Didn't you just say—"

"I said we prodded him to *call* Kevin, to see if there was something left. I didn't say I hoped there *was* something left. We just thought—well. Partly we just thought it would be interesting to see what happened— so you're right, we probably *are* spending too much time with Uncle

Calvin—but mostly we just thought Ben should be doing *something*. He wants to be in a relationship, but they never seem to last, and we thought he was just getting kind of tired of trying, like maybe he was going to give up. So—Kevin. Better than nothing?"

"He seems like a decent guy." More or less.

"Absolutely. If he'd been a total jerk, we wouldn't have suggested Ben give him another try."

"And it seems to be going well." Liam reached for a wrapped gift, trying to disguise how much he was hoping to be contradicted.

"Seems like they're right back where they used to be." Dinah accepted the gift from him, peered at the card, and said, "Nipple cream. Guaranteed."

"Pardon?"

"Aunt Maggie is obsessed with my nipples. I guess hers were really a problem when she was nursing, and she's made it her life mission to ensure that nobody else suffers like she did."

"That's noble."

"But kinda weird." Dinah slipped the wrapping paper loose, peered at the gift, and nodded. "Write it down. Aunt Maggie. Nipple cream."

"Do you think—" Liam stopped. He'd been about to ask whether Dinah and Seth would be interested in seeing more of him. He'd have found a better way to phrase it, he hoped, one that didn't make it sound like discussion of Dinah's nipples had led him to propose a threesome. But then he'd realized it wouldn't work.

Seth was a good old friend. Dinah was lovely. There was something undeniably positive about being around them, being around Calvin, being in North Falls itself. But would Liam actually be able to enjoy any of it if he knew he could turn around at any second and see Ben and Kevin together? Ben and anyone, really. Anyone who wasn't Liam.

"Do you think I'm totally irrational?" he asked instead of his original question. "Am I 'in crisis' or some other psychobabble?"

"What do you think?" There was just enough of a twinkle in her eye to let him know she was aware of the therapist cliché in her question.

"I think I've gotten everything I wanted at work. I got it in kind of a strange way—kind of a bad way, maybe. I just pushed my way in. But still, I won. I'm in."

"Yay?"

"It should be 'yay,' yeah. So why isn't it?"

She reached for another gift. "That's a really interesting question. What do *you* think the answer is?"

He snorted and took a sip of scotch. Before he could come up with anything more useful than *I've been missing Ben for the last fifteen years and now that I'm actually seeing him again I have no idea how the hell I'm supposed to walk away*, the front door opened and Seth came in, a somewhat bedraggled toddler in his arms.

"Tamara, can you say hi to Liam?" Seth prompted. "You remember him from the other day, right?"

Tamara raised an eyebrow and looked Liam up and down. "Raspberries," she finally said. Then her gaze fell on the presents, and her body tensed with electric interest.

"They're boring, sweetie," Dinah said quickly. "But if you want to come help unwrap them, that'd be great. They're things to help us get ready for your new brother or sister."

And that was the end of the soul-exposing portion of the evening. Probably a good thing, really. Liam ended up in the backyard with Seth, drinking beer while wrestling with some raspberry sprouts that had survived the earlier apocalypse, and they were fine together, friendly enough and working in companionable silence. But there was no invitation to deeper conversation, and that was okay; it was fair. Seth was Ben's.

Of course, Dinah was Ben's too, according to any metric that made sense.

Nobody in North Falls was Liam's. Possibly nobody anywhere.

But what the hell was he getting worked up about? An old boyfriend who didn't want him back? Big deal. He was Liam Marshall, up-and-coming New York City architect and man-about-town. His career was soaring, he had no shortage of interest from men who were, by any objective standard, way the hell more eligible than some small-town schoolteacher carrying a grudge about something that had happened a decade and a half ago. Liam was fine. He was good. Great, even.

By any objective standard.

By a subjective standard? By his *own* standard?

Well. He didn't think he should start thinking about that. Not until he was safely at home, or at least in a guest bedroom where nobody would stare at him if the damn tears came back again.

CHAPTER TWENTY-ONE

BEN SPENT Sunday alone, mildly hungover and completely humiliated, and it was *all* Liam Marshall's fault.

The lack of Kevin was definitely Liam's fault. Obviously and completely.

But normally Ben could have hung out with Seth and Dinah on Sunday—their post-party brunches were such a tradition there was barely any need for discussion. Except that Liam had stayed with them after the party, and he would probably stick around for the meal. And Ben had seen more than enough of Liam Marshall for one weekend.

For one lifetime, he told himself. Liam was done, finished, out of Ben's life. Kevin was the future, as long as Kevin calmed the hell down and decided he actually *wanted* a future with Ben.

If not Kevin, then someone else. It didn't really matter, as long as it wasn't Liam fucking Marshall.

Ben made it through most of Sunday without wavering from that stance and turned it into his mantra as the week wore on. *Anyone but Liam. Anyone but Liam.*

By Thursday, when he walked into the long-delayed meeting with Peyton, his aggressive student, and Larissa, her even-more-aggressive mother, the words were imbedded firmly in his mind, a low buzz of denial behind everything he did. Wake up in the morning, *anyone but Liam*, go for a run, *anyone but Liam*, eat his breakfast, drive to school, greet his students, get through the day, *anyone but Liam* rumbling along in the background of it all.

But that background chant was finally silenced, at least temporarily, on Thursday after school when he looked up from his marking and saw Peyton and her mother stalking through the classroom door. Peyton lean and scowling in jeans and a baggy flannel shirt, her mother more rounded but with similar clothes and the exact same expression on her face. Ben needed to keep his full attention on the task at hand if he was going to survive the meeting.

"Hey, Peyton," Ben said, working his best "friendly but in charge" tone as he stood up and made his way around his desk. "And Mrs. Dale. Thanks so much for—"

"Ms.," she growled.

Shit. Stupid mistake on his part—he had no idea if Peyton's dad had married her mom, but he sure as hell wasn't in the picture anymore, and getting the honorifics wrong was a horrible start to a meeting. "I'm sorry. But—thanks for coming in. I really appreciate you—"

"You're not going to appreciate me for long." She looked at the three plastic and metal chairs he'd arranged around a student desk near the door and shook her head as if displeased with the accommodations. "We might as well sit down."

And just like that, she was in control. She went on the offensive immediately, demanding to know why her daughter was being insulted, what was being done to punish the other student, and telling Ben how sick she was of her daughter being judged just for standing up for herself.

Ben made himself really listen. He absorbed the anger, the protectiveness behind it, and the love behind that. An angry parent was a parent who cared, and that was a hell of a lot better than the apathy he saw far too often. Not that he enjoyed being yelled at in front of a student, but he could take it.

And when Ms. Dale finally wound down, he was ready. "Peyton's a great kid," he said, and he meant it. "She's doing well academically, and I love seeing what she's reading and talking to her about it. I think she has some really mature insight into a lot of the stories."

Yeah, that knocked Mom back at least temporarily. Damn, Ben was going to be able to pull something useful out of this meeting after all. "Socially, I think she's struggling a little. Peyton, does that sound right? I know you were friends with Marlys, right? But since she moved away, is there—"

"I have enough friends."

"And we're not looking to you for help with any of that," Ms. Dale growled. "You're her *teacher*, not her social secretary. You teach her what you're supposed to and leave the rest of it alone!"

"Well, the role of a teacher is a bit more complex than that. Students can't learn well if they're unhappy, or if—"

"They can't learn if some asshole boy is bullying them and calling them names, that's for sure!"

Ben managed to keep his sigh internal. "I agree. And as I said, there have been consequences for that student. But he's not the only student that Peyton's had trouble with this year. Peyton, you and I have talked about this—I always feel bad talking about a student as if they're not in the room, but is it okay if I review some of the things we've discussed?"

"You don't need to." Ms. Dale looked at her daughter and her angry face melted, just for a moment, into something warm and gentle. "Peyton tells me everything. She's told me all about your deep breathing and your drawers for feelings and all the rest of it. And we both think it's crap."

"It's about self-control. About being smart and protecting yourself and not letting your emotions take over."

Ms. Dale stared at him like he was an alien. "Protecting herself? Not letting her emotions *take over*? That's bullshit. She's eleven years old, and she's strong and tough and she doesn't need to *protect herself*, not from her own damn feelings!"

Ben was losing control of the conversation again. "I agree that she's strong and tough, but the world can be a hard place. I think we need to help her figure out how to not get hurt—"

"*Not get hurt?*" He would have thought her glare was at maximum level before, but apparently Ms. Dale had the ability to turn things up to eleven. "Of course she's going to get hurt! She's been hurt already." She glared at Ben as if he should have known that, but whatever the injury was, it hadn't been in Peyton's file. Then she turned to her daughter. "But after you get hurt you get back up and you keep fighting. Right? Your dad was an asshole—I should have protected you better. You could have given up after that, but you didn't." She turned back to Ben. "She *didn't*, and she *won't*. She's been hurt, and she'll be hurt again and again, because that's what life *is*."

Ben stared at her, trying to sort through the words and the emotions behind them. Emotions from Ms. Dale, but also, strangely, from himself.

Ms. Dale shook her head fiercely. "My daughter's going to *live*. She's not going to hide away from everything—from *herself*. She's going to feel it all, and live it all, and she's going to get hurt, but the times in between the hurt will be fantastic. She's not going to turn herself into some prissy little robot. She's not going to whimper, she's going to fucking *roar*. And if Ty Connelly or any other asshole thinks he's going to call her names, she's going to make him regret it."

Yeah, Ben had absolutely lost control of the meeting. He wished he'd recorded it, wished he could play it back and analyze where things had gone wrong. But in the meantime he said, "Ty Connelly is quite a bit smaller than Peyton, physically. She might be able to intimidate him, but sooner or later she'll run into someone bigger than her and tougher than her."

"Yeah, she'll lose sometimes. So what? She should give up before she even tries, and go through the rest of her life being afraid?"

"She should figure out a smarter way to handle things! If she'd come to me and told me Ty was picking on her—"

"If she'd gone running to a man to solve her problems even though she can solve them herself?"

"I really don't think this is a feminist issue."

"Feminism? I don't have time for that. But I don't need a man to take care of me, and neither does my daughter."

"The police," Ben suggested. He was pretty sure he was letting himself be led far, far from where the conversation should be headed, but he didn't seem able to stop himself. "If someone was breaking into your house, you'd call the police, wouldn't you? That's kind of my role in the classroom, or at least one aspect of it."

"If the same asshole kept breaking into my house and the cops didn't give him more than a slap on the wrist each time, and he came back and broke in again? It wouldn't take long before I stopped calling the cops and started loading my gun."

Yup, he'd walked into that one. He wanted to defend himself, talk about how Ty *had* received consequences, how Peyton's refusal to back down made it much harder to see her as a victim who needed to be protected and therefore harder to treat Ty's behavior as bullying—he wanted to say all kinds of things. But he was finding himself distracted by the words echoing in the back of his mind. Not the old ones about *anyone but Liam*. Something new, something he'd just heard from Ms. Dale. *That's what life is*. Life is getting hurt, and then standing back up and getting hurt again. But not being a robot. Being alive. *Roaring*.

"I appreciate your perspective on this," he said, and maybe she could tell that he meant it, because she didn't snarl in return. "I want to think about it all. But I need to warn you—there are school rules, rules I agree with and support, banning violence. If Peyton gets physically violent with another student, especially when there's a teacher *right there* willing to help her find a different solution, then all the talk about roaring and standing up for herself isn't going to keep her out of trouble with the office. Or with me. And maybe that's okay. Maybe getting detention or even a suspension is just one more adversity for her to overcome. But I don't think there's a need for it. I hear what you're saying about being willing to stand up for yourself, but I also truly believe that you have to pick your battles. Sometimes the best thing is just to walk away from a fight."

"And sometimes the best thing is to fight." Ms. Dale held his gaze, waiting for him to object. But he didn't. Sometimes the best thing *was* to fight. After a moment, Ms. Dale stood up and straightened her work shirt. "You think about what I said, and—we'll think about what you said." She took a step toward the door, then turned back around and spoke quickly, as if the words were being forced out of her mouth and she couldn't control them. "Peyton likes being in your class. She says you're a good teacher. All the breathing bullshit she could do without, but—she likes you. And she's a good judge of character." She looked him up and down and added, "Usually."

With that, the two of them stomped out of the room, as fierce and independent and stubborn as they'd been when they arrived.

Ben sat quietly in the classroom after they were gone, and he couldn't help noticing how empty the space felt without their intensity and vitality. Empty, even though he was still there.

"Liam fucking Marshall," he said out loud. He wasn't quite sure how to trace his current state back to Liam Marshall, couldn't precisely track the connection through all the switchbacks and false trails, but he knew it was there. He knew this all came back to Liam somehow.

He pushed himself to his feet, the student desk rocking as his thigh hit it. He grabbed his keys and phone out of the drawer of his desk and left the pile of grading behind as he strode out of the building. Into the Toyota, then downtown, all without a single coherent thought. He pulled into the small parking lot of the small-engine shop and sat staring at the windows. The sign on the door said Closed, but that didn't mean Uncle Calvin wasn't inside. He shut down at five, most days, and spent another hour or two on the day's more complicated tasks, the ones he couldn't work on earlier when he was likely to be interrupted by customers.

He probably didn't need to be interrupted by his angsty nephew either. And what was Ben hoping the old man would say, anyhow? Did Ben even know what he wanted to talk about? What question he wanted to ask?

Well. Yes. He did know that, as a matter of fact.

He pushed his way out of the car before he had time to second-guess himself and rapped on the front door of the shop. After thirty seconds or so, he rapped again and saw movement in the shadows inside. Uncle Calvin appeared on the far side of the glass, unlocked the door, and stood back as Ben pulled it open.

"Am I a coward?" Ben demanded. "Am I running away from things because they're scary? Things that—that could be good? Or great, even? Am I settling for something less than what I could have just because I'm afraid of trying and failing? Of being hurt again? Is that what I'm doing? Am I *roaring* enough?"

"Well, those are all good questions." Uncle Calvin frowned. "Except for the last one. That one's just strange. But for the others—I think those questions are best answered while drinking scotch by a campfire. And probably best answered by *you*, not me. But if you want me to provide the scotch and the campfire, I can do that."

"Yes," Ben said before he could change his mind. "I want the scotch and the campfire. Please."

"Okay." Uncle Calvin wiped his hands on the rag he always had tucked into his waistband when he was working. "I need to get some of this oil washed off me before I go anywhere near an open flame, so I'll go home and shower, and you'll go pick up pizza for dinner. I don't care what kind, but make sure there's something green on it. We'll meet at my place."

Ben nodded. He wasn't sure he wanted to have this conversation, really, wasn't sure he wanted to feel the way he was feeling. The strange buzz in his brain, under his skin, the excitement of something new and scary on the horizon—something he might not be running away from.

No, he wasn't sure he liked it. Not exactly. But there was something about it, all the same. Something familiar, a reminder of other times he'd felt this way, and the good things—and bad things—that had happened after the feeling.

It was being alive, he was pretty sure. This was what Peyton's mom had been talking about. This riot of energy, uncontrolled and unfocused, with so much potential to cause damage and chaos, also had the ability to create something wonderful. But only if he was strong enough to let it keep flowing.

"I'll get pizza," he said. "Yeah. Okay." He stepped back away from the door and looked at his uncle. "And you'll get cleaned up, and we'll talk." All pretty obvious. But then Ben added, "Hurry. Please." Because he wasn't sure how long his nerve was going to hold, and he really, really wasn't sure what would happen if it broke.

Uncle Calvin nodded sagely. "I'll be ready when you get there." He smiled, quick and true. "I've been waiting for this conversation for a long time."

CHAPTER TWENTY-TWO

IT WAS a big party, in every sense of the word.

Lots of people. Lots of rich people. Lots of rich, famous people. Actors, politicians, patricians of old-money families, nouveau riche citizens looking to make their mark in the cultural landscape, all dressed to impress and mingling in a Tribeca ballroom.

It was a rich hunting ground and Liam was a wolf—no, wolves hunted in packs, didn't they? He was a—not a lion, he was pretty sure they hunted in packs too. A jaguar? Yeah, he was a jaguar—shit, were they the spotted ones or the black ones? No, he was a panther, a real one, not a mountain lion calling itself a panther, and he was stretched out on a branch, ready to drop down onto unsuspecting prey and—

And sink his teeth into their necks? Jesus, he sucked at analogies.

He wasn't any sort of animal. He was just an architect ready to charm old clients and meet new ones. He was at the party on business. *Everything* was business now. For the past week he'd thrown himself into his new role at the firm, and already he was seeing results. Sure, he was also seeing some pretty nasty bags under his eyes from not getting enough sleep, but he'd let Allison doctor him up with some Preparation H and concealer—now that she was his employee, he was happy to be friendly with her again—and moved on.

The night was all about meeting and greeting, making an impression. So when Eric Wilton, the Hollywood A-lister with a house that had been featured in *Architectural Digest*, smiled at him, Liam scooped another glass of wine off the waiter-held tray and crossed the room to introduce himself. Wilton was out and proud, so maybe he wanted to get laid, or maybe he wanted another award-winning home design. Either way, Liam was interested.

At least, he damn well *should* be interested. And if he went through the motions, surely he'd kick himself into gear and *get* interested. Maybe he was just chasing another shiny thing, but what the hell else was he supposed to do? Sit still and wait?

No. He couldn't let himself be still, couldn't let himself slow down enough to think. He walked straight up to Wilton, offered his hand, introduced himself, and started in on the small talk. The evening was a fund-raiser for arts programs at inner-city schools, so that made conversation easy. Sure, yeah, art's important. Architecture? Well, yes, that was his own passion—he said "passion" without wincing at all—but of course architecture was best understood as practical art, just as engineering was practical science—

And Wilton actually seemed into it. He mentioned famous architects, recent projects, his own ambitions for his properties, and he did it all with a mix of bashful charm and genuine enthusiasm that should have been both heart-softening and dick-hardening.

If Liam had known Wilton would be at the party, he would have read up on him and had a better idea about his personal life. As it was? Even if Wilton had been straight he still would have been totally worth Liam's time. He was something more than shiny. He cared about architecture, was interested in ideas, had a rare sensitivity—

"Sorry, am I boring you?" Wilton asked. He wasn't being snotty; he was genuinely concerned that his rapture over what he'd seen on his recent trip to Kazakhstan wasn't interesting. "It's probably something you'd need to have seen in person. None of it was really all that *good*, I don't think, from a design perspective, but there was just a great energy to it, a sense of potential and excitement—sorry. I'm getting started again. But tell me about your firm. What are you working on now?"

Perfect opportunity. Name-drop a couple projects, mention the Taybec Briggs project to show things were always active, then segue into a discussion of how the firm sometimes took on smaller projects, even residential projects, if the client was someone sufficiently interesting, sufficiently artistic—*sufficiently famous*—and let things happen from there.

It would have been easy, and it was exactly what Liam was supposed to be doing. Bringing in clients, giving them what they wanted. Building the company, building his reputation. Building a damn building.

And maybe building a relationship too. The thing with Ben was over. For good this time, whether Liam liked it or not. And Wilton—Eric—was a prize by any standard. Liam needed to move on.

"I've found myself thinking about different kinds of architecture lately," he said. Not a great idea to talk to the prestigious potential client about something totally unrelated to the firm. That meant this wasn't about business. "Maybe more like your Kazakhstan experience."

"I'm not sure I follow," the actor said, but he raised his eyebrows and smiled in an invitation to continue.

"I think maybe I'm interested in smaller projects. Like small-town houses. Nothing architecturally grand about them, often mass-produced from a common plan, but over the years they get customized in little ways, reformed to better suit their occupants. I was at a house last weekend with three porches—small house, probably twelve hundred square feet or even a bit less, but three big porches—and I remembered helping to build one of them when I was a kid. My friends and me, scrambling all over the place with handsaws and our dads' cordless drills, putting in way too many screws in one corner, hardly any somewhere else. It was the summer before we started high school, and when we poured the concrete footings we all tossed in little mementos of our childhoods like we were memorializing our own lives—"

He stopped. What the hell was he doing, spilling all this crap to a stranger? But Eric nodded thoughtfully. "The best architecture is for people," he said slowly. "That's the ultimate point. If a building can be beautiful, that's important, but it also has to be functional, and it has to *mean* something. There has to be emotional resonance as well as intellectual and aesthetic appeal."

"Damn. We should get you writing copy for our promotional materials."

"I really care about design. If my career had taken a different turn… well, who knows? You can spend your life wondering about all that, about what might have been, or you can just go ahead with the life you've got."

"The life you've got seems pretty damn good, at least from the outside."

A quick smile, easy and relaxed, genuine enough that Liam honestly couldn't tell whether he was imagining the hint of sadness. "I can't complain."

"Is that your big what-if question?" Liam asked. Taking the conversation from architecture to something more personal. If Eric went along with it, that'd mean something. "Actor or architect? That's the one you wonder about?"

"It's one of them." Eric shrugged, and it was like a physical manifestation of his decision to open up. "A couple relationships I wish

I'd handled differently. I wonder what would have happened if I'd come out to my grandfather before he died—it wouldn't have gone well, I'm sure of that, but I wonder if that would have been a good thing overall. Like, maybe that was a fight I needed to have. Maybe it was a fight *he* needed to have." He took a mouthful of wine, swallowed it, and smiled ruefully. "I'll never know. I guess that's the point, right? How about you? What are your big ones?"

"Relationship," Liam admitted. Not too smooth to talk about an old guy with a potential hookup, but he didn't seem to care about being smooth, not right then. "First boyfriend. I screwed it up when I got greedy. I was a stupid kid, thought I could have everything, have Ben *and* fuck around with anyone who caught my eye." Not just sharing that he was hung up on another guy, but revealing his history as a cheater too. Interesting decision.

"First boyfriend?" Wilton nodded slowly. "I think just about everyone screws up their first relationship. And I guess most of us regret it too."

Was that all this was? Was Liam's crisis nothing unusual, just typical angst and regret?

He thought about Ben's smile, his honesty, his strength. And everything that went with Ben. His uncle, his friends, North Falls itself.

"I've seen him a bit over the past few weeks," he admitted. "It's got me kind of—well. I think maybe I was kind of messed up all along, but it's got me kind of *admitting* I'm messed up."

"You going to keep seeing him?"

"No. It's over." Liam gave his smile more confidence than he felt. "His choice. But being with him, and his whole circle of friends, helped me understand what I'm looking for. I want a relationship. Someone to really care about, to trust. So—I don't know. I guess now I just need to get off my ass and try to make that happen."

Eric nodded slowly. "That sounds like what I'm looking for too," he said. His smile was gentle and easy. "Maybe we should spend some time together? Get to know each other a bit better and see where that goes?"

It was a good suggestion. And there was only one reasonable response to it. Liam just needed to pull his head out of his ass and forget about Ben, and he could walk through this new door, explore this new opportunity—start building his new life.

THERE WERE actual paparazzi outside the building, and real reporters too. Ben's original plan—well, "plan" was probably a little generous, but his original idea—had been to just show up, dart inside, catch Liam's eye, and take it from there. He didn't have Liam's home address, after all, and a phone call seemed a bit too mundane, too noncommittal, for the conversation Ben wanted them to have.

Still, maybe a phone call would have to do. He could call Liam and ask to meet him. That would work, surely, and it was a scheme that was much less likely to get Ben roughed up by aggressive bouncers than anything he could arrange at the stupid ballroom.

Ben should just go. He could give Liam a call, leave a message— no. Not a message. If Ben couldn't talk to Liam in person, then at *least* he needed the directness of a live phone call. But Ben could go somewhere and wait. He could get a hotel room, even, and call Liam the next morning. Everyone would be well rested and happy. Absolutely, that made sense. Leave, hotel, sleep, phone, happiness. Excellent plan.

But Ben couldn't seem to make his feet move.

Liam was right inside that building. Not that Ben had seen him go in, but Liam had told Dinah he was going to this event, so it was a pretty good guess.

And beyond that, Ben just *knew*. As if he could sense Liam's presence even through all the crowds and concrete.

He ignored the voice that reminded him about Liam's many visits to the North Falls area, all of which had occurred without Ben's mysterious senses picking up any hint of his presence. That was different. Somehow.

Because Liam was inside that building. Ben knew it. And he also knew he couldn't trust his nerve to hold if he walked away. He'd almost turned around five times on the drive to the city, almost given in to the murky doubts that threatened to overpower the tiny flame of hope in his heart.

If he walked away now, if he had to face a night alone in a hotel room, torturing himself with all the reasons he was stupid to even think about taking a chance on someone like Liam? He couldn't get through that.

So he stood still, and he waited.

Cars began pulling up, collecting women in gowns and men in tuxedos, whisking them away to the next stop in their glamorous evenings. Ben edged closer to the front doors. He worked his way through the crowd of photographers until he was at the metal barrier that separated the glittering folk from the hoi polloi.

He shouldn't be there. He was making a mistake. He was going to get hurt, and he knew it. He couldn't stand it. But he couldn't leave.

He was frozen in agonizing indecision when Liam appeared in the building's doorway, and just like that, the uncertainty left him. Liam. Beautiful and smiling, so polished in his tuxedo, so relaxed even in the crowd and under the flash of so many cameras. So, so many flashes.

And shouts. Voices calling "Eric! Eric! Over here, please! Eric!"

Only then did Ben notice the man walking beside Liam, close enough to make it clear they were leaving the party together. Together. Liam and Eric Wilton the fucking movie star, both poised and handsome, both smiling, Wilton waving to the crowd, to the cameras.

It made so much sense. It was so much more natural, more in keeping with the expected order of the universe. Liam and a movie star. One golden creature with another, and Ben should slink back to his small-town world and his small-town life. It would hurt, of course. It already hurt, a weird aching tension in his chest, a swirling in his brain that no amount of deep breathing would dispel. But it was a *private* hurt, at least. Ben could spare himself the public humiliation of—

"Liam!" Shit, that was him. Yelling. He was yelling Liam's name. He was.

Still, with all the paparazzi, all the calls for Eric Wilton's damn attention, Liam hadn't heard him. It wasn't too late. Except—

"Liam!" More of a bellow this time. And, damn it, Ben had come this far. He was going to go the rest of the way. Painful humiliation was better than giving up without a fight. "*Liam*! Hey, Liam!"

Liam still didn't hear him.

The metal barrier was about waist-high and there were security guards on the other side of it, but not all that many. None directly between Ben and Liam.

And Ben the law-abiding, Ben the elementary school teacher, Ben the careful—Ben jumped the barrier.

It was shocking how quickly the security guards moved in. Also shocking to feel the crush of other spectators following his lead and crashing over the barrier themselves. The chaos, the excitement, the press of bodies, the strong arms locked around his body—well, his neck—and squeezing against his throat—

And Liam was still moving away from him. Eric Wilton had grabbed him by the arm and was tugging him toward a waiting limo, saving him, rescuing him, so the two of them could go off and live in perfection together.

But perfection was a trap. Ben knew that now. Calm, peace, serenity—it was lovely, and necessary, but struggle and anticipation and excitement were necessary too. Did Liam know that? Ben thought maybe he did, or at least maybe he had.

But now? Liam was leaving with another man.

And Ben's serenity was *gone*.

He wriggled at least partly free, pushed and struggled until he was upright, called Liam's name once more, saw Liam half turn before Wilton reclaimed his attention and directed him to the open limo door.

Liam was leaving. Ben had built up his courage, come all the way to the city, risked himself, exposed himself, and Liam wasn't even noticing his efforts. Liam was leaving with another man, and Ben would be alone. He'd lose Liam again.

He *couldn't* lose Liam again.

And right there, in the crush of paparazzi and autograph-seekers, celebrities and security, Ben roared. Nothing as coherent as words, just frustration, anger, need—passion. He roared, and heads turned toward him. *Liam's* head turned toward him.

Eric Wilton turned too, but *fuck* Eric Wilton. This wasn't about him. Now that Liam was looking at Ben, this wasn't about anything or anyone that wasn't the two of them.

"Ben?" Liam's voice was carried away by the commotion, but the word was clear anyway. Ben had been seen. Recognized. Acknowledged. And maybe that should have been enough, but damn it, it wasn't.

He squirmed free from the grip of a guard who'd clearly been surprised by the volume of Ben's cry and stumbled forward. "Liam!" he called.

And Liam was stepping toward him, although he looked more concerned than amorous. "What the hell's going on?" Liam yelled. He shook his head, grabbed Ben's wrist, and tugged him forward.

Before Ben understood what was happening he was being shoved into a limo, soft leather upholstery cushioning his graceless sprawl. He stayed still for a moment, one arm and leg on the seat, the others on the floor, trying to figure out what he'd just done.

As the vehicle began to move, he struggled gracelessly onto the bench and stared at the two men opposite him. Liam was staring back. Eric Wilton, on the other hand, looked smooth, polished, and slightly amused.

"Am I the only one thinking 'threesome'?" the actor asked.

Ben closed his eyes and tried to find a moment of peace, but there was none to be had. So he opened them, looked at Liam, and said, "I hope you are. But I've screwed all this up badly enough, making the decisions myself. I think I have to put myself at Liam's mercy now."

CHAPTER TWENTY-THREE

IT WAS strange for Liam to have Ben in his apartment, as if past and present had collided into a not quite coherent whole. Strange, but not bad. Not necessarily.

"Eric Wilton's a good guy," Liam said. Maybe it wasn't kind, but maybe he wasn't feeling all that kind. He paced restlessly around the living room while Ben stood and stared at him. "And he's gorgeous and sexy and he'd be good for my career. And I walked away from him tonight. No, wait. I didn't walk away. I had the fucking nerve to ask him to give me and another guy a ride to my apartment in his damn limousine. So if this is another one of your teases, Ben? If this is another hello-goodbye, push-me-pull-me mind fuck? You should expect me to *not* be impressed."

"It's not that," Ben said. He sounded strained, as if he was operating on too much adrenaline and not enough sleep. And he kind of looked that way too.

"So what is it?" Liam was suddenly almost as tired as Ben looked. "What are you doing here?"

"I came because—" He stopped and turned away.

"Yeah. Great. You came because you didn't want the angst to be over. You don't want to actually *do* anything, don't want to have anything to do with me, but you want to make sure I keep on—"

Ben moved fast for someone who looked so worn out. Across the room in only a few steps, jerking to a stop in front of Liam, raising a hand toward his face, then catching himself and lowering the hand before saying, "I want you. I want—us. I don't know what—no, I *do* know what was in the way. I was scared. Scared of being hurt. Again."

Liam stood frozen. It sounded like Ben wanted—but it had sounded like that before. And Ben had pushed Liam away those times. Who was to say he wouldn't do it again?

"And now *you're* scared," Ben said. There wasn't much humor in his short laugh. "For good reason, just like I had good reason. But at some point we just have to—don't we? Don't we just have to get past that? I know I'm no one to talk, but I think I'm right anyway."

"Could you—" Liam swallowed hard. "I need you to spell this out for me. You're here because…."

"I'm here because I want to be with you. I have no idea about the details. I mean, you live in the city, I live in the sticks, and that's not too convenient. And there's no way I'm going to be good for your career, so if that's what you're looking for in a guy, I guess I'm not a prime candidate. But… I miss you. I've been missing you for fifteen years, but I managed to convince myself I was missing a memory, a dream, an idealized version of someone who never really existed. But you came back, and—fuck, Liam, you're *not* ideal. You're a pain in the ass and you make me crazy and you *totally* destroy my Zen. But I still miss you. I still want you. *You.*"

Ben stopped talking and took a half step backward. "Shit. Sorry. That was a lot. And I'm totally embarrassed now, and I want to start running away or making up a cover story or doing whatever I can to make myself feel less open, less vulnerable, less… less honest. Because it would be really, really nice if I was feeling a bit calmer right now. But I'm trying not to do any of that. I'm trying to be brave."

"You're doing a good job," Liam said. His voice was huskier than he'd expected. "You're right. It is scary, and I've given you every reason to not trust me. But for what it's worth? I absolutely, completely learned my lesson. I did something—well. I was going to say unforgivable, but I'm really hoping that isn't quite true. But unforgettable, at least. For me. I'm always going to remember what I did, and I'm *never* going to do it again."

"Okay." Ben nodded. "Okay. But—you will hurt me. Not on purpose, but you will. And probably I'll hurt you too. That's just what happens. Maybe nothing big, but even if it is, I can survive it. You can survive it. It's better to take the chance than to sit around afraid to try."

"Who've you been talking to? Calvin?"

"Partly. But not just him." Ben shook his head. "I can tell you the whole story, if you want. But I feel like I'm maybe going to pass out from stress pretty soon. Could you just—can you tell me? Am I too late? You were right about Eric Wilton. Well, I don't know if he's a good guy, but the rest of it? I can't really compete with—"

Well, no words would tell Ben what he needed to know. Liam stepped forward instead, wrapped a hand around the back of Ben's neck, tugged just a little, and kissed him. Slow and deep, with every bit of truth and love he could summon. And Ben kissed him back with just as much sweet sincerity.

Which was nice. It was more than nice. But it wasn't enough.

Liam pulled free long enough to ask, "Can you stay? You're not going to take off? And I mean, *stay*. Not forever, I get that—we'll have to figure all that out. But for breakfast at least. Maybe lunch, or even dinner? Like—stay a while. Don't run away, and don't push me away. Can you do that?"

Ben's eyes were wide, but he nodded. And Liam believed him.

There was no rush after that. They stayed in the living room for quite a while, clothes on, kissing and swaying in a sort of music-less dance. When they needed more skin, more contact, they made their way to the bedroom and lay down on the bed, and Liam wedged his thigh between Ben's just as he used to, decades earlier when they still weren't ready to go too far.

Ben's lips, his cheeks, his ears, his neck, his chest, his rib cage— Liam needed to explore every part, needed to touch and kiss and taste and let himself sink back into the new/old familiarity. He needed to hear Ben's whispered words, his gentle huffs of laughter when Liam found a ticklish spot, his sharp inhalations when Liam's explorations found *other* kinds of sensitivity.

The cool light of dawn was leaking past the curtains before they were completely naked, and it was full day by the time Liam finally let himself sink into Ben's body and complete their dance. They moved together slowly, almost sleepily, easy and gentle even as their climaxes built. At the end, as Ben gasped into Liam's mouth, as they arched together and then apart and then together again, they were as close to perfection as they'd ever been together. Maybe as close as they ever could be.

They dozed afterward, comfortable and cozy, until hunger drove them to the kitchen to forage for sustenance. They stood together, staring into the fridge as if it held the secrets of the universe, until Ben said, "You don't have any food."

"There's cheese. And milk. I'm well supplied from a dairy perspective."

"You need some fruit. And some grains." Ben leaned back into Liam's arms. "I'll bring groceries next time I come."

Such a simple statement. Such a simple promise. But it was enough to make Liam's chest ache in a wonderful way. "Okay," he agreed, turning to bury his lips in the crook of Ben's neck. "You'll bring groceries. In the meantime, should we order in?"

"Breakfast? Does breakfast get delivered?"

"This is New York City. *Everything* gets delivered."

"Okay. You order us food. I'll have a shower. And I'm going to have to give Uncle Calvin a call. He'll want to know how things turned out."

"Not with details, I hope?"

"Oh, I'm pretty sure he'd want any details I cared to share. But, no, I won't give him much. Do you have stuff you need to do today?"

Liam had work. Lots and lots of it. But he shook his head. "Not 'need,' no. Not if you're still okay to stick around."

Ben smiled. "You're going to have a hard time getting rid of me."

"I'm not even going to try," Liam replied. And he didn't.

EPILOGUE

"Ben!" Liam's mother enveloped him in a hug, and Liam's father was right behind her, then all around her, enveloping them all in a sort of uber hug in which boundless enthusiasm made up for limited reach.

"Hi," Ben said as soon as he could wriggle a little bit free. "Thank you so much for inviting me down here!"

"Oh, thank *you* for coming," Lillian, Liam's mom, said. "When Liam suggested it, Richard and I were over the moon! We've missed you so much!"

"I missed you too." Not as much as he'd missed their son, but, still—the Marshalls had been a second family to him, and Christmas cards and occasional emails hadn't made up for the loss of visits and phone calls. "I'm not sure how to handle the next part—I feel like I should be offering condolences or something, but I get the idea you'd rather have congratulations?"

They looked temporarily confused, then Lillian said, "Oh, the divorce!"

Ben exchanged a look with Liam. *Oh, the divorce! That old thing—I'd forgotten all about that!*

"Congratulations are appreciated," Richard said firmly. "And I'm really glad to have the two of you here to share the celebration with us. It seems appropriate, somehow. Lillian and I may not be married anymore, but we're still part of each other's lives. And the two of you were apart for quite a while, but now you're back together because you never really forgotten each other. Formal relationship labels aren't the important thing, are they?"

"Hear hear," Calvin said as he, Seth, Dinah, and Tamara climbed out of their own rental car. "We get too caught up in the details and forget to appreciate the important things." He stretched his arm out, offering the cooler he was carrying to Richard. "Important things like Dan Stuart's kielbasa!"

"Oh!" Lillian cried in excitement. "And we're so happy you could all come see us as well! Seth! I can't believe you're a daddy! And your beautiful wife, and your precious little girl! And Calvin." She sounded less excited for that last bit. Still interested, but more—cautious, maybe? Preparing to be amused but also worried about being shocked? It was a reasonable reaction to Uncle Calvin, Ben was pretty sure. "Thank you so much for coming."

"And for wrangling the kielbasa," Richard said with more enthusiasm. He took the cooler and led the crowd toward the house.

Ben and Liam hung back a little. "Is it weird?" Ben asked. "I mean—it seems weird to me. They still seem totally content, totally in tune with each other. Why the hell are they splitting up?"

Liam shook his head. "I don't know. I guess—I guess maybe they want something more. Fuck it, I think they want 'passion.' I can run away from that damn word all I want, but maybe Tristan wasn't completely wrong. Maybe being 'content' isn't enough. Just because they're older doesn't mean they're dead, right? They still have a lot of life to live, and they want to be intense about it."

"Intense with other people."

Liam nodded slowly. "I guess?"

They were at the house then, kicking sand off their shoes before climbing the white wooden stairs to the wraparound porch. A moment to appreciate the ocean view before Lillian was in action, shepherding her guests to their respective rooms, giving them a rundown of the events for the weekend, and generally displaying a level of energy that should have been too much for someone half her age.

"Have we considered the possibility that your parents are breaking up because your mom has developed a serious cocaine problem and your dad just can't handle it anymore?" Ben asked when he and Liam were safely in their room.

"Nah. You watch. She'll burn out by nine o'clock and he'll just take over, being the gracious host until the last guest has finally stumbled off to bed. He's at least as coked up as she is."

And the evening went as Liam had predicted. After dinner on the patio they all went down to a campfire on the beach, but Lillian was yawning before the sun was fully down, and she snuck away shortly after dark. Dinah took an exhausted but reluctant Tamara up to bed, and the men were left watching the fire and the water.

"You got sharks down here?" Uncle Calvin asked.

"Sure," Richard replied. "It's the ocean. There are sharks. But we don't have many serious attacks—just nips, generally."

"That right?"

"Well, maybe more than a nip. But not fatal."

"And whatever doesn't kill you makes you stronger," Calvin mused.

"I don't know how much stronger you'd be if you were missing a foot or something," Ben interjected. He did *not* want his uncle getting too adventurous on this trip. "If you want to swim, swim, but don't go *looking* for sharks, okay? Don't, like, rub yourself in bacon before you go in the water."

"So careful all the time," Calvin scolded. "You've got to live a little, Ben."

Ben felt the gentle squeeze of Liam's hand around his own. "I'm living just the right amount, thanks."

"Smug bastard," Seth said.

"Maybe we *should* do more," Liam said suddenly.

"What?" Ben turned to face him. "You'd better not be talking about sharks and bacon."

"No. But—"

"Oh." The same thing they'd been talking about for the whole six weeks they'd been back together. Their future, and how exactly they were going to make it work when they were living hours away from each other. If it were short-term, it wouldn't be a big deal. But Ben didn't want to live in the city; his occasional weekends there were fun, but he didn't really feel at home. And Liam? Well. Liam seemed happy as a clam in North Falls. But his work wasn't there.

"Liam could be an architect anywhere," Ben told the others. He wasn't sure if this was a conversation fit for public consumption, but he really couldn't consider the other men around the campfire as "public," could he? "But he can't be a *great* architect unless he's in the city. That's where the clients with all the money are, and for the really big, exciting projects, you need money. So—you know. He needs to be in the city. To be great, to do what he wants to do with his life. The city. He needs to be there."

"No, I don't," Liam said quietly.

Ben frowned at him. "What do you mean? You just—you just said maybe you should do *more*. What does that mean? Is New York not enough? You need to go to Paris or Dubai or something?"

"Whoa, slow down." Liam's smile was gentle. "That's not what I meant at all. I didn't mean more professionally. I meant… *more*. You and me. Like living together? I know it's fast, but it's not like we don't know each other pretty well already. And I feel like—I don't want to waste time. I want to *be with you*, you know?"

"Yeah." Ben did know. He wanted the same thing. The details? Well. He'd just have to make the details work, he supposed. "Is there somewhere other than right downtown? I know you like the hustle and bustle, but could we—I don't know, somewhere quieter? A bit less central?"

"I was thinking of North Falls," Liam said, sounding genuinely confused. "You don't want to live in the city—you've told me that already."

"But you need to—"

"No. I don't. My career… it's not the most important thing, not by a long shot. And it's not like I'd be moving to Antarctica. It's s a bit much for a daily commute, but if I have to go down to the city for a couple days a week, I can do that no problem."

"And Tristan's going to agree to that?"

"I doubt it. But I think that's okay. I've walked away from that firm once. I can do it again."

"But your projects…."

"I'm getting really interested in residential design. It's not as glamorous, not as high profile, but there's a lot of room for creativity. And I was thinking about doing some writing too. Like, helping people understand architecture with coffee table books or whatever. I like photography. And you can travel over the summer—I could work on getting my photography up to standard this winter, and next summer we could travel together. Take pictures of buildings. That'd be fun, right?"

"Like Terry," Uncle Calvin said, and Richard nodded in agreement.

Liam frowned. "Terry?"

"Terry Franks," Ben said. Was it possible? Could this work? "He died earlier this year? Oh, yeah. You were kind of at his funeral. But before he died, he was based in North Falls but he traveled pretty regularly. He wrote antique books."

"Books *about* antiques," Uncle Calvin clarified. "Not old books."

"How could he *write* old books?" Seth asked. "I know he traveled, but unless someone thought he *time* traveled, I'm not sure how his books could be old."

"Terry Franks?" Liam said. He seemed to be talking just to Ben, now, which was really just as well. "I thought he was—damn. I actually thought of how small his life must have been, how—I don't think I actually used the word pathetic, in my mind, but I might as well have. But now I'm hearing…. Wait. Am I hearing that he *wasn't* all that pathetic, or am I hearing that I'd be just like him if I moved back to North Falls, and that'd mean I *would* be pathetic?"

Of course Uncle Calvin couldn't stay out of the conversation for long. "You've got a pretty high opinion of your opinion, son."

"What?" Liam asked.

"You think Terry Franks gave a shit whether you thought he was pathetic or not? Sixty years from now when you've lived a full and interesting life, you think you're really going to care what some snot-nosed kid thinks about you? I certainly hope you won't."

"Wait," Liam said.

But his father was involved now, and waiting didn't seem to be an option. "You need to live your own life, Liam. You need to do what's right for you, not what *other people* will think is impressive."

"*Screw* other people!" Uncle Calvin crowed.

Seth leaned in. "Not literally. Don't go screwing other people just because Calvin said so. He was speaking figuratively."

"Thanks for the tip," Liam replied. Then he turned to his father. "But—isn't it—don't you want—"

"Liam. Do you remember when your mother and I told you we were getting a divorce?"

"It was only a couple months ago. Yeah, I remember."

"I told you we weren't looking for your approval, or even your opinion. And that goes both ways. You need to live your life for *you*. You and Ben, maybe. But not for me, or your mother, or the people you went to school with or your neighbors or the world. Just *you*."

"Terry Franks lived that way," Uncle Calvin said. He seemed serious, although of course there was no way to be sure. "And Terry had a pretty damn good life."

"So—" Liam looked blankly at the people around the fire, and Ben fought the urge to step in, to help out, to do whatever he could to make

Liam less confused. Possibly this was something Liam should figure out for himself. "I was already going to move to North Falls." He turned to Ben. "Not in with you, necessarily. If you think it's too soon, that's fine. But the town? Yeah, I was going to move that far. And I knew it might hurt my career. But I was okay with that, more or less. So—this conversation hasn't really changed anything. But—I feel like it has. What's that about?"

"Maybe now you know you don't have to be ashamed," Uncle Calvin suggested.

"More than 'not ashamed,'" Richard said. He beamed at his son. "You should be proud. You're not quitting anything. You're not running away. You *won*. You're a principal in a major New York architecture firm. You've made it. Walking away now? You're walking away with pride, looking for a new challenge."

"Living with Ben," Seth said. "Yup, that could be challenging."

"Shush," Ben told him. Then he turned to Liam. "I'm not proud of you."

"Uh—what?" Uncle Calvin leaned forward. "That's not quite the feel-good message we were shooting for, hoss."

But Ben ignored him. "I'm not proud of you because 'pride' makes it sound like I'm taking some kind of credit for things. I'm not *proud* of Elon Musk for combining entrepreneurship with environmentalism, and I'm not *proud* of you for having a great career *or* for being ready to walk away from that career. But I'm—" Ben squeezed Liam's hand. "Damn. I'm impressed. Whether you go on and build artistic skyscrapers or cozy, functional houses for people to raise their families in, I'm impressed. And *whatever* you do with your career, if you're in North Falls? If you're with me? I'm happy. More than happy. And if you're proud of yourself? That makes me happy too."

"I think I might start cooking meth," Liam said. "Just as a sideline to see me through, financially. Anyone got any objections to that?"

"A man's gotta do what a man's gotta do," Uncle Calvin said.

"Your mother worked hard to teach you to cook. I'm sure she'd be pleased to see you putting it in practice," Richard said. Ben honestly wasn't sure if the man knew what meth was or not.

"I've never tried meth," Seth said. "Would you be offering free samples? Or maybe some kind of pyramid marketing scheme?"

"I'd still love you," Ben said. "I'd kick your ass and throw you out and yell at you a lot. But I'd love you."

"Okay," Liam said slowly. "I'll put the meth idea on the back burner, but I'm sticking to the idea that we should do more. Like—live even deeper, even richer than we are. You, Ben. You and me? I want that for us." He leaned back and the firelight danced across his face. "But all of us. My dad, my friend, my—" He stopped, glanced at Calvin, then said, "My uncle. By blood or not, I don't care. You're mine, whether you like it or not."

"I don't object," Calvin said.

"Okay. So, all of us. We can all live deeper and richer together. Does that sound possible?"

"It sounds like something Dinah's likely to kick my ass over," Seth said. "Can you give me some details before I commit to anything?"

"Nope. No details. But no long-term commitment either. For now?" Liam stood up. He pulled his shirt over his head and dropped it on the sand. "For now, we swim. The sharks should know better than to mess with us. And if they don't, we'll teach them a lesson in manly fashion. Who's with me?"

Ben stood up. He hadn't needed to think. Of *course* he was with Liam. Always.

Seth was the next to rise. "I'm not gay. I don't have to worry about pleasing the damn picky male eye. I'm sorry if I'm not as ripped as you guys are." He pulled his shirt over his head and slapped his belly. "But I'm a good floater, and I'm ready to go."

Uncle Calvin looked at Richard. "This younger generation," he said. "They don't understand what it's like to be a little older."

Richard nodded. "They don't know about sore joints."

"Low energy."

Richard stood up. "Failing eyesight and hearing."

Uncle Calvin stood up as well. "Increased craftiness," he said, and he and Richard took off together, sprinting for the ocean, barely stumbling as they pulled off their shirts and tossed them to the breeze.

Seth ran after them, whooping so loudly it might have been heard up at the house, if anyone was awake to listen.

Ben turned to Liam. "Do you actually want to swim, or were you just trying to get rid of them?"

"I want to swim. I don't want to get rid of them." Liam pulled his own shirt over his head. "But since we just so happen to have a moment to ourselves...."

His lips were salty from the sea air, his skin warm compared to the cool night breeze. He was Ben's. He'd been gone for too long, but now he was back. And he was damn well not getting away again.

KATE SHERWOOD started writing at about the same time she got back on a horse after a twenty-year break. She'd like to think she's far too young for it to be a midlife crisis, but apparently she was ready for a few changes!

Kate's writing focuses on characters and relationships, people trying to find out how much of themselves they need to keep, and how much they can afford to give away. She tries to find a careful balance between drama and humor—she wants readers to have an intense experience and feel drawn into the book, but she also wants them to enjoy the time they spend reading.

Website: www.katesherwoodbooks.com
Email: kate@katesherwoodbooks.com
Blog: www.katesherwoodbooks.com/?page_id=451

CHASING
THE DRAGON

KATE SHERWOOD

When mercenary Jack Hunter stumbles upon Christian Manning servicing a client in a back alley, it stirs feelings he's kept deeply buried. Hunter becomes Christian's knight in shining armor when he rescues him from an attack and takes him to his secluded cabin to heal.

Being stuck in the cabin over the winter gives both men a chance to get their lives in order. Christian is struggling to break his heroin addiction, and Hunter needs to get away from the organization he helped start years before—a group of people who don't appreciate being told no. It's a toss-up which goal is more difficult. Their new starts spark a relationship between them, but nothing good comes cheap. Despite the complications, Hunter wants more, but Christian is resistant to making that commitment. When Hunter's private security company threatens them, only nurturing the fragile trust they formed at the beginning of their love affair will save them. But for two men with very dark pasts, relying on each other might be easier said than done.

www.dreamspinnerpress.com

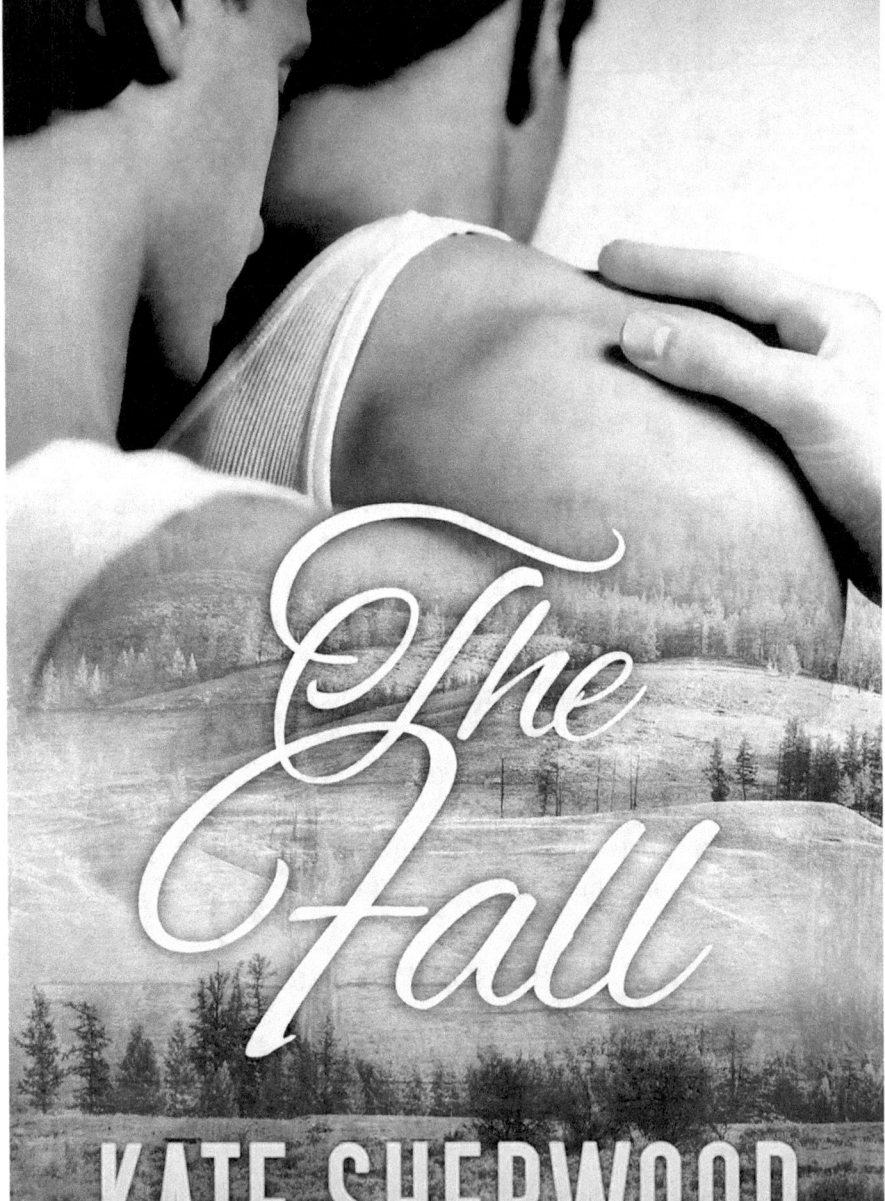

The Fall

KATE SHERWOOD

Every relationship leaves something behind. Dumped by his sugar daddy, part-time model Scott Mackenzie somehow ends up owning an abandoned church in rural Ontario. He dreams of using it for gay weddings, even if he'll never have one of his own.

Joe Sutton is trying to keep his family together after his parents' deaths. Between the family ranch, his brother's construction company, and commitments around town, he doesn't have time for a relationship. But Mackenzie is hard to ignore.

As both men fight their growing attraction, challenges to Mackenzie's business threaten their relationship. If he can't make it work, he'll have to crawl back to the city in defeat. But the only solution involves risking the ranch Joe loves, and each man has to decide how much he'll sacrifice for the other.

www.dreamspinnerpress.com

Kate
Sherwood

IN TOO
DEEP

At first glance, Cade and Aiden hardly seem like a match made in heaven. Their worlds couldn't be further apart. Cade is quiet, serious, and determined to succeed; Aiden's a party-loving frat boy. Cade comes from a rough home and worked hard to get the scholarships that make it possible for him to attend college; Aiden's had it all thrown in his lap by supportive, kind, and wealthy parents. Cade wants nothing to do with Aiden, but from the moment they meet, Aiden is determined to find a way to bring their different worlds together.

Aiden manages to persuade Cade he's a decent guy, and a tentative friendship becomes much more. But a trip to Aiden's family cottage puts Cade in the path of a ghost from his past, and a dark secret he never expected to face again. Cade did what he had to do to escape his dead-end life, but now he sees he didn't leave it as far behind him as he thought.

www.dreamspinnerpress.com

www.ingramcontent.com/pod-product-compliance
Lightning Source LLC
Chambersburg PA
CBHW070124260626
47160CB00004B/1619

* 9 7 8 1 6 4 0 8 0 5 2 6 2 *